Céline Chancelier

ALL THE STARS WE FOLLOW

A novel

*To my grand-mother Paulette and
my great grandmother Augustine Noëlie.*

PART ONE

1

Saturday is market day in Uzès and, on the third Saturday of July, the pretty Place aux Herbes was heaving with locals and tourists meandering around the plane trees and the colourful market stalls set around the central fountain. At ten, the sun was already high in the deep blue sky and the heat stifling. The heatwave was here to stay. Léa smiled. This was summer in Provence. You had better like it.

Her woven basket in one hand, she entered the square by a side street, a lane by any other name, with three pretty archways. It was the quickest way for her to get to her favourite fruit and vegetable stall. Yet, she had to swerve to avoid people pushing and shoving to get a better look at what was on display, parents with pushchairs, dogs excited by the smells and straining on their leashes. It was chaos, but she loved it. When she finally made it to the stall, the lady who ran it was red in the face from the heat, her fine mousy hair stuck to her head as she shouted to people to come and buy the best cherries this side of the Pont du Gard all the while serving and keeping track of her customers. She recognised Léa instantly and smiled to her.

'What can I get you, my lovely?'

'Some tomatoes, a melon and some white peaches please. And some spring onions,' she said, handing the woman her basket.

'Too hot to make ratatouille, hey? I wish this heat would stop. It was over thirty-seven degrees in the fields yesterday. Imagine picking fruit in that heat!' She shook her head and winked. 'I've put some mint and basil for you in the bag. Just put them in a little water. Don't tell anyone!' she said with a big laugh, handing Léa her basket.

Léa stopped to buy some sweet fougasse from Aigues-Mortes, a soft orange water flavoured sponge cake sprinkled with sugar and cut from a rectangular tray, from a girl who stood in the same spot every market day. A little indulgence, but as her granny used to say, life has to be lived. She stopped to look at the brightly coloured hibiscuses a man was selling near the shop with the toy cars in the window. She felt tempted to buy one but her bag felt heavy already and she worried it would get damaged by the crowds before she got home.

She joined the queue at the cheesemonger instead. He recognised her and waved to her, finishing with a flourish. She was still wondering how the coral-coloured hibiscus that had caught her eye would look like against the ochre wall of her little courtyard when the guy in front of her startled her out of her reverie by turning around abruptly, almost crashing into her. Did he look surprised or annoyed to see her? Léa could not have said. He had deep blue eyes that bored into hers and for reasons she could not have explained; she noticed the broad shoulders, the short undulating black hair. He looked vaguely Italian with his branded polo shirt, well-cut cargo shorts and an expensive watch but without knowing why she marked him out as a Brit instead. He was tapping his foot, arms crossed, looking annoyed. Obviously, he was not used to the market trader way of doing business in Provence. They will happily engage in conversation regardless of who you are. Forget about being served quickly; you just have to go with the pace of life.

A young woman, wearing a tight emerald green dress, huge gold loop earrings, a Hermès Birkin handbag on her well-sculpted arm and a wide floppy hat joined him as he turned away and put her arm in his. Léa almost giggled when she saw the girl's shoes, a pair of high-heeled gold sandals. Not the most practical footwear when walking around the cobbled streets of Uzès. The woman put her head on his shoulder, and she wondered if she was his daughter. She looked young enough to be.

The cheesemonger, Pierrot, a jovial, rotund man with one of those huge moustaches that curls at the ends, finally came up to the man and the woman and she asked him in English for a selection of cheeses. He gave at her a quizzical look followed by a Gallic shrug.

'*Je comprends pas.*[1]'

He made a gesture for her to show him what she wanted, but she looked just as puzzled as he was. Léa stepped in, thinking otherwise they would be here all day.

'Maybe I can help?' she said, repeating the questions in French for the cheesemonger. He beamed at her and turned back to the couple. The man in front of her stepped back, studying her as he did so. 'You speak English?'

The contempt in his voice irritated her. The woman glanced at her stoney-face before declaring that she could manage, but her companion ignored her.

'I spent twenty years in London so hopefully I can help yes.'

The beginning of a smile formed on the man's lips. 'Touché.'

'You should tell them to get some Pélardon,' said Pierrot. 'It's the best I've had in ages.' It was always the best he had had in a long time but Léa dutifully obliged, telling the couple that they should get some local honey to go with it. They nodded, and a few minutes later they had melted in the now dense crowd.

'They're funny, these people who think we all speak their language. How many languages should we speak to satisfy everyone around here? I tell you crazy!' he said, raising his hands above his head theatrically.

Pierrot put the mozzarella she had asked for and a Pélardon she had not in a plastic bag and, as she extended the money, he waved her away smiling. '*Bah, c'est cadeau. Tu m'as bien aidé.*[2] If you ever need a job, let me know. I could do with someone like you now that my son has gone to university.'

Léa smiled, thanked him and said with a wink that she would

---

[1] Je ne comprends pas.
[2] It's a present. You helped me a lot.

think about it. Her savings on the cheese went on the hibiscus instead. Her phone buzzed as she moved away. It was a text from Michel. Could she meet him at the café? It was important. She did not bother replying. After stopping to buy some dry-cured ham; she walked to the café on the corner of the square where they usually met.

Michel was sat at a table outside under a large umbrella drinking a Ricard when she arrived.

'A bit early, isn't it?' she said, plumping herself on a chair next to him in the shade. As she did so, she noticed the couple she had helped were having coffees at the next café under the arches. The woman had just planted a rather sensual kiss on the man's lips. She was not his daughter then. Léa noticed that he had not moved and looked annoyed. Maybe he did not enjoy being kissed in public.

The waiter who knew her well came to get her order, kissing her on the cheek as he did so. 'An espresso with a glass of water?' he asked her cheekily before going back to the café without waiting for her answer.

She felt hot and sweaty despite the light dress she was wearing and wondered how the woman with the tight green dress could look so picture-perfect. She had noticed that she was wearing full make-up and wondered how it was not running in the heat.

'What's up?' she asked Michel, who was looking at his phone. They had met two months before, at a co-working space, just a few days after she had moved to Uzès. She had been looking for a place to work outside her house, somewhere with a decent internet connection and where she could meet some people too. She had been overjoyed to find a collective of independent workers in such a small provincial town. Michel, who ran a recruitment agency from another desk and, as she had later discovered, several more or less legal businesses, had been the first to introduce himself. He was funny, flamboyant and generous and had made a point of introducing her to lots of people in town. They had become firm friends.

'Got a job for you.'

'Don't tell me! Pierrot the cheesemonger has asked you to hire him to help him on the markets!'

He looked at her, smiling. 'Darling, please,' he said in his unique over-the-top style, 'I don't send people like you to work on markets.'

He picked a cigarette from the packet in front of him on the table and held it between his long fingers just as an espresso and a glass of water appeared as if by magic in front of Léa. 'No, it's much better than that.'

'There's nothing wrong with working on markets. I'm just not sure I could stand the smell of cheese all day long though,' she added before taking a sip of her coffee while he lit his cigarette.

With Michel, better could mean many things. He had offered her a job in a small supermarket a few weeks after they had met, saying it would be a brilliant way for her to meet people. She had laughed at him then and said no. Having just arrived in Uzès; she had thought she had enough savings to keep her going until she sold her London flat.

'Well, as luck would have it, I need to find a French teacher to help a thirteen-year-old boy improve his French language skills. The kid is British, so you need to speak both languages if you see what I mean. The perfect job for you.'

'I don't need a job, Michel, as I've told you before. What I need is to find a story, something I can write a novel about.'

'Well, you never know it could give you ideas.' He paused, dragging on his cigarette. 'It doesn't matter anyway because you've got the job.'

He had noticed her surprise as he continued before she could talk. 'They need someone to start as soon as possible and I've got no one else who can do the job apart from you.'

She was not speechless for long. 'Michel, I could probably teach English but I'm really not sure about French.'

'You write French better than I do despite having spent the last twenty years of your life in England, so please stop the modesty Léa.'

'Kids are not my forte,' she started, noticing that the foreign man was looking in their direction. She had the feeling it was her that he was looking at and felt like covering her bare legs. She pulled at her skirt.

'He's thirteen. There are lots of things you can do with a thirteen-year-old.'

'And you would know how?'

'My cousin Fred has a kid the same age.'

'Who you entertain often?' she said, sarcasm in her voice. She had never heard of Fred or his child and did not put it past Michel to tell her a white lie to sell her the assignment.

He pulled on his cigarette and looked at her, his eyes smiling. 'The thing is babe, this job is super well paid. We're talking 4,000 euros for a month. I'll give you 3,000.'

'And what do they expect for that sum exactly?'

Michel cleared his throat and fixed something on the table. 'They want you to spend four hours a day with him every day except at the weekend.'

She looked at him in disbelief, her anger rising. 'I can't spend four hours a day with a teenager. I don't do babysitting and I've got work to do.'

'Yep, but you told me yourself you needed money until they sold your London flat. And remember that in a place like here, a sum like that goes a long way.'

He was right. The few savings she had had dwindled steadily since her move back to France. The London flat she shared with her ex had found a buyer, but the contract was still up in the air. She would not see her share of the deposit for another few weeks at the very least. Her earnings from her work as a translator and editor would not be enough to make ends meet once her savings were gone, and finding work had proven more difficult than she had expected. Luckily, she was only paying a nominal rent on the house she lived in, though this was because the owners were looking at selling it and needed someone to move out at short notice. And once they had sold the house, she would need to find a flat or house and it would be expensive even outside of tourist season. This was Provence. To make matters worse, it was now high summer and within a week, most companies she could expect freelance work from would shut down for the traditional three-week August holiday. She threw her head back and breathed in deeply. What did she have to lose? Surely looking after a teenager could not be that hard.

As she kept quiet, Michel moved forward in his seat.

'Listen Léa, I understand you might not want this job but I need your help. At least until I find someone else. You'd do me a huge favour. It's summer now, and business isn't exactly booming. And it'll be worse in August. 1,000 euros would help.'

She had known for a while that Michel was living small contracts and his boyfriend's salary so the speech did not surprise her but she let him stew a little longer. She finished her espresso and shook her head, a couple of curls falling forward.

'Give me some time to think about it.'

'How long?' did he ask, playing with his lighter.

'A few days?'

'They need someone to start at 10am on Monday. I need an answer today.'

She struck the armrests of her chair, her voice rising.

'Monday morning? When did you plan to tell me Michel?'

'It's not my fault if they only confirmed late last night,' he said while picking up another cigarette.

She sighed heavily, pinning a curl back.

'What's his level of French?'

Michel shrugged. He had obviously no idea and had not asked. She sighed again before getting up.

'Is that a yes?' he asked, holding the hibiscus while she put her basket on her shoulder.

'Don't know. I'll call you this afternoon.'

2

Uzès is a small town, and it only took her a few minutes to go
from the market square to the house Léa was renting, but her
dress was sticking to her skin by the time she reached her front
door.

Inside, the coolness almost surprised her. She left her basket
and the hibiscus in the kitchen and opened both the kitchen
door and the double doors in the lounge that gave onto the
small courtyard. Thanks to a large oak tree planted near the
dividing wall, the courtyard was half in the shade in the middle
of the day. She took the hibiscus and put it on the antique white
metal table and admired it for a while. It would be perfect
against the ochre wall in that lovely green glazed pot she had
brought back from London.

She looked around with pride at the freshly painted wall and
little lights she had installed. The only thing that was left to do
was to spruce up the borders running along the walls. It was the
in-kind payment she had offered her parents' neighbours when
they had kindly agreed to let her stay for a nominal rent until
they sold the house.

She wondered who would buy such a house. She could not
see it being bought as a holiday home. It was highly desirable
because of its situation right in the middle of the 'quartier
préservé' in Uzès which meant that there were no electric poles
or disfiguring road signs but it was fairly small - a lounge-
dining room downstairs with a long thin kitchen and a small

toilet and two bedrooms and a bathroom upstairs. Because of the size of the walls, it was quite dark inside despite some walls having been painted white. She could imagine it being a little damp in the winter months, too. Her father had told her that the people who owned the house had inherited it from an old aunt. In Léa's mind, it explained why it had been refurbished to the bare minimum with just a coat of paint and a few commodities so that it could be rented to holiday-makers. The flagstones on the ground floor had been cleaned, and the wooden floors in the bedrooms polished. It was rustic and probably not what affluent travellers would be expecting in this posh area of Provence.

But to Léa, the greatest feature of the house was the little courtyard at the back. It was only six by ten metres and could be accessed by double French windows from the lounge and a door from the kitchen. Besides the tree and the borders, two weather-beaten white iron-wrought chairs and a round table completed the picture.

After spending twenty years in London in tiny, poky flats with no outdoor space, she just loved the fact that she could come out at any time of the day and sit outside, from sunrise to sunset.

She looked at the house and wondered not for the first time if she could buy it one day. A church bell somewhere rang. Eleven o'clock. A beep on her phone brought her back to reality.

Sorry to insist but can't find no one else to put forward for the job. Have you decided? Please remember it is super well paid! Jobs like these don't grow on trees around here.

Michel. She knew he would try again, but she had hoped it would give her an hour or two to think about it. She bit her bottom lip. She should have told him no straight away rather than procrastinate. The doorbell rang. Her answer would have to wait a little longer.

The light blinded her when she opened the front door, so much so she did not recognise the postman straightaway.

'Hello, Madame Pasquier. I have a registered letter for you.'

Léa recognised the British stamp and her heart jumped in her chest. Could it be that her London flat had sold at last?

As she closed the door, she could feel her heart beating hard in her chest. Her hands were clammy and shook as she tore the envelope. The letter was from the agent, but it was not good news. The potential buyer could not find the money and so they were back to square one. They were still hopeful to find her a buyer soon; it was only a matter of time, etc… The usual sales pitch.

Tears started running before she could stop them, and she slid slowly against the wall until she was down on the flagstones. She stayed there a while, her head between her hands, crying. This was harder to take than expected. Selling the flat was not only meant to end a painful period of her life but to enable her to live decently in Provence. But three months later, all the promises they had made her were just that promises.

She felt in limbo, waiting for this sale to come through before she could finally launch herself into writing a book, buy a house, settle down. All she seemed to have been doing since moving back was surviving, living from dead-end jobs which had enabled her to make her savings last until now.

But more than anything else, this letter was a personal humiliation that she could not ignore. It artificially prolonged a relationship that she had wanted to forget. William. She had left him in March because he loved another. Ten years of life together, of love given for nothing, to discover on a chilly morning a text that explained a lot about his business trips and his work nights that seemed to last long into the night. She had felt so stupid not to have understood sooner what had been going on right before her eyes. She smiled through her tears. There was solace in that letter, though: he was in the same situation, unable to buy another flat with the woman who had taken her place.

She sighed and raised her head. She would get there, even if it would take her longer than she had hoped. She had never given up; she was not about to now. And, in truth, she was happier here in France than she had been in London for many years. Yes, she had loved that city fiercely when she had first moved there because everything felt possible if you tried. And it had worked for her for a while. First a job as an assistant in a small independent publishing house, then going up the ladder slowly, moving companies, going from one middle-management post to another, meeting her boyfriend, finally being able to rent a flat and not share after ten years, buying a place of their own. Long before she left William, she had known that she would soon have to head somewhere else, do something else. But coming 'home', to France, had long felt like an admission of defeat, of failure. She had left to build a better life all these years before. Awake at night, she had wondered how she could justify to those she had left in France her return. And yet, in March, because of something she had missed the signs of, it had happened and she had gone back to France with little more than she had left with twenty years earlier.

Léa stood up slowly and dried her tears with the back of her hand. She stepped in the courtyard and looked at the hibiscus. Its orange flowers were just as beautiful as before. Given the circumstances, though, this had been a small folly, and she would have to rein in her expenses in the coming days. Unless… Unless she agreed to take that job that Michel had just offered her. Her little grandma, who had gone too soon, often said that sometimes a door closes so that another can open. Take opportunities where they are rather than where you want them to be.

But how could she teach French to a teenager when teaching had never attracted her? She had never given private lessons, not even when she had been at university. And how could she teach a language that she did not know as well as before? Twenty years spent living and working in London had made her lose her French a bit. It was coming back but no parents who cared about their child would have agreed to let her teach them French.

3

Mark Hunter was a tough man to please. A highly successful hedge fund manager, he expected the best from everyone, from his employees to his kids. When he had asked his personal assistant to book a villa near Avignon in Provence for six weeks, she had known exactly what he was looking for and had made sure everything would be as he expected things to be. He smiled as he surveyed her find and made a mental note that she should receive a generous bonus for doing such a perfect job.

The house was located at the edge of a tiny honey coloured village five kilometres out of Uzès. It was an area he knew a little for having spent a magical three days there when he had been a student, thirty years before. Then he had been travelling with a group of friends on an allowance given to him by his father. They had spent most of their money on food and booze and slept in some pretty awful places. But then, he had been in love with a girl. He sighed. The situation could not have been more different this time around.

Max, his eldest son, Freya Abbott, his current girlfriend, and himself had travelled by private jet to a small airport near Nîmes the day before. The latest Range Rover had been waiting for him at the airport and they had made the twenty-minute journey to the house by themselves, their luggage following behind.

The large bastide dated back to the eighteenth century according to the estate agent and was set on a hill overlooking a valley of fields and vines. The owners had modernised the old building with care. The walls and beams throughout the ground floor had been sanded but left bare, giving it a rustic feel. Chic furniture in white and muted grey tempered this. The kitchen was state-of-the-art and the cook, Manuela, had been waiting for them when they arrived. A large terrace ran around the south side of the house, most of it shaded by a wisteria covering a pergola. He shaded his eyes and looked at the swimming pool shimmering in the sunshine in the garden below. He could hear his son splashing in the pool and make out the shape of Freya on one of the sun loungers.

He walked around the house and to the ornate wrought-iron gate, which opened onto a lane that joined the main road a little further on the right. He turned around and slowly walked back towards the house. It was almost seven and the soft evening light played on the golden colour of the stones. The smell of lavender and rosemary baked by the sun all day was pungent in the air. He took a deep breath, trying to lift the heaviness that weighed upon him. It would be a good holiday. He had to believe that it would.

Back on the terrace, the young woman who would be their cook and cleaner came and set a plate of antipasti on the coffee table before asking him what he would like to drink. He asked for a glass of one of the whiskies - with ice and no water - he had had shipped to the house together with several cases of wine before they arrived. She was back almost immediately.

He sat in one of the comfortable dark grey rattan armchairs on the terrace, took a sip, and looked over the valley. The stress of the last few weeks hit him like a wave, and he had to close his eyes. He hoped he would not have to go back to London. He needed some time to breathe and to find out what was missing in his life.

He was starting to relax when Max arrived from the swimming pool dripping water all over the flagstones. It annoyed him, but he told himself not to scold him. The psychotherapist had said it was important.

The fact was that Max worried him. A tall and gangly boy,

with deep blue eyes and soft curly dark brown hair, he looked like a younger version of himself. But this was where the similarities ended. In character, Max could not have been more different. While Mark had been an outgoing child and teenager, not afraid of trying anything, Max was extremely shy. This was not new. He had been a quiet boy even as a toddler, and losing his mother when he was just nine had not helped. His schooling at a prestigious school for boys in London had seemed to compound the issue and make him not only shy but withdrawn. Mark had tried to get him out of his shell and encourage his pursuits, but after a while the constant silent battles had just felt pointless and they had both slowly retreated to their corners. The only positive was that his son was highly intelligent. Unfortunately, it had turned out to be a problem at school where he had been picked on and bullied. Max had begged him to change schools, but so far he had made no decision. Should he tell him to stick to it and fight or yield and find another school? It was another decision that needed to be made. Soon.

Looking at him now, he wondered how one could have children that were so different. His second son, Tom, who was staying at his widow's parents for the next three weeks, was the complete opposite and so much more like him, although in looks he had taken after his mother. He felt much closer to his five-year-old than to his eldest son and wondered, not for the first time, if Max and him would ever get closer.

'How was the water?' he said, trying to sound cheerful.

The boy grinned. 'Great Dad.'

'Sit down for a sec. On a chair, please.'

Mark moved forward in his armchair, arms on his knees, his fingers touching lightly. 'I am thinking of getting you some French lessons while you're here.'

Max looked down, his bottom lip quivering, and Mark felt anger rising in him. He would have preferred the boy fighting him rather than this limp response. Why couldn't he just be a teenager? He breathed in, trying to calm himself. 'Ms. Watkins, your French teacher, said you've got a gift for the language and she believes that you could be fluent soon if you just practice a little this summer.'

He paused again, looking at his son. He was fixing something on the floor and knew he would not meet his gaze.

'What do you think? I've been told the woman who would teach you is lovely and funny and speaks fluent English. She apparently lived in London for many years before moving back here.'

Somewhere at the back of his mind guilt rose, and he added, 'so you should have plenty to talk about.'

Max finally looked up to him, shivering.

'Are you cold, Max? Go and get dressed before you catch a cold.'

The boy swallowed hard before getting up. 'When do I start?'

This was better that he had hoped, despite the resignation in his son's eyes. 'Don't know yet. Monday, probably.' He paused. 'I'm sure she'll be great.'

He dearly wished it would be the case when he saw his son walked head down into the house. He finished his whisky and went into the lounge to find the bottle and make a call.

4

Freya Abbott looked at herself naked in the standing mirror of the bedroom. She may soon turn thirty-three, but she looked good. Not an ounce of fat on her, long lean limbs, which the fake tan she had had sprayed on in an expensive beauty salon in Mayfair helped looked even better. She grabbed a skintight black dress she had bought especially for this trip and sighed. If only Mark had rented a villa on the Côte d'Azur instead of this place in the middle of nowhere. Uzès might well have been in authentic Provence with its pretty villages, but nightlife was non-existent.

As far as she could remember Freya Abbott had always had what she wanted. And Mark Hunter had fallen into that category as soon as she had set her eyes on him. They had met at a dinner party given by Alex Stevens, her god-father, and she had decided there and then that she would sleep with him. Alex had introduced him as a banker, but working in the financial industry she had known exactly who he was. A very gifted and well-respected financier, and a very rich man at that.

It was not that she had fallen in love with him. Looking at him sitting on the terrace, she did not feel love. But she had known then that to be seen going out with someone like him would open doors for her who was arriving from her natal New York and that the perks would be great too. She had not planned on their affair to have lasted more than a few months, which was time enough for her to get what she wanted from him, but five months later they were still seeing each other and she was fine with that. The reasons for this state of affair were simple: they had great sex, something that had surprised her but had also transformed what she saw as her making "a small sacrifice" for her career and bank balance into a pleasure rather than a chore, and they were keeping each other at arm's length. He had never asked her to stay at his house, always sleeping at hers and leaving very early in the morning, and had not promised more than taking her out and buying her whatever she wanted. Their little arrangement had worked well and even though she had not always been faithful to him - she had needs after all and a few nights a month of great sex were far from enough for her - it had so far given her pretty much everything she had wanted.

She had been careful to appear coy and not greedy, knowing that the greater prize was winning his influence on some deals she was working on. So far that had not worked as well as she had hoped, but she knew people thought that if she could bed him - he was seen as having become a true bachelor since his wife's passing - she could get anywhere. It had not done her professional reputation any arm, and she was pleased to see the face of some women when they went out together.

It was only in the last few weeks, since hitting thirty-three, that she had wondered if she should not try to get more out of this relationship. She had never wanted to be married and had no desire for children, but she could see what being married to a man like him could do for her. She would have nothing to worry about for the rest of her life, and he would not prevent her from working. Mark was one of those men who liked their women active, well-groomed and sharp. And if it did not work out between them, she could always divorce and cash a huge cheque, possibly even half of his fortune. The payout even with a pre-nuptial agreement would be substantial. Gone were the days of the little poky house she had lived in with her mother when her father had died unexpectedly, leaving them almost penniless.

She had expected some resistance on his part when she had suggested one night that maybe they could see each other more often. He had been dead against it at first, but then out of the blue; he had asked her if she wanted to come with him for ten days to this place he was renting for the summer in the South of France. Convinced that they would live it up on the Riviera she had shown as much enthusiasm as she could, imagining their life in Cannes or Saint-Jean Cap Ferrat where she could show off her expensive wardrobe. She had even gone as far as dreaming of lounging by the pool all day, getting drunk and making love in the afternoon before going dancing all night. Except that a few days before they were due to leave, she had realised that Max, Mark's eldest son, would be with them and that had made her very cross. She had met both boys the weekend before and while she had found the youngest, Tom, funny and lovable like a puppy, Max had been quiet, even resentful towards her. She had told Mark who had dismissed it as teenage behaviour but she had not been so sure and now; she was stuck with him here. She could see it was more than just teenage behaviour. She did not like him, just as he did not like her. She felt that he could read her intentions towards his father and worried that he could scupper her plans if he wanted to. The only positive thing as far as she could see was that father and son did not get on well.

She looked out the window to Mark again and wondered if she should find an excuse and go back to to London. He looked distant even since they had arrived. Even during their love-making session the day before - he had not touched her since - she had felt him distracted, like he was not there. She was sure he had even avoided her kiss at one point. She could make a scene and say she would leave if he did not look after her better, but she knew him well enough to know that he would not stand for it. Her survival instinct told her to be patient. She would find out in time what was behind his moods. And she had plenty of tricks up her sleeve to make him beg her for more.

5

Sunday morning was sunny and Mark woke up early. Seven feels like a luxury when you are up at five thirty every day. He looked at the naked form of Freya lying on her stomach next to him. Her skin looked silky in the soft morning light, but he did not feel like touching her. They had had another blazing row the night before as she wanted to party in Nîmes and he did not. It was not the first, and he knew that it was unlikely to be the last. She had stormed off to their bedroom long before he had gone upstairs. When he had finally joined her, she was asleep.

He had drunk a lot more than he should have, and yet he felt strangely clear headed that morning. He got in the pool and powered through length after length, feeling the cool water glide along his body, his muscles burning. After a while he turned on his back and lay still, looking at the sky. It was pure blue with just a couple of wispy clouds moving south. He could feel the warmth of the sun on his body. He thought of Max. Maybe telling him he would take French lessons during the holidays the night before had not been his finest hour. He could almost hear Sarah, his widow, telling him he needed to spend more time with him, that he could not expect to connect with the boy by expecting him to be like him. His personal assistant had told him that the guy at the agency had assured her he had the perfect person for Max. She spoke English and was lovely; he had said. Floating around the pool, he hoped she would be as good as she had been described. He could not face spending days after days on his own with his son. He just could not.

He had wondered as soon as she had said 'I spent twenty years in London' if it was her, the teacher his personal assistant had found for Max. He had turned around when he had seen the cheesemonger waved to someone behind him more out of curiosity than anything else and there she was, the woman in the coral-coloured dress who had caught his eye just a few moments before. For once in his life, he had been speechless, bewitched by her dark brown eyes under perfectly arched eyebrows. He had wanted to say something but Freya had turned up in her tight dress and ridiculous shoes and he had turned back and tried to focus on her. She had been complaining all morning that he was not looking after her. Having tried and failed to bring him back to bed after he had gone swimming, she had been both clingy and sharp. So focused he had been on the woman behind him, he had only vaguely heard her say something like this was not the Côte d'Azur, that people looked shabby, that the cobbles were damaging her Manolos. He had wondered then - like now - why he had asked her to come and had cursed himself for not finding something to say to the beautiful stranger behind him while they were waiting to be served. He had felt the hairs on the back of his neck rose as his thoughts had turned to her again. She had come to their help and again he had found himself unable to say anything of substance. It was probably for the best if she was going to work for him this summer.

As Freya kept complaining about her shoes, he had suggested they stopped at a café more in the hope of seeing the beautiful stranger again than because he cared about her shoes. And she had appeared again. She had kissed a guy who seemed to have been waiting for her on the cheek and they had laughed at the large pot plant she was carrying. There had been something sexy, earthy about her. Her dress had gone up her thighs a little as she carried a heavy bag on her shoulder, revealing toned, sun-kissed legs. She had waved and said 'Ciao!' to her companion and disappeared from view in one of the side streets. He had wished then, he had been on his own to offer his help to help carry her purchases home. Why had he invited Freya to come here?

Lunch back at the house after the market had been a sorry affair. Max had not said a word and Freya had picked at her food like she always did. He had felt like telling her to stop and eat. Her stick thin arms and bony shoulders stuck out and, suddenly, it felt unhealthy. But the tension had not gone between them, and he had thought better than to push it. The heat had been intense on the terrace under the wisteria and they had all retired to the house: Max to a corner of the lounge with his tablet and Freya had gone upstairs.

He had moved to the library, hoping to find a book to read before going up to their bedroom. Freya had been lying half-naked on the bed. She had looked asleep, and he had watched her a while standing by the window. He had been about to walk away when she had called to him.

'Mark?'

'What is it?'

She had got up and walked to him in that feline way of hers. Her arms had gone around his neck and he had felt her breasts pushing against his chest, the smell of her heady perfume. She had kissed him deeply. 'Come to bed,' she had whispered. He had resisted until the warmth and softness of her body had eroded the last of his willpower and Freya's expert hands had done the rest. He had kissed her back and pushed her onto the bed.

He had hoped that sex would ease the feeling of emptiness that seemed to be a constant with him of late. It usually did. And maybe for a few fleeting moments it had. But as he had laid next to her, his eyes fixed on the ceiling, he had wondered how long this affair could go on. He had always known it would come to an end and had made no secret about it. It had been like a commercial transaction between them. She wanted to be seen on the arm of a successful man, and he had needed sex for relief. Still, at the back of his mind, he had hoped that this relationship would fill a void too, but like all the others since his wife had died; it had not. The picture of the woman on the market had come back to him. She had been floating around in his mind all along.

Thinking about it now, floating around in the pool, something stirred in him. He could see in his mind's eye her curves under her dress, her sun-kissed skin. He wondered what it would feel like to touch Léa Pasquier.

6

Sunday afternoon and Léa kept pacing up and down the courtyard. This offer of a job that she had accepted, and for which she should have been grateful for, still grated on her. It was not so much the last-minute offer from Michel which annoyed her although, thinking about it, she was not pleased about that. It was something else. Something deeper. No, she could not do it. She would not do it.

She picked up her keys and let herself out. Outside, the heat of the day radiated off the old townhouses and pools of sunlight played on the cobbled lanes as shadows lengthened. She was still trying to come up with what she would say to Michel when she rang the bell of his flat. He lived just outside the old city, in a dead-end lane on the top floor of a two-storey building that had seen better days. The door opened, and she launched herself into her speech.

'Michel, I'm sorry but I just can't take this job. I've thought long and hard about it and…'

A tanned hand touched her arm as the dangling beads behind the door revealed the smiling face of Luca, Michel's partner.

'Sorry to disappoint you my love but Michel is out.'

'Where is he?' Her voice came out harder than she had wanted to and she forced herself to breathe.

'At his Dad's, in Arles.'

He moved aside and smiled that big smile of his. 'Come in. I think you need to tell me what this is about as I have no idea.'

She hesitated, but having come all this way, she did not feel like going straight back. Maybe Michel would turn up if she waited a while. She slipped between Luca and the wall and moved towards the light of a small terrace on the other side of the flat.

'Put the papers on the floor and make yourself at home. Give me two secs and I'll be back.'

Léa did as she was told and settled in a comfortable rattan chair. She could hear Luca in the kitchen just off the terrace, but felt too deflated to wonder what he was doing. Had Michel guessed that she would have second thoughts and had gone out so that she could not speak to him? She knew that there was no point in calling him. He would most certainly not pick up the phone.

Luca came back with a bottle of rosé and two glasses, which he placed on the small table between them.

'Luca, that's lovely but really, I should leave you in peace...' He waved her with his free hand and poured two glasses before putting the bottle back in a terracotta cooler.

'Tell me what you think of this one.'

She picked up the glass and smelled the wine before taking a sip. It was cool and round with hints of red fruits.

'It's good. Where did you get it from?'

'The Lubéron. I chose it myself. It's for the restaurant.' They clinked their glasses before taking another sip.

'Your Dad must be proud.'

He shrugged. Theirs was not a family where you gave compliments freely. You worked hard, and that was that. But she saw in his eyes a bit of pride.

She had met Luca shortly after Michel when he had invited her for a drink and introduced him as his partner. They could not have been more different. Michel, skinny, loud and of a nervous disposition; Luca, built like an ox, quiet and taking life as it came. Luca was the son of Italian immigrants who had fled Mussolini before the Second World war and settled in Uzès. To survive after the war, his grandparents had opened a restaurant that his parents still ran. He had expected to take over from his father when he had reached retirement age late the year before, but the old man was still there and very much in charge. Léa knew Luca had plans to modernise the restaurant, but so far his father had not allowed him any say in the running.

'What's this job about then?' he said sitting back in his chair, his glass of rosé in his large hand.

Léa sighed. What could she tell him? She did not want to put Michel in a tough position.

'Michel offered me a job yesterday.' She paused. 'Starting tomorrow morning.'

He said nothing, and she felt obliged to continue. 'It's teaching a thirteen-year-old British kid French.' She looked away. 'I didn't want to do it but I had a letter about my London flat yesterday.' She paused. 'The sale's fallen through so the money would be good. But I'm just not sure I can do this.'

There was a silence and all she could hear was the hum of the city and the cicadas.

'Why not?'

She looked at Luca and took a sip of her wine. 'I'm not good with children. I don't have any you see. And I've never taught French.'

He said nothing.

'Oh, I don't know Luca! I accepted the job because I need the money, but I don't think I can do it. What am I going to do? I have to spend four hours a day with this boy!'

A tear ran down her cheek, and she wiped it away with her hand. Before she could say anything, Luca was next to her on his knees, his arm around her shoulders.

'Hey, why do you worry so much? You'll be fine. It's just nerves. It doesn't matter that you don't have children or that you've never taught French. If they accepted you, then it doesn't matter to them that much.'

She wanted to say that she did not think Michel had explained that to the employer, but he was shushing her and for a moment she just felt safe in the embrace of this gentle man letting her cry on his shoulder. After a while he took her hand.

'Léa listen. You need to stop begrudging your talents. You

really do. You're good, girl! Come on, you lived in another country on your own for twenty years! What on earth are you afraid of? You need to get out there and be proud of yourself. I know Michel probably embellished the whole thing, but he had only your best interests at heart.'

She shook her head, but he continued. 'No, he did. He is a good salesman, I give you that, but he also knows, like I know, that you're brilliant. You deserve that job. You deserve to do well. Man, if I'd done only half of what you've done, I'd be shouting about it from the rooftops. You've got to believe in yourself, Léa.' He wiped a tear from her face and kissed her hair.

'But what if I fail?'

'Why would you fail? If it doesn't work out, it's not necessarily because of you. It's a like recipe. Everything has to come together. The ingredients, the temperature, the expertise of the chef. But why wouldn't it? You've got to give it a try. It's just nerves.'

She put her arms around his neck and hugged him. 'Thank you,' she whispered.

He pulled away and she could see the shyness returning to him. For all the bravura speech of the last couple of minutes, he was a quiet man.

'Just promise me you'll go to the interview tomorrow?'

She nodded and dried her tears. He poured more rosé in their glasses.

'Now come with me to the kitchen. I'll cook something for you.'

They moved to the compact kitchen, which was bathed in the orange glow of sunset. Léa sat on a stool, her glass in front of her. She had never seen Luca cook before and was fascinated by the dexterity with which he prepared several dishes. The room soon smelled of onions, garlic and oregano.

'Where did you learn to cook?'

He smiled and shrugged. 'In my grandma's kitchen. When I was small, I wasn't allowed in the kitchen at the restaurant, so I'd spend time with her and she'd teach me all the Italian recipes that she knew. I loved it. Just her and me in the kitchen.'

'Why don't you cook at the restaurant Luca?'

'Wait until you've tried it, you may not like it!' he said with a laugh. 'Dad wants to keep the restaurant as a pizzeria when I think it should become an Italian restaurant.' He shrugged, his eyes fixed on the worktop.

'Did you go to cooking school?'

He laughed and threw his head back. 'Hell no! I was sent to a catering college when I was fifteen, but I knew everything there was to know already about laying tables and serving customers. A proper cooking school would have been better, but it was too far and my parents needed me to help, so I stayed here. Maybe if I had, I could fight my corner a little better. But then again, maybe not.'

'What will you do when your Dad finally retire and leave you to run the place?'

He stopped cutting red peppers into thin strips and looked at her. 'I'd like to change the restaurant a bit, you know. But it'll depend on the money and whenever my father finally hangs his hat.'

'Have you always known what you wanted to do? I mean, when you were a child, did you know?'

He looked at her, surprised. 'Yes, no, I don't know. I guess I didn't have much of a choice but I've always loved cooking and looking after people so it's kind of natural. What did you want to do when you were a kid?' he said, putting the terracotta dish in the oven.

She pouted. 'I've dreaded that question all my life. I didn't know and I still don't know.'

'You had no idea at all?'

'I had ideas but nothing fitted with what was expected of me.'

'Expected?'

'I did well at school and I felt everyone expected me to go into a profession like lawyer or doctor. But isn't it what happens to all of us?'

He shook his head. 'I do what I like. If I'd wanted to do something else, I'd have gone for it. Life's too short.'

'Even with your parents expecting you to take over the

restaurant?'

'They never expected me to do anything. If anything, I think they'd have preferred that I didn't go into the restaurant trade. It'd have made the transition easier for them.' He sipped more of his wine before sitting down next to her on a stool. 'Is this why you went to London? To be free of expectations?'

Léa smiled. 'You know me far too well Luca!' clinking her glass against his. 'I guess so. I just knew I wanted to work in publishing, London was my escape.' She was lost in her thoughts. 'I guess coming back here is another escape. Maybe I don't want to face things.'

'I think you just need to give yourself some time. It'll be when you least expect it that the answer will come to you!'

They laughed, and she felt better for having talked to him. It was not the first time that she noticed that he had this emollient effect on her. Luca lived in the present with the set of circumstances that were his. She had to learn to be more like him, to stop letting her thoughts grow into those uncontrollable paralysing fears. She may not have had time on her side, but she had possibilities.

7

Léa did not sleep well that night. The heat was intense, and her mind kept racing. She could not help but think she knew nothing about children and even less about teenagers. She had hoped that putting some ideas on paper would help, but it was not enough to cast her doubts away. When her mind finally exhausted itself, it was four in the morning and she felt groggy when the alarm clock went off at seven. She dressed carefully. She chose a blue skirt that fell just under her knees and a white broderie anglaise top with fluttering sleeves. A pair of espadrille wedge sandals and her gold bracelet - her lucky charm, a present from her beloved grandmother - completed the look. She twisted and pinned her curls in a loose bun at the back of her head and applied as little make-up as she could get away with.

Downstairs she made some toasts and a cup of tea and sat in the courtyard reading her notes, but she could not focus. She looked up again on her phone where the house was. Arpaillargues-et-Aureillac was the village, just west of Uzès.

Michel had told her to use his car for the day and she drove carefully out of town. The sun was already high, and she put on the air-conditioning. The image of the impeccable woman at the market on Saturday came back to her. She smiled to herself. She could avoid turning up a sweaty mess, but that kind of perfection was out of her reach.

She found the house more easily than she had hoped and

parked the car under a tree in a lay-by on the main road. She checked herself in the mirror again before walking up the dusty lane to the house. A beautiful iron-gate stood between two solid walls. She took a deep breath and rang the bell. It buzzed shortly after and she walked in. A gravel path surrounded by fragrant borders set among mature trees led up to a heavy wooden front door.

Mark had been up early again. He had a swim, breakfast and had called his London office, then Hong Kong. When he hung up, the clock on his phone showed almost ten. The bell rang shortly after.

As he walked to the door, Manuela came out of the kitchen saying it was the French lady. He smiled and told her he would handle this. He was about to shout for Max, but the boy was at the door already. He smiled to him and ruffled his hair. He felt excited as he was about to open the door. He was not a betting man, but he thought he knew who would be behind the door.

The heavy wooden door opened and Léa looked up. She recognised him instantly and opened her mouth, but no sound came out. He smiled and extended his hand. She took it. It was warm and firm.

'We meet again. Mark Hunter.'

She saw the young man next to him look up at his father with a puzzled look.

'We do, Léa Pasquier.'

'This is my son, Max. Max, this is Léa, your French teacher.'

Léa turned to the boy and smiled as brightly as she extended her hand to him. 'Hello! Or rather, bonjour!'

He took her hand and shook it limply, his eyes not meeting hers. She heard him say a muffled 'Bonjour'.

'Come in,' Mark said, moving aside. 'I need to have a chat with Léa. Go and play. We'll come and find you later.'

Seeing the man she had helped on the market had put Léa ill at ease, but the way he spoke to his son infuriated her. He had just dismissed him without an ounce of warmth. She felt crossed when she saw the boy walk away, his head bowed. They heard him go up the stairs. Mark Hunter looked at her.

'I don't think he is too keen, I'm afraid.'

She could not help thinking she would not be either if she was in the boy's shoes. They walked over sand coloured flagstones and passed a beautiful stone staircase with an elegant black metal railing before walking into a large lounge with low grey sofas. He led her to the terrace through opened French windows and pointed to an armchair while he sat opposite her on a sofa. Dappled light came through the beams of the pergola where a wisteria and a bougainvillea grew. A woman appeared with a pitcher of water and lemon and asked if there was anything else they wanted.

'Water will be fine thank you,' said Léa crossing her legs. She felt slightly nauseous and wished once again she had said no to this job. She caught his eyes going up her legs and smoothed her skirt over her knees while returning his gaze. He would not unsettle her. He was wearing a checkered white and dark blue shirt with dark blue cargo shorts. It all looked expensive in an understated way that made her feel a little shabby.

'Thank you for accepting to do the job at such short notice. I didn't think I'd find someone so quickly, and it's just brilliant that you speak fluent English. My son Max is rather shy as I'm sure you've noticed.'

She nodded and wondered if he had heard any of her conversation with Michel on the place two days before. She had not heard him speak French at the market, but she had not given him a chance too either. She preempted the next question.

'Tell me about him.'

He saw what she was doing and liked it. He liked people who could think on their feet. How would she deal with her lack of teaching experience? He looked forward to that part of the conversation. She was also prettier than he remembered. He just wished she would relax a little and turned on the charm.

'Max turned thirteen three months ago. I'm not sure if you've been told but my wife died a little over three years ago and as you can imagine, it's been hard for him.'

She wondered how it had been for him. She had detected no hint of sorrow in his voice.

'He's not the most confident of boys, but he's very bright and doing well at school. He got top grades in French this year and I thought it would be good for him to benefit from his time here to improve his language skills even further.'

'A month is a long time.'

'Five weeks actually.'

He saw the surprise in her eyes. 'You haven't been told?'

'No, I haven't.' Another piece of information Michel had omitted to tell her.

'Is that a problem?' He hoped it would not as he was starting to thoroughly enjoyed himself.

'It's fine.'

He smiled warmly, and she knew the battle was about to start. She did not avert her eyes. Now that she was here, she might as well give as good as she got.

'So tell me about your teaching experience?'

She smiled before replying. 'You haven't been told, have you?'

She paused, but he did not move. 'I'm not a teacher, I'm a writer and an editor. The agency thought I could probably teach your son French thanks to my fluency in English and writing skills. If you don't feel that's good enough, I would completely understand. I told them as much myself.'

She was prepared to walk away, and he admired her for it. There was nothing that annoyed him more than people who desperately clung to something or caved in at the first hurdle. He shook his head and returned her smile. She would not get away that easily.

'I'm sure you'll do a brilliant job.' He knew as soon as he said it that it sounded patronising and was about to make amends when a woman's voice called him from the lounge.

'Mark? Mark, where are you?'

There was a silence before the woman appeared at the door. Léa recognised her instantly and forced herself not to gawp at her attire. She was wearing a tiny dark blue bikini with a long, sheer navy chiffon cover-up and two very large gold bracelets on each wrist. Her long, straight, black hair was glossy and her make-up as immaculate as it had been two days before.

'Freya I told you I was busy this morning.' His voice was hard and clipped. Léa turned back to him and saw a muscle twitched in his jaw. When he looked back at her, there was anger in his blue eyes that made them appear almost black. She smiled to him and heard Freya's heels clicked on the stone floor behind her. His gaze followed her before focusing again at Léa.

'Where were we?'

'I have something to ask you,' Léa said. She saw the curiosity and the warmth in his eyes return.

'Would you mind terribly if one or two days a week I took your son into town? The best way to learn is by listening and practising, and there are so many things to see in and around Uzès.'

He seemed to hesitate, and she was about to continue when Freya who had sat next to him and put a thin arm in his as if to say 'he is mine', unexpectedly came to her help. 'I think it's a splendid idea, Mark. Max needs to get out of the house. He can't stay cooped up in here for five weeks.'

Léa saw anger flash in his eyes. 'You don't have to give me an answer right away,' she said hoping to pour oil over troubled waters.

He raised a hand as if he was capitulating. 'No, it's fine. I'll give you some money for that. It'll do him good to get out of here.'

Léa thought the same, but not for the same reasons.

'Unless there is anything else you need from me, how about I go and find him?'

'Let me show you—'

'Mr Hunter.' He looked at her, and she felt again as if she was being tested. 'I think it's best if I find him on my own.'

He agreed silently, his eyes locked into hers. 'If you go back through the house and take the stairs to the first floor, his room is the second one on the right.' He hesitated a little before continuing. 'Manuela has been told that you would stay with us for lunch so whenever you're ready just come down.'

* * *

After Léa had left, Mark turned to Freya. Anger and resentment rose in him in equal measures and he got up, concerned that he might otherwise punch her. He walked to the edge of the terrace, taking deep breaths. She was up, her arms folded across her chest in a provocative pause as he turned to face her.

'Who is this woman? Wasn't it her who you spoke to at the market on Saturday?'

His voice had a hint of menace when he spoke. 'I told you I was busy this morning, Freya. I don't appreciate you turning up when I speak to someone from outside.'

'Why? You're sleeping with her?'

He shook his head. 'What are you talking about? I've never met her before in my life.'

'Let me get this straight, this woman made fun of me when I tried to buy something on the market the other day and you were all smiles with her and she turns up again today and I'm supposed to think there's nothing between the two of you?'

He did not reply. What was the point? She could think what she wanted, he did not care anymore. He turned around and walked towards the house.

'Mark!' she shouted as she came after him. But he kept moving and was by the French windows when she grabbed his arm to stop him. He turned to face her slowly. Her eyes glistened, but he was insensitive to her attempt to regain control by playing the victim. They stood facing each other in the full heat of the midday sun.

'Mark baby, I'm sorry. I am, I really am. But you've been acting so strange since we got here. Nothing seems to satisfy you. And then she turns up,' she said, making a gesture towards the house, 'and you're suddenly all smiles. What am I supposed to think?'

She put her hands on his chest, but he moved away. 'I just don't know what to do.'

'I don't know either Freya. But maybe if you behaved better, things would be easier.' He saw the hurt in her eyes but walked away to the library which he had transformed into his office and le himself fall into one of the club chairs. A little later, he heard the tyres on the gravel outside. She was gone. He felt himself breathing more easily.

The image of Léa sat in front of him earlier came back and he closed his eyes. There was nothing fake about her, and he had enjoyed their sparring. But it was something else that had caught his attention. Something he had noticed on Saturday, too. He could not quite put his finger on it, but she intrigued him. He was not entirely sure how to handle her, and he had to admit to himself that he quite liked that. It was a challenge. He could not wait to see how she would get on with Max. For his son's sake and strangely for his too, he hoped it would work out.

Freya stood there watching him walk out of the room. She was angry, but she knew better than to show her temper. She had known as soon as she had mentioned the woman who was now Max's teacher that she should have said nothing, but she had been so incensed when she had seen her through the window she could not keep her mouth shut.

Was he having an affair? The idea seemed ridiculous. She did not think he was capable of two-timing someone. It just was not his style. But there was still a lingering doubt at the back of her mind. She had noticed how enraptured he had been when she spoke to her. The good news was that she would take the brat out a few times a week so she would have Mark to herself. She smiled. He did not know what would hit him. She looked at her fingers. One of her nails was chipped - she would have to complain to the expensive manicurist she used in London - and needed to get it seen to as soon as possible. A trip to the hairdresser would not go amiss either. She picked her phone up and checked what was available in Nîmes. There was no point trying Uzès. What she had seen on Saturday had confirmed that this place was far too provincial for her.

8

Léa went up the stairs slowly, wondering what she would say to Max. She had so little to go on and knew almost nothing about him apart from the fact that he was thirteen, bright and had lost his mother. Strangely, she felt for him too. It must have been strange to be stuck here with his father and his glamorous girlfriend. Given her outburst, Léa bet that she did not like the boy one bit.

On the threshold of the boy's room, she knocked on the door. It was opened, and she poked her head in.

'Hello.'

A small voice told her to come in and she stepped in what was a very large room with two single beds on one side. The walls were painted a light coral colour, and she saw kids' chairs and books on a small table in a corner by one of the windows. A few clothes laid folded on a chair. The lack of chaos surprised her.

Max was sat cross-legged at the head of his bed. He did not move as she came in. She asked if she could sit on the bed next to his and he nodded, his blue eyes framed by long dark eyelashes following her.

'Shall I tell you a bit about me and then you can tell me a bit about you?' said Léa. She felt unsure of herself but knew better than to show it. He nodded, and she started describing her childhood in Paris, then her life in London, her travels. He gradually became animated and before she had finished her story, he was talking about places in London they both knew.

'Now it's your turn, tell me about you?'

A look of terror spread on his face. 'In French?'

She burst out laughing. 'No, let's start in English. We have to spend five weeks together you and I so there'll be plenty of time to speak French.' He relaxed but seemed stuck.

'Tell me about what you like to do.'

She thought it would be best to stay away from school and family given the issues so she stirred the conversation towards sports, films, TV series. A bell rang somewhere, and the boy's eyes lit up.

'Lunch is ready.' He stopped and looked at her in disarray. 'You're staying for lunch, right?'

'Oh yes! You're not getting rid of me like that.'

She followed him downstairs, and he led her to a table on the terrace. A large spread of salads and cold meats had been laid out on the table, but neither Mr Hunter nor his bikini-clad girlfriend were there. The woman she had seen before appeared and introduced herself in French.

'Je suis Manuela. I cook and take care of the house for Monsieur Hunter,' she said, hands on her hips. 'He told me you should not wait for him and start lunch.'

Léa extended her hand to the woman and thought that both of them were the help here. She was glad she was not the only one.

* * * * *

The heat was intense at 3 p.m. when Léa parked Michel's car on the ring road just outside the historical centre. She had agreed to meet him at their usual café on the Place aux Herbes and walked slowly, looking for shade. She needed some time to think about that family and the boy she had just met. By the time she got to the café, she wished she had had time to go home to take a shower and change; she was in a foul mood when she sat down in front of Michel. A glass of rosé was waiting for her on the table. She wondered if it was in anticipation of her giving in.

'So how did it go?' he said, his eyes shaded by his sunglasses. She knew him too well now not to notice the nervous tics like the tapping of his foot on the ground, the fingers playing with his cigarette packet. Still, he had a smile on his face which she did not like. She slowly took a sip of her rosé, enjoying making him wait for an answer.

'Strange family if you ask me.'

'Who cares, they are paying us well.'

Well, it's not you that has to work with them, she thought, but kept the remark to herself. 'You didn't tell me it was for five weeks.'

'A month, five weeks, what's the difference? Think of the money you will make in five weeks - 4,000 euros, give or take.'

She had thought of that and little else while driving back. She was still in two minds about the job, but the money made it hard to turn it down even if she kept telling herself that she could make ends meet without it.

'You did not tell them I was not a teacher.'

Michel smiled. 'They didn't need to know, darling. At the end of the day, they needed someone for their kid quickly and I don't think they cared that much about your qualifications.'

Léa thought he was probably right there. Something Mr Hunter had said came back to her. He thought she would be perfect because she spoke fluent English. 'I feel like I'm going to be a babysitter for the next five weeks, Michel. I'm not sure I like it.'

He shrugged. 'At least he isn't a baby and you won't have to change diapers.'

She kicked his shin under the table.

'Ouch! What was that for?'

'It'll teach you for making fun of me.'

'I'm not.' He paused, took off his sunglasses and looked at her. 'The thing is, I'm grateful for your help on this.' There was a silence before he continued. 'So, are you going to do the job until the end?' He did not say that he needed to know, but she knew that was what he meant.

She moved back in her seat and sipped a little more rosé. She had made her mind while walking to the café: she would not leave Max on his own with that awful woman.

'Yes. If only because that poor kid needs a friend.'

'Pray tell,' he said hooked.

Freya was certainly the villain of the piece, but she was not sure about Mark Hunter either. It was only when she got home later, sitting outside in her small courtyard, that she thought about how he had made her feel. He had been polite and well-behaved except when he had looked her over. She had not been sure if this had been out of an appreciation for her body or the cheapness of her clothes compared to his girlfriend's. He had spared with her but had not baulked when she had replied without flinching. She rather had the impression that he had enjoyed the little battle that had played out between them. Just like he had enjoyed seeing her face when he had opened the door; she had not missed the self-satisfaction on his then.

Yet there had also been a sharpness to him. Not with her, but with Freya. A hidden anger, barely controlled. But then they were a very odd couple. He looked like he was someone in control of his life who should have been married to some well-to-do woman. He had mentioned that his first wife had died and perhaps Freya was just a bit on the side until he found the one. Not that it mattered to her. She had no chance with him and he was not her type. She was also just a few months out of her own relationship disaster and was not ready to start anything new. Hell, she did not even know what she would do in a couple of months from now.

But Mark Hunter and the rich girl just looked wrong for each other. There had been a discordance between them ever since she met them on the market. He had shown no more affection towards her today than he had done when she had kissed him at the café. It was like he did not want to be with her.

And then, Max had only been too eager to share the gossip with her. His father when he had introduced her to him had said that Freya was his best friend Alex's god-daughter, who was also Max's god-father. They had not met until recently because she had been living in the US with her American mother, her British father having died in a car crash when she was very young. Max has also said that both his Dad's mother and sister did not like her. They saw her as a gold-digger, even if she was a high-flying banker or trader - he was not sure - in London. Like them though, he hoped his Dad would get rid of her. Léa wondered how easy that would be. She looked like she would hang on to him for dear life. And although Léa had only glimpsed bits of their lifestyle and heard bits and bobs from Max - they had arrived by private plane and the large Range Rover in the driveway had been waiting for them at the airport - she could understand why Freya would do so.

9

Lying on the bed, his arms behind his head, the light falling, Max felt safe in the darkening room. He liked it that way these days. Obscurity gave him the permission to think about his mother all he wanted. He still missed her every day. It might have been three years since she had passed away, but the pain was the same. Sharp, numbing. He felt almost hollow at times like if, with her going away, there was nothing left inside him, no substance, no love, nothing. He was just an empty shell without her presence and her love.

But even thinking of her every day had not prevented him from losing the memory of her. He felt as if she was ebbing away from him a little more every day, disappearing in a big black hole. It was terrifying. It was an insult to her memory that he could forget the contours of her face, the sound of her voice. So every night, as night fell, he attempted to think of her face, her eyes, the way she used to smile to him. Sometimes when he was lucky, he could almost hear her voice, smell her perfume. But it was getting harder and harder. There was just no denying it.

Outside, the sound of the cicadas had stopped. There seems to be no one in the garden, and yet he knew that his father had not come up. Something was up between him and Freya. Of that he was sure.

He sighed. What a strange day it had been.

He had been worried, maybe even a little afraid, of being

stuck with an old lady in musty clothes, like his teacher, Mrs Watkins, before Léa had turned up. He feared being stuck indoors for four hours each day doing French grammar when all he wanted was to play in the pool. The relief had been physical - he could almost feel it still - when his father had opened the door and this smiling woman had greeted him.

Léa. He could not tell how old she was, but she felt like an older sister rather than a teacher. She had promised that they would do practical stuff rather than sitting indoors and had got his father to agree to her teaching him in Uzès two days a week. He had doubted her at first. His father would never agree to let him or his brother out of sight without a trusted aide. Except that there was no-one filling that role here.

An odd thing had happened when his father had opened the door to Léa. They seemed to have met before. Where could that have been? She had said she had lived in London, but he was pretty sure she had not moved in the same circles as his father. He would have to ask her. Maybe she would tell him. What was sure was that she was not his father's type.

Looking at the stars in the clear night sky - you could see so many here in Provence - he wondered what his mother would have made of her? Would she have liked Léa? He did not know, but tonight, he had hope.

10

Wednesday morning and Léa left her house earlier than she needed to. She did not want Max to wait for her or his father to change his mind about leaving him with her in Uzès. The sun was already high, and it would be another scorching day in Provence. She nodded to a few people she knew and crossed the Place aux Herbes before turning right on rue Jacques d'Uzès. She had ten minutes to spare and decided to nose around the shop windows lining this busy street.

She saw them arrive before they saw her. Mark Hunter stopped his car just at the entrance of the pedestrian street and Max stepped out. She smiled to him as she moved towards him and waved to his father, who nodded. She noticed that Max did not look back. His shoulders were down again, and his face closed. She wondered what could have happened since she had left him the day before.

'How are you this morning?' she said as brightly as she could.

He shrugged as he seemed to fix something on the pavement, and she forced him to look at her. 'How are you doing?'

'Ok. I guess.'

She put her hands on her hips and gave him a conspiratorial look once she knew his father's car had gone. 'What happened? Is it Dad or his girlfriend?'

He looked up, and she saw the beginning of a smile form on his lips. 'A bit of both.'

'They won't be bothering you for the next four hours so let's go, I have plenty of stuff planned for you to do. And we start with a bit of French. How do you call a street in French?'

He answered *rue* as she took him by the arm and pulled him gently along the street. She made him repeat the word until the pronunciation was correct. She had four hours to make him smile again and hopefully regained a little confidence.

She took Max to the medieval garden right in the centre of the city. He had confided to her the first time they met that he loved history. As they took the narrow cobbled lane that led up to the garden and the two towers, Léa explained in simple French what he was about to see.

'The botanical garden was recreated about twenty years ago and shows what plants people used in the Middle Ages to cure the sick, for example.'

'I learnt about that in a book I read. The bark of... What's the name for birch?'

'Bouleau,' said Léa, impressed that he knew the French equivalent of bark.

'That's right, well the bark from birch was used to cure headaches,' he said in shaky but correct French.

'Très bien!' she said clapping her hands as they entered the pretty garden set around the remnants of a small castle. She saw him smiling, and it warmed her heart. All this kid needed was a little encouragement.

She picked up a leaflet in French and gave it to Max. 'Let's see if you can tell me what this is about. The bit about the castle there,' she said pointing to the top of the page, 'but first, let's have a look at the garden and see what plants you recognise.'

Léa loved that secluded garden in the middle of the city. There was always something to discover, an idea for her to pick and try to reproduce in her small courtyard at home.

'Saffron, that's the most expensive spice in the world.'

'Do you know that it comes from crocuses, those colourful flowers that are some of the first to flower in the middle of winter?'

'The purple and yellow ones? Wow! Did you see the magic plants? It's like in Harry Potter!'

'So tell me about this castle, what do you understand from the description?'

He read it again and bit his lip. 'Huh, it was a small castle with two towers. One was sold to the évêques… a religious order?'

'The bishops.'

'In the thirteenth century and they exchanged the other with the French king, Charles VIII. Then, the towers became tribunals and prisons until 1926.'

'You'll see marks left by prisoners inside. Come on, let's go up the tower.'

It was Léa's least favourite part. The staircase to go up the King tower was narrow and only one person could go up and down at one time. Going up, except for the exertion of walking up a hundred stairs, was not the worse. Coming down on the tiny uneven steps always gave her cold sweats.

At the top, she breathed in deeply. It was a gorgeous day with not a cloud in the deep blue sky. From the various maps, you could see points of interest in Uzès and its surrounding areas. Léa pointed out towards the direction of where Max and his family were staying.

'Where do you live?'

'In town, near the Duché. You see, the stout tower with the high walls and the coloured tiles? That's the Duché.'

'Is there a Duke living there?'

'Yep. We'll visit it one of these days. Come, let's go down and have a look at the prison cells.'

'Freya said that I shouldn't be there, and that she hopes Dad will send me back home.'

Léa had finally got Max to say what was bothering him after an hour of touring the shops and the streets. They were sat at a café, one of her favourite, away from the crowds in a small lane near the Place aux Herbes. He had been hard work but by getting him to talk about other things; she had finally got to what she wanted to know.

'Are you afraid that he will?' she said while looking at him playing with the straw in his Coca-Cola.

He shrugged. 'I don't know. I don't think he will.'

'Do you want to go back?'

Suddenly, he was animated and shook his head vigorously. 'No, I don't. I like it here.'

'Good! Then there is nothing she can say or do that will change that. And I don't think your father will send you home now that he has paid me to get you to learn French for five weeks.'

This was not completely true as she had not been paid yet, but this little white lie meant nothing to him. His eyes lit up.

'No, he wouldn't, he can't stand wasting money.'

He was grinning now, and she looked at him more closely. Although he was tall for a thirteen-year-old, you could still see the child in the roundness of his face. He had freckles on his nose that the sun was making more visible. She would have to remind him to make sure he put some sunscreen on in the morning. She bet no one at home had thought of that. She found it difficult to understand why you would bring your child here and spend as little time as possible with him and let that woman bully him. But maybe he did not know. It was none of her business of course but she would have a word with Mark Hunter if Max ever complained about Freya's behaviour again. Someone had to take that child's side. In the meantime, she had to instill some hope in him.

'You know, there is nothing she can do to take your place in your father's heart so you shouldn't be afraid of sticking it up to her.'

'But Dad likes her.'

Léa shook her head. From what she had seen she was not so sure, but he was just too young to understand that.

'He may do, but you're still his son, so you're way more important to him than her.'

He looked down again. 'I don't think he likes me very much.'

She put her hand on the table towards him. 'Max, that's not true.'

'He'd like me to be more like Tom. I know.'

Her heart broke, but she went on. 'How's Tom?'

He looked up at her again. 'I don't know. Not afraid, I guess. Of anything.'

'And are you afraid?'

He nodded.

'Of what? Of your Dad?'

He nodded again.

'He doesn't hurt you, does he?'

He shook his head. 'No, nothing like that but he can get angry when I don't reply quickly enough.'

'Ah! He is a little impatient then,' she said with a sarcastic tone. 'Yes, I can see that quite well now.'

He smiled, and she wanted to tell him that he should not be afraid of his father, but she also knew that it was not that simple. She took out a small paper bag from her handbag and gave it to him.

'This is for you.'

'What is it?'

'Open it.'

He opened the paper bag cautiously and took out the notebook and blue pen. He looked at her, surprised.

'When I was your age, my little grandma gave me a notebook and a pen just like these and told me to write in them every day stating what was wrong and always ending with three positive things that had happened to me during the day.'

'Like a private diary?'

'Like that yes.'

'That's for girls!'

She smiled. 'Not necessarily! Everyone can write. There are male artists, musicians and writers who write every day. Try it. What have you got to lose?'

'Will you read it?'

'Absolutely not! It's for you and you only. Hide it or write in French or in code in it if you wish! Or keep it and write nothing in it!'

As they walked back up the rue Jacques d'Uzès to meet his father, Max suddenly remembered the money he had given him. He pulled open his backpack as if something was burning inside it and took it out.

'Dad asked me to give you this.'

She took the envelope and looked into it. There was at least five hundred euros. She took a hundred and extended the envelope back to him. He looked at her stricken, shifting from one foot to the other. 'I can't do this.'

'Do what?'

'Give Dad the envelope back with most of the money in it. He will be cross with me.'

She smiled. 'Okay, leave it with me. I'll give it back to him when I see him.' She saw his shoulders lift with relief and it pained her. It would take time for him to get his confidence back, but she would not give up.

11

Mark saw her as Max stepped out. He could not help but notice the tanned legs in her laced-up espadrilles, her light yellow shirt dress going up a little where she carried her handbag. Her curly hair was up and held by a clasp at the back of her head, showing her graceful neck. He felt a stab of envy when she walked up to Max, smiling brightly. He thought about parking the car and going for a wander in the historic part of the town but he did not want Léa to think he was checking up on her on the first day she was taking his son into town.

She had been in his thoughts since their meeting three days before. He had gone to bed thinking of her and had woken up thinking of her. There was something about her that stirred something in him. She was so different from the other women he was used to having around him. All were highly sophisticated, power women with egos to match while there was something disarmingly natural about her. A kind of what you see is what you get and I-don't-care-if-you-like-it-or-not. And yet he remembered her twice, first at the market café and then, when she had been sat in front of him feeling a little uncomfortable when his gaze had looked her down. He had found that sweet, cute even. The thing was, he liked the curves of her body a lot more than Freya's skinny frame. He realised as he turned down the drive to the house he had never asked himself these questions before.

Freya was lounging by the pool under a large white umbrella, in a black bikini and an enormous pair of sunglasses, reading fashion magazines when he came back from Uzès. She was wearing a large chunky gold bracelet that he thought inappropriate. He moved a sun lounger next to hers under the umbrella and let his towel and books fall on the chair. She looked up to him from her magazine.

'Shall we go to Nîmes this afternoon? I can't stay here all day. It drives me mad.'

He took his polo shirt off and moved towards the pool. 'Not before I pick up Max at two. But afterwards, why not?'

'Can we go without him?' she said, but he barely heard it as he dived into the cool blue water, an image of Léa standing on the pavement in his mind. When he emerged on the other side of the pool, she had sat up on the lounger, her hands over her long legs, her sunglasses over her hair.

'Mark please.'

'Freya, I can't leave my son on his own all day. You know that. I told you before we came here. If that doesn't work for you then you're free to go. I understand.'

She was pouting, and he knew she would not leave as it would have meant accepting defeat.

She got up, took her sunglasses off and moved to the pool, her lithe and toned body shimmering in the heat. Many men would not have resisted her and, in truth, he had not when she had offered herself to him. She had flirted with him at that party months ago and he had felt flattered. It had been easy, and until recently it had worked well. He would see her now and then, they would have dinner or got to a party and then he would go to her place. They would have sex and then got their separate way the next day. Since the death of his wife, it had been the only kind of relationships he had wanted: intelligent women who, like him, wanted nothing complicated. No promises of everlasting love or marriage. Just a few outings, maybe a long weekend somewhere. He was happy to pay and be generous as long as he was not asked for more than that. The other women he had gone out with before Freya had had enough at some point and had found men who offered more - one was married now - but that had not made him change his mind. He did not want a long-term relationship. So Freya's neediness since they had arrived in Uzès grated on him. He suspected that she was hoping for a lot more than he was prepared to give and had misread his intentions. The only reason he had asked her to come to France with him had been his fear of being alone with Max for two weeks. He could see the stupidity of that now as he looked at her getting gingerly into the water. As she finally released herself from the edge of the pool, he promised himself that he would put an end to this soon. She would not ruin his holiday.

She swam to him and put her arms around his neck.

'Babe, I'm sorry, I know you want to spend time with Max but we need time to ourselves.' Her voice was all sweetness and light, but he did not budge, his hands gripping the stone rim of the pool behind him.

'Maybe we could go out tonight? Have dinner in town?'

He did not reply, and she kissed him, her body touching his, her legs rubbing against his. All he could think was what it would feel if it was Léa that was there kissing him.

'Sure' was all he could find to say when she released his lips. He pushed her arms and her body away from him, sliding under water, getting as far from her as possible.

Mark drove back into town shortly after two. It was quiet at that time of the day, most people were either napping or staying in the shade as the heat was at its highest. Thirty-nine degrees said the screen on his dashboard. He was not going to park but found a space and decided that a walk would do him good. He lost himself in the pedestrian cobbled streets of the old town before spotting Léa and Max at the end of the street she had picked him up on earlier. They were joking and jostling and he stopped to look at them for a minute. Max was laughing and looked happier than he had been for a long time.

As he approached them in the sun-baked street, he noticed the change in his son. Gone was the bright smile, and the relaxed demeanour. Léa, at least, was smiling and extended her hand.

'Sorry, I got lost. I couldn't remember which street it was, every street looks the same!'

'No problem. I was quizzing Max on what he learned today.'

There was a light sheen on her face and an auburn curl escaped from the clasp and fell forward. She moved it behind her ear and he saw a curiosity in her eyes that had not been there before. He thought of asking her for a coffee but nothing seemed opened around them.

'Are you coming to us tomorrow or do I bring him back here?'

'I'll come to you. Is 10 tomorrow morning still good?' she said, looking at Max. He nodded, smiling at her.

'And try to do an exercise or two tonight, we'll have a look at them tomorrow okay?'

She kissed and hugged him and whispered something in his ear that made his son giggle. He felt excluded from their connection and the pang of jealousy he had felt that morning reared its head again.

She left them and they both looked at her walking down the street until she disappeared.

12

It was only when she got home that she remembered the money and kicked herself for not having given it back to Mark Hunter. Oh well, she could use some of it when she took Max out in Uzès. It was what it was for, after all. She would make sure to keep the receipts and give them back to him at the end of the five weeks.

Michel called just as she was getting changed. 'How did it go?'

She waited a little before replying, looking herself up in her underwear in the full-length mirror of her bedroom.

'Good. I think I can help that poor kid.'

'Learning French, you mean?'

'Yes, but not only. Someone needs to give him some love and his confidence back.'

'That's not your job, Léa,' said Michel. She could hear him puffing on his cigarette.

'But I will do it all the same. His father won't do it.'

'Well, that's his problem.'

'No Michel,' she said, 'it is my problem too. I can't let that child being bullied by his father's girlfriend just because he's indifferent to him.'

She twirled in front of the mirror and pulled her stomach in. She could do with losing a few pounds. France had been a little too good to her since her return.

He sighed. 'As long as you know what you're doing and his

father doesn't find out. What's the problem with his girlfriend, anyway?'

Léa smiled. Curiosity got Michel every time. 'She's a bitch who's only interested in his father's money if you know what I mean.'

She heard Michel chuckle. 'It's the truth, Michel.'

'Do you want to come for a drink tonight? Luca is desperate to know how you're getting on.'

She thought about it. There were things she wanted to do like writing. 'Can't do tonight, but how about tomorrow night instead?'

Later, as she looked at guidebooks for things to do in and around Uzès, she could not help reflect on Max. His high intelligence was so clear to her. He picked things up with lightning speed and could talk about subjects that most teenagers would not have been interested in. There was a touching innocence about him. He was ill-equipped to deal with people because he believed the best in them. She knew only too well how that could be misconstrued by others and how quickly you could become their punchbag. It infuriated her though that an adult such as Freya could bully him. This was just criminal and made her want to scream. She had no right to treat him that way. But she knew too that Max would need to build his own shell to protect himself from people like her or his classmates. Over-protecting him would serve no purpose. He needed to learn how to deal with people like these.

He was very lucky. He came from a very well-off family who could afford the best education for him and the best holidays too. Yet the tragedy that he had known when he was still a little boy seemed to have cut his wings. Would have things been different for him if his mother was still alive? She had tried to get an idea of her, but between Max's adoration of his mother and Mr Hunter's few words on the subject it had been difficult to build a picture of the woman. She suspected though that she had adored Max, protecting him from the world and from his father's more harsh views of life.

She thought of her little grandma and her line about taking

opportunities where they are come back into her head. She smiled to herself as the darkness fell in the courtyard. How true she was! Who would have thought that she, Léa, who had never shown any interest in children, would take a teenager under her wing? But she was sure of it now: her role that summer was to enable Max to fly, to grow into the beautiful swan that he could be.

* * * * *

Mark had given up and taken Freya to Nîmes for some "serious" shopping as she had put it the next day which suited Léa perfectly as the atmosphere in the house was a lot lighter when they were both out. It also gave her the freedom to chat with Manuela, whom she learned had been born in Uzès but whose family was originally from a tiny village in Andalucia, Spain. Max looked more relaxed too, and she wished she had taken her swimsuit to go for a swim with him.

When she left by mid-afternoon, driving back to town in Michel's car, she felt lighter than she had for a long time. She was not sure why that was, except maybe that she was helping someone else and that felt good. She spent the rest of the day at home, writing in the coolness of the lounge, the light streaming from the courtyard before meeting with Michel and Luca. The other thing this unconventional family had given her was fodder for her book, and for that she was very grateful.

'So what's the news then?' said Léa as Luca made his way between the chairs of the café on the place aux Herbes.

He was beaming. 'Dad is retiring.'

Léa jumped up and embraced him. 'That's brilliant! You must be so happy!'

He sat down as the waiter came to fill up his glass with the rosé Léa had ordered.

'I couldn't believe it you know when he called me at lunchtime to tell me,' he said shaking his head as they clinked their glasses.

'When do you start?'

'He'll stop at the end of the week so Saturday night will be his last.'

Léa frowned. 'So soon? Is something wrong?'

'I thought that too when he told me earlier. I reckon something's happened, but he won't tell me. He's like an old mule, stubborn to the core.'

'Did you speak to your Mum?' Léa knew that he was much closer to his mother.

'Couldn't today, but I'm planning to have a chat with her tomorrow. I know something must have happened for him to relinquish control so quickly.'

'But are you happy?'

He nodded vigorously. 'Hell yeah! I've been waiting for this almost all my adult life. I'm prepared and I know what I can do.'

'What will be your first action?'

He looked at her sideways. 'Is that the management executive speaking?'

'Old habits die hard! But come on, you said you wanted to change things, so what's the first thing you will do?'

'There are so many things I want to change you know but the first thing? Let me see… The checkered tablecloths!'

They laughed. Luca had lobbied his dad to get rid of them for many years, he had told Léa. He hated that fake Italian vibe that pretended to be traditional. It just looked dated to him.

'Then I'll change the food. I'm fed up with the Europeanised pasta and pizza we serve. I want to go back to authentic stuff. The stuff we ate when we went to Italy when I was a kid. Dad thinks it wouldn't work, but I've argued the opposite for years.'

'I can't wait! I know you'll do well,' as she kissed him on the cheek. 'To your success!'

Léa saw them first as they crossed the Place aux Herbes and touched Luca's arm. Michel was late, but how she wished he had been there to see.

'Here's my boss and his girlfriend. And please don't smirk at her dress,' she said as Luca chuckled.

'Do you think she clocked that we are in Provence here and not on the Riviera?' he asked, half choking on his rosé.

She avoided his eyes, knowing she would not be able to stop herself from laughing, and looked at them behind her sunglasses. If Freya had not got the sense of the place yet, Mark seemed to have slipped into it with an abandon which made him look almost like a local. Cargo shorts, a polo shirt that showed his broad shoulders, white trainers. Except that his were all coming from top brands. She noticed the expensive watch was not there either. He must have finally slipped into holiday mode then. Even his skin had gone a warmer colour than when they had first met. She felt a stab of envy at Freya, a longing for someone to take her hand and walk these ancient streets with.

They sat at a different café and she looked at the woman who had become Max's nemesis. Her floaty yellow dress was rather inappropriate, but Léa had to admit that she was wearing it well. She had the body for it, long, tanned legs - fake-tanned surely, thin arms but enough of a chest to fill the very low top of the dress. She could never look that good, even if she put herself on a diet. She had lumps and bumps everywhere, but then she was not twenty- or twenty-five as this woman surely was.

'Why do you think older men go for younger women?' she asked Luca.

'Hey reassurance you know?' he replied with a shrug and a gesture of his hand that made her giggle. 'Although it doesn't seem to be working for him. He doesn't look happy,' he continued. 'Their body language is all wrong if you ask me.'

Léa smiled. Michel would not have noticed, but Luca had, just like her.

'It's been like that ever since they arrived. They seemed to have little in common.'

'Life's too short,' said Luca before changing the subject.

* * * * *

Mark was downstairs when Freya came down from their bedroom. He was in a foul mood and felt like cancelling this dinner outside. The trip to Nîmes had been a disaster where she had wanted to just spend money while he had wanted to have a wander around. He had even wished he had taken Max with them so that the two of them could have explored *les Arènes*. With his passion for history, Max would have loved that, he had thought, as they had stopped for lunch in a restaurant just in front of the ancient monument. By the time they got home, it was four o'clock, and he had missed Léa. Not that it mattered he told himself. He did not need a report on how his son was doing, but he was a little curious nonetheless.

Max had been a lot more opened when they had came in and they had gone swimming together under the scorching afternoon sun. They had splashed about and used fins and snorkelled, and he had wished that Tom had been there too. Just the three of them. Their small family. As he got in the shower, he reflected that he had organised this holiday badly and should plan for Tom to join them. By the time he was downstairs; he was on the phone to his widow's parents, but the conversation, as usual, did not go well. His father-in-law accused him of taking the boy away from them when they already did not see their eldest grandson, to which Mark replied that it was their own fault, that they had pushed him away. He hung up, annoyed with himself for having snapped and knowing that he would not get to see his youngest son for another two weeks. A promise was a promise, his father-in-law had told him. He wished he had never agreed to letting them have Tom in the first place.

He had not heard Freya come in, so lost in his thoughts he was as she put her hands around his waist. 'Babe I'm ready.'

He turned around and saw her wearing the dress she - or rather he - had bought in that expensive shop in Nîmes today. It was not the money that bothered him but the incongruity of the garment, a yellow floaty number, with a long skirt slit up on one side to the top of her thigh and thin straps that showed her bony shoulders. It just did not fit with the place or the dinner he had planned. And once again she was wearing far too much make-up, and he had to refrain from asking her to take some off. At least, she had put on flat sandals, remembering the cobbled streets of the old town. He somehow longed for the off the shoulder dress Léa had been wearing the day before. Something less flashy.

Mark had noticed Léa when they had walked into the square but had directed Freya to another café where he could observe her in a more discreet way. She was wearing an off the shoulder dress in what looked to him like an Indian print which showed her shoulders and tanned legs. Her hair was loose for once, her curls flowing around her, gold loops just barely visible. She looked stunning. He wondered if the guy she was with was her boyfriend, but something about him made him think it was not the case. They were sharing a bottle of rosé and were picking at olives and smearing tapenade[3] on small pieces of bread. The atmosphere at their table looked joyous in sharp contrast to him and Freya. He suddenly felt like walking over, leaving Freya on her own and sitting down with them, just buying drinks and enjoying their company.

But he could not. He tried to focus on Freya but conversation was hard going. Everything they seemed to say to each other sounded like recriminations, and dinner seemed like an even worse idea now than earlier in the day. He drank his Ricard, and the alcohol slowly made him relax. He looked up at the sky. It was still deep blue, in sharp contrast with the golden stones of the buildings. He wondered what it would be like to live here, how things were during the winter months or the autumn. It was difficult to imagine the city in the rain or even cold given the heat and glorious sunshine that had been bestowed upon them since they had arrived. For the first time in days, he felt like London was really far away.

---

[3] A traditional mix of black olive, capers, anchovies grounded will olive oil to form a paste and served on small pieces of bread.

13

Mark looked at his son sideways. He looked happier than he had been for a long time as he recalled what they had done with Léa that day. It was Léa this, and Léa that, but he loved it. He caught glimpses of Léa in what his son said and marvelled at how quickly she seemed to have given him some of his self-confidence back.

'And she got me to try this sweet cake called *fougasse*. She said the best one is the one you can buy on the market.'

'Did you like it?'

'Hell yeah! It's like a sponge cake with orange flower water in it and sugar sprinkled on top.'

'I must try some of that.' Freya made a face, but he pretended not to notice.

'Jeez Max, if you continue to talk about this woman I'm going to think you've fallen in love with her,' she said making eyes at Mark.

He looked at her and knew she had done it on purpose because she was not the centre of attention. The scene about Léa the other morning was still fresh in his mind. He looked at his son and saw that despite the tan he had gained in a week; he had reddened to the roots of his hair.

'What was that for exactly?' he said, his eyes boring into Freya hoping to salvage the situation.

'Well, that's true, isn't it? It's all about Léa this and Léa that these days between the two of you. Why am I even here?' She made a theatrical gesture before leaving the table.

Mark sat back in his chair.

'I'm sorry Dad, I…'

'There is nothing for you to be sorry for. Come on, tell me more.'

He looked at his son, but he could see that the charm was gone. They finished their dinner in silence.

There was no sound in the house. Max got up from his bed and looked at the window. His father was still sat on the terrace. He had not moved since dinner had been over. He wondered what he was thinking. He had wanted to talk more about Léa after Freya's outburst, but had not dared. But now he wanted to. He wanted to reach out to him. He had seen the interest in his eyes when he had talked about her and wondered… Maybe… It was worth a try. Freya would not last long at the rate she was going. And maybe if he could make him see…

He got out of his bedroom in the semi-darkness and walked on tiptoes to the stairs. There was still no sound, and he went down the stairs, careful not to make any noise. A hand stopped him as he was about to cross the lounge. He turned around and saw Freya. She was wearing a grey silk bathrobe, and her long hair was loose.

'You go back up. Right now!'

He stood up. Léa had told him not to be afraid of Freya. She had nothing on him.

'No. I need to speak to my Dad.'

She must have sensed that he would not be bullied this time and changed tack. She bent down, the top of her bathrobe opening a little, and he glimpsed a breast. He felt himself turning red again.

'Please. It's important that I talk to him first. Could you wait until tomorrow, maybe?'

He nodded. She made a sign for him to go back up the stairs and put her finger on her lips.

He went back up to his room and stood at the window. He saw her sat down on his father's lap and put her hands around his neck. He could not see, but he could well imagine the robe becoming undone. He realised then that she had not said sorry to him for what she had said at dinner.

Mark did not move when Freya slithered to him and sat on his lap. He looked at her seeing right through her.

'Mark baby. I'm sorry I was wrong to say what I did earlier. He is your son and I know he means the world to you. But I need you too.'

He looked at her but did not reply. His hands stayed on the arms of his chair. She kissed him on the lips.

'Come upstairs. I'll make it up to you.'

'Go away, Freya.'

But she kissed him again. 'We could make love here if you want,' she whispered, letting her dressing gown fall to her waist. He pulled it back on her shoulders.

'Leave me alone.' His voice was stone cold as he pushed her up.

She stood in front of him, fists closed tight against her legs.

'You're unbelievable, you know that. When I think of everything I've given you.'

He looked up at her, a sarcastic smile on his lips. 'Are you sure it's not the other way round Freya?'

She left in a huff and he stayed there, not moving, lost in his thoughts.

Mark had no idea how long he had stayed outside. When he finally went upstairs, he looked inside his son's room. He was asleep. He moved quietly and went to sit on the other bed. He looked at him. For the first time, maybe the first ever, he felt close to him. He pulled the sheet up on his shoulder and lay down in the other bed. He had made his choice.

14

The light falling on the bed woke Max up. He sat up straight when he saw his father lying on the other bed in the clothes he had been wearing the night before. He had thought after Freya's little seduction he would go up to her, eventually. But he was there. Suddenly he got worried. Had something happened? He jumped out of bed and shook him by the shoulders.

'Dad! Dad!'

Mark woke up with a start. 'What? What's going on?'

He looked around, trying to remember where he was.

'Why did you sleep in my room, Dad?'

Mark smiled and kept his eyes closed. 'Because I felt like it. I wanted to try the bed.'

He opened one eye and saw the suspicious look on his son's face. He burst out laughing, catching the boy and bringing him close, tickling him. He could hear him giggle while he begged him to stop. They looked at each other, and he held him tight, kissing his hair.

'I love you, you know that?'

He pulled him back. 'How about we go for our morning swim? It must be about time.'

Max smiled brightly. 'See you in five.'

* * * * *

Freya woke up and knew Mark was not in their bed. He had not slept there last night. She knew that too. Her little seduction had not worked, and yet she did not think he was sleeping with the French woman. He just seemed to be in a place where she could not reach him at the moment. And it annoyed her no end. It was one thing to be somewhere with no life and no friends if the guy you were with looked after you, but it was another to be left to fend off for yourself and on your own most of the time. This was no fun.

She got up and looked at herself naked in the mirror. She looked damn near perfect, even if she was saying so herself. She had seen how Léa had looked at her and knew she could never have a body like hers. Not to mention the clothes. This poor woman dressed like a peasant at best. The one thing Freya granted her though was that she had glorious hair and lovely curls. Shame she could do nothing about the rest.

She moved to the window and saw Mark and Max come back from the swimming pool. They were laughing, and Mark was ruffling Max's hair, teasing him about something. The boy was beaming, lapping all the attention that was lavished on him. But she would not play that game. Oh, no. Mark had not liked her outburst the night before, but she had only told him the truth. For all she knew, Léa was after the son and not the father. Maybe she should tell him that. See how he would react.

Her eyes strayed on Mark though, and a wave of desire engulfed her. He was two years shy of fifty, but he was still a very sexy man and she yearned for him to come up and put his arms around her. Of all the lovers she had had, and she had had a few, he was the most attentive but also daring. Nothing seemed to phase him, and that had been one reason it had worked so well between them. He enjoyed her, and she enjoyed him, and neither of them had any qualms about sex. But right now he was sat at the breakfast table with Max. Manuela, another one who had fallen under his spell, came by and poured coffee for him while he chatted to her. Freya could not hear what he was saying but knowing him he would just be as interested in her as he would be in some high flyer. It infuriated her. His wealth gave him the right to treat people as he wished, and she had never understood why he treated people inferior to him with so much respect. They were there to serve him, not to have a chat with him.

She hesitated about going down to have breakfast with them. She could do with some coffee, but she decided to wait for him. Her little seduction the night before had not worked, but she would be damned if he would not yield to her this morning once she had tried what she had in mind.

* * * * *

'What time is Léa coming today?'

'She said 9.45,' said Max, looking his father in the eye before smearing butter and jam on a piece of baguette.

Mark sipped his coffee while looking at his son. He seemed to have grown since they had arrived in Provence. Maybe it was because he looked more confident about himself or in his relationships with others. Whatever it was, Mark knew it had a lot to do with Léa.

'Dad, do you think you can love two people the same way?'

The question had come out of the blue, and Mark was so surprised that it took him a few seconds before he could reply.

'Why do you ask?'

Max shrugged and looked at him, smiling. 'I don't know. I just wondered if it's possible, that's all.'

'I think so. I love you and your brother the same. Same with your grandmother.'

'But it's not the same, is it? I'm your son. What if you love someone you're not related to the same as someone you are related to?'

'Why not? There is no law against that. You can love anyone you want.'

He looked at his son who was shaking his head, his eyes fixed on his plate. He was not sure he believed him, but he seemed happy with the answer. Where was this question coming from and who was he speaking of? Léa? Had he fallen in love with Léa? It seemed so far-fetched that he put it out of his mind. He looked at his watch.

'You might want to get ready soon. It's 9.20 already.'

Max shoved the last bit of bread in his mouth as if his life depended on it and ran inside the house. Mark breathed deeply. The scent of the wisteria was coming through already. With the sun on his shoulders, he felt happy. Just happy.

15

Mark went up shortly after Max. As he opened the door, he saw that Freya was not in bed. He did not know where she was, and he somehow hoped she was not around. She was not who he wanted to see.

He moved to the window and looked out. He was starting to love this place. The slow pace of life here, the fresh air, the warmth of people. What would it be like to live here all year round? He could not do it, but he enjoyed the daydream just for a minute. Him, the kids and… The image of Léa came to him and he smiled. That would be interesting.

The door of the bathroom opened behind him and he turned around to see Freya. She was naked, and he knew somehow that she had something planned. He could read it in her fiery dark eyes. She moved up to him and smiled.

'Where were you last night?' she told her hands going up his shoulders, touching his face. He could feel her breasts brushing his chest, the warmth of her body, that perfume she wore.

'Freya…'

'Take me,' she whispered, 'you know you want to.'

It would have been so easy to take advantage of her. He had done it before and she was offering herself to him. But he found that he could not. He could not even bring himself to touch her. He pushed her gently away.

'No Freya. I can't. It's over between us.'

'I don't want it to be over,' she said moving back to him, her body pressed against his while her hands moved down his back, fingers pulling at his shorts. She kissed him before he could move away. He tried to resist, but lust stirred in him. Before he knew it, his hands were on her waist and he was kissing her back.

'Dad! Léa is here.'

The shout from Max outside their bedroom brought him back to reality, and he pulled away from Freya.

'I can't do this. Sorry I've got to go.'

He moved to the door before she could say anything, grabbing a shirt left on a chair as he did so. He turned around, his hand on the doorknob.

'Get dressed. You and I need to have a chat when I'm done downstairs.'

'Mark if you leave now to see…'

She did not finish. He had closed the door on her.

'Have you got everything?' asked Léa.

'I've got to tell you something super cool,' said Max. He had a big smile on his face and Léa wondered why he was so happy.

'You'll tell me in the car. Are you ready?'

'I told Dad you were here. He probably wants to…'

He did not finish as his father came running down the stairs. Léa could not help notice he was buttoning his shirt and wondered what he had been doing. He smiled to her as he stepped down the last step. He was about to say something when Freya came running after him. 'Mark! You come back right now! You have no right…'

He did not turn around, but Léa saw him winced. She tried to smile, but it felt all wrong. They were obviously having problems.

'Come on Max, let's go.' She did not want the boy to be in the middle of a dispute between his father and Freya, who was waiting behind Mark halfway up the stairs, her eyes boring into her.

He turned around at the bottom of the stairs. At least she was wearing something, he thought.

'As soon as I'm done here.'

'No, now!'

He heard the front door close and sighed. He was about to move away, but she grabbed his arm.

'Leave me alone, Freya.' There was a hint of a threat in his voice, but she did not budge. He would not get rid of her that quickly. She had far too much to lose, and they both knew it.

'Are you sleeping with her?'

'Who?'

'The French teacher,' she said with as much contempt as she could.

He burst out laughing, and that released the tension he had felt just a minute before. But there was no going back now, he knew exactly where he was.

Freya felt like slapping him as he stood there laughing and shaking his head.

'So, are you sleeping with her yes or no?' she said, wrapping her négligé more tightly around her body.

He stared at her. 'This is not about her. This is about you and me. It's over.'

She started saying something, but he put his hand up to stop her. 'Don't argue please. I'm tired of the arguments.'

'You asked me to come here, I thought it was serious between us.'

'It was never serious between us Freya and you know that. I never made any promises to you.' He paused. 'It was a mistake to ask you to come here and I'm sorry about that. But we both need to move forward.'

'Move forward?' She was almost shouting. 'It's so easy for you, isn't it? You use women like you use tissues! I should've known…'

He pressed his fists against his body. It was taking all his self-control not to hit her.

'I've never used you, Freya. You wanted to be with me and I with you. We both knew from the start that this was never going to be a long-term relationship.'

'I didn't know that!' she screamed.

'Yes, you did. Alex told you about me. You knew I'd been out with a few of women after my wife had died and that none of them had been more than a fling. And you also know this because you know one of them very well. I even have it on very good authority that she warned you about the affair.'

She looked at him, her mouth half-opened, not sure what else she could say.

'And then I know that you've been sleeping around too,' said Mark.

'Well, it's not like we slept together every day,' she replied, trying to sound nonplussed.

'I agree. This is why you also know that this was never serious between us.'

There was a silence as she tried to find something to say. She wondered how he knew she had been sleeping with someone else.

'It was never serious between him and I. It's just that I needed more of you and you…'

'I don't want to know. What you do with your life is your problem. But this is where it ends between us.'

She suddenly felt abandoned, like the child she had been when her father had died suddenly, leaving her and her mum with little. And the more she looked at him, strong and calm, the more she realised she wanted him. More than she had before. Badly.

'Mark I love you. I'll make it up to you. Please don't leave me.' She grabbed his arm, but she knew before she finished her sentence that his answer would be no. He was not the kind of man who could be swayed. If he could resist her naked, then…

'I can't Freya and you don't love me. And I don't love you either. We both know that.'

He took her hand away from his arm and locked his eyes in hers.

'I want you to leave. Today.'

She looked at him with shock all over her face. 'Leave? And to go where?'

'Wherever you want. I'll pay for it. Just let me know.'

'I don't want to leave Mark. I…'

'I want you out of here today. I need to focus on my son.'

He turned around and walked to the front door. When he opened it, Léa and Max were gone.

16

'I want a flight to Cannes,' said Freya as she burst in on Mark in the library. He looked up to her. She was dressed in skinny white jeans, a blue silk blouse and some colourful high-heel sandals.

'There is no scheduled flight between here and Cannes. But I'm sure I can get you on a train.'

'I want a private plane.'

'No, but I can get you a first-class seat on a fast train down to Cannes.'

'You heard me, Mark. I want a private plane.'

He looked at her, his blue eyes boring into her. 'Ok, then you organise it yourself.'

'Your PA can do it.'

He shook his head. 'No, she has much more important things to do,' he said looking down at his computer screen.

'You said you would get me what I wanted if I left.'

He sat back, crossed his arms and looked at her. 'Yes, but within limits. That's just bonkers.'

She had her hands on her hips in a provocative pose. 'You get me what I want or I'm not leaving.'

'You don't order me about, darling. And you will leave today, whether or not you want it.'

Freya knew she would not win against him and, in truth, she did not want to spend another night here. If she could not get him, she could at least have some fun down on the Riviera. She pursed her lips.

'What about a car?'

'You want to drive down there?' he said, puzzled.

'I want someone to drive me down there, babe.'

'It's probably a good four hours, Freya. The train is quicker.'

'Yes, but it's better than to be on a train with lots of other people. And anyway, you owe me this. You said you'd pay.'

Mark thought about it. It was not the cost that bothered him, it meant nothing to him. It had more to do with losing face in front of her, but he guessed that the reason she wanted this was to show her friends that she could still arrive in style. For all he knew, she would probably lie too about their relationship. That was the price to pay for her to be out of here. He let the silence continue awhile, his gaze lost somewhere above her. He heard her tap her foot. Patience was not Freya's strong point.

'So?'

He focused on her at last, sarcasm in his eyes and in his voice. 'Very well.'

'And I need a place to stay in Cannes, so book me a suite at either the Carlton or Eden Roc in Antibes.'

'No.'

She knew straightaway that there would be no negotiations about this, but she tried nonetheless. 'I need somewhere…'

'No Freya. I know exactly where you're going and you don't need a suite anywhere. Don't take me for a mug.'

She wondered if he had overheard her organise her stay at friends of hers who had a villa between Cannes and Antibes. Or was it Alex who had told him she had close friends there? He would hear from her that godfather of hers when she saw him next. He was supposed to protect her and have her best interests at heart and not try to break her relationship with his best friend.

'When can the car be there?'

'No idea. Need to make some calls.'

'The sooner the better Mark,' she said with as much disdain as she could before turning around and going out the door.

'Indeed, darling, the sooner the better,' he said as the door closed.

The car arrived shortly before lunch, but Mark did not come out of the library to see Freya out. He wanted her gone and never set eyes on her again.

17

The car broke down in the middle of nowhere, somewhere between Comps and Montfrin as they were coming back from Arles. She just managed to pull over into a lay-by as the engine seemed to die.

'No, no, no!' she screamed to herself.

This was the last thing she needed. She had omitted to tell Mark Hunter that she was taking Max further afield, worrying that he would say no if she asked. She had sworn Max to secrecy on the way to Arles in the morning, something he had only been too happy to do. She turned to face him, worried that he would be scared but he smiled to her.

'Now that's a proper adventure!'

She was glad he took it that way because she felt a little lost. She started by calling Michel; it was his car after all, surely he would have insurance and be able to sort something out. Unfortunately, her phone had no signal.

'Max, do you have a signal on your phone?'

'Yes, I've got two bars.'

She made a face but took the phone and dialled Michel's number. He did not pick up the phone, and she left a message. She noticed as she hung up that Max's battery was almost out of juice. The clock in the car said it was 3 p.m.. She was expected to bring Max home between three thirty and four. This would not happen. Should she ask him to call his father, given that she had taken the boy on this little trip without asking for his permission first?

'Ok, I think we'll have to walk to the nearest town and find a garage, otherwise we may be here all afternoon.'

They got out of the hot car and Léa took the water bottles she had bought before they left Arles, congratulating herself on having thought of that. They started walking towards the town they had just passed. The sun was high in the sky and she was worried Max would get heatstroke or something. But he kept moving and did not complain once. She noticed his great loping walk after a while and knew that he was enjoying himself.

In Comps, she found a garage and possibly because she was a woman; the owner agreed that she could use the phone. She called Michel, and this time he answered. He was annoyed but not surprised that his old car had broken down and asked her to put him onto the mechanic. While they chatted, she noticed the posters of naked women on the wall above the desk and caught Max looking at them. He saw her looking at him and blushed. She pulled him gently out the room and they found a spot in the shade on a low wall outside.

The mechanic came back and told her she was lucky. He knew Michel; they had been at school together apparently and he would go and pick the car up for her and see what could be done. She looked at her watch and winced. It was just after 3.30 p.m.

'Do you need to be somewhere, love?'

'Me no, but this lovely boy yes. His father will worry if I don't bring home quickly. Do you know where I could get a taxi by any chance?'

He looked at her like she was talking Chinese and scratched his balding head with his oil-stained fingers.

'Taxi, huh? Around here, don't know. Where do you need to go?' He gestured at the two of them.

'Aureillac.'

The man smiled at them.

'Let me go and pick up the car and then I'll drive you and the boy back. I'll be back in thirty minutes at most. Where did you say again you left the car?'

Léa explained and saw that he knew exactly where it was. He was off almost immediately, leaving the two of them there, his garage opened and no one else around. She wondered if there was maybe someone upstairs above the garage or at the back, but nothing moved. Only the sound of the cicadas and a few cars zipping along the road behind them.

She looked at her phone, but she still had no signal. She could have sent it flying so angry she was, but she put it back in her purse.

'You should try to call your Dad Max. He'll be worried by now.'

The boy grinned. 'I can't, I've got no signal. Look,' he said, showing her his phone.

'I'm sorry. I didn't want our adventure to end like this.'

He shrugged. He was getting more gallic by the day.

'I don't mind. I'm better here with you than at home with Dad and Freya. When they fight, she takes it out on me.'

Gone what the excitement he had shown in the morning when he had told her the dispute he had witnessed the night before between his father and his girlfriend, asking Léa if this meant it would be over soon between them.

She smiled sadly and wished Mr Hunter would sort himself out. Why did he need that woman around? Couldn't he see how badly she was treating his son? She could not believe he did not know. A father surely, like a mother, would know.

'Don't worry, I'll take the blame for this. And your Dad can shout at me as much as he likes, he doesn't scare me.'

'Really?'

She read the amazement in his eyes and hoped she would be true to her word in front of Mark Hunter. 'Nope, not one bit!' she said with more force than she felt.

It took much longer than thirty minutes for Monsieur Pellan, the mechanic, to come back with the car. Then, he had to find a place for it in his garage - to Léa's astonishment there were three other cars being serviced inside - and close the place before they could squeeze in the cab of his van and be on their way. He talked all the way, asking her where she was from and if the boy was her son. He had noticed he had an accent, he said, but she did not so he had been wondering.

'No, I'm just his teacher. He's British, but he speaks good French,' she said, putting a protective arm around Max.

'British, hey? So many of them around here in the summer. They're buying all the good houses. A tragedy for young people like you.'

She smiled but said nothing. It was not completely false. The house prices in the area were high, but then again you were in Provence, as she kept reminding herself, in one of the prettiest areas to boot.

They got to the house close to five. He left them at the gate wishing them *une bonne soirée*. She offered to pay for the petrol, but he waved her away. She braced herself for what was to come.

She knew as she stepped inside the house that this would not be good. Mark came in from the lounge at the same time as Manuela.

'I'll handle this,' he said, dismissing her with a wave of his hand.

The woman looked at her, and Léa knew he had been worrying and probably pacing around. She wondered where Freya was. Surely she would have enjoyed her discomfiture.

He gestured for her to go into the lounge and ordered Max to go upstairs. But the boy did not move.

'Max, upstairs.' His voice was hard and cold.

'Dad, it's not Léa's fault…'

'I don't want to argue with you. Go upstairs!'

Léa gave Max a gentle tug. 'Go upstairs. Don't worry.'

'No, I'll stay here with you,' he replied, sticking close to her.

There was a determination in his voice that surprised both of them. Mark gave up first and walked into the living room. When she followed he was standing in the middle, hands on his hips, a deep frown on his face.

'Close the door.'

She did as she was told, although she wondered what for given that all the windows were open.

'Where have you been?'

'I took Max to Arles today. Unfortunately my car, or rather Michel's from the agency, broke down on the way back about halfway between Arles and here.'

'And it didn't come to you that you should've called me to let me know?'

'I had no signal and Max didn't have any either. You know how it...'

He cut her off.

'Let me get this straight. First you take my son on an unauthorised trip. I don't recall you asking me for permission to take him to Arles? Then, you take him in a car that is obviously not fit for purpose and, to top it all, you tell me you couldn't call me to let me know? It's five thirty. He should've been here at three thirty at the latest. What do you think I've been doing for the last two hours? I was that close,' he said, making a gesture with his fingers, 'that close to call the police.'

'I'm sorry. I can only apologise. It was my fault, and it's true that I should've told you about taking Max to Arles, but you looked busy this morning and I just thought it'd be fine and we'd be back on time.'

'And that I needed never to know.'

'Something like that.'

He could not believe that she had just said that. She had not budged since she had come in and no matter what he said; she seemed to take it in her stride with a calmness that infuriated him even more.

'How did you get back then?'

'A kind man, a mechanic who went to fetch the car, took us back here, Dad. And it's not all Léa's fault, I...'

'I didn't ask for your opinion, Max. I'm speaking with Léa here. I want you to go upstairs.'

'No.' The answer was loud and clear and Léa thought for a minute he was going to hit his son.

'Max,' said Léa, 'please go upstairs. It's best if your Dad and I sort this out.'

She pressed his hand and saw his blue eyes filling up with

tears. She smiled to him. He left them giving his father a heinous look that pained her.

Mark took a deep breath. 'Is this what happened?'

'Yes. I did ask if I could call a taxi, but he told me there weren't any in the village.'

'And you believed him?' He looked sceptical.

'I had no other way to check whether this was true or false, my phone still had no signal.'

'Ah yes, the famous phone!'

He turned around and walked to the French doors before coming back.

'I tell you what. I don't think this is working out, this French teaching. It's probably best if we stop there.'

She held his gaze. 'I understand and I agree with you. This isn't working between us. It's a shame really because it's working for Max. He's made a lot of progress and you should be proud of him. However, if you permit me before I go, I've one more thing to say. It may be none of my business, but if you value your son, you need to tell that girlfriend of yours to stop bullying him.'

'I don't need your advice,' he snapped back.

Léa shrugged. 'Of course not. You know best.'

She turned around and went out of the lounge, closing the door behind her and then out of the house. It only occurred to her when she was out of the gate that she had no transport to get back home. She would have to walk the four kilometres or so. Oh well, at least it would give her time to calm down.

As she was about to turn onto the main road, Manuela's husband was turning into the lane. He stopped and leaned out the window.

'Ah mademoiselle Léa! So happy to see you! How are you?'

She felt still flushed from her conversation with Hunter, bits of what he had said to her swirling around in her head.

'OK, thanks. Would you know how I can get back to Uzès? Unfortunately, my car broke down this afternoon and...'

'Come in, I'll take you back.'

'But Manuela, she's probably expecting you...'

'Don't worry. She's fine, she's cooking. I was just bringing her some stuff she asked me to deliver.'

Léa smiled and got in the car next to him. She had not met him before, but by the time he left her just on the edge of the medieval city; she knew he had been in the army, that he had retired because of an injury and was now *un homme à tout faire*, a handyman of sorts, and if he could be of any help, he would always be pleased to help her. Walking home, she realised his words had soothed her somehow, and she was less angry. There were still some lovely people in this world. Not all was lost.

18

Mark looked down at the swimming pool from the higher part of the garden. The blue water was rippling gently under a light breeze, sparkling in the sun. He walked down the stone steps and walked to the edge of the pool. Max's flippers laid discarded on a lounger. The air was full of the noise of the cicadas.

He looked at the water again. It seems to call him. Cool, blue, inviting. He removed his trainers and walked around the stone border to where he knew the water was a little deeper. He took a deep breath and dived. The cool water ran along his body, enveloping him. He let himself fall to the bottom of the pool and stayed there a while, his white linen shirt billowing around him. He waited until he could not stand it anymore and pushed himself back up. He emerged gasping, arms shooting into the air. He moved onto his back, feeling his clothes dancing around him, pulling his body up to keep himself afloat.

He looked at the sky. It was deep blue, immense. He felt himself becoming calmer as if the water was washing away the pains and the ills of the days, the months, the years.

Freya had left, and that was good. A weight had lifted off his shoulders when the car she was in had gone out of the gate. He could see how poisonous her presence had been. The thing was, he had never wanted things to go this far with her. She had been a distraction, someone to relieve tensions with. Yes, he had used her, but she had used him too. He felt no guilt about it and pushed her out of his mind.

His reaction to Léa's adventures that day looked over the top. He knew that she would never had put Max in danger. But she had stood up to him, not afraid to show his reaction as ludicrous, and he had taken the bait. He did not mind that she had criticised his relationship with Freya. Somewhere he knew he had had it coming, but it had hurt because what she said had felt true. He had been unaware of the bullying, but it did not surprise him. Her shining brown eyes flashing with anger came back to him now, the pink of her lips. She had been so close to him at one point; he had felt the heat of her body on him, her perfume. She stirred something deep, visceral in him. He wondered, not for the first time, what it would be to touch her, to taste her. He let the thought play on his mind a little longer before letting himself go under again. When he finally got out of the water, he felt like cleansed of all guilt.

He walked to the house, his clothes dripping, a smile on his face. He felt like he was a child again, doing something he knew was naughty. On the terrace, he grabbed a towel that had been left out to dry on the back of a chair. He looked around, but apart from the cicadas, there was no one. He took off his wet clothes, standing naked in the sun. He did not care who saw him. It oddly did not matter anymore. Laughter started rising in him as he left the towel on the back of a chair and ran naked into the house and to his bedroom.

In the shower, he thought of Max and decided that he would take the boy out after dinner. They would go into town, have ice-cream and walk around. He would explain why he had been angry with Léa but that this would not stop the way things had been. He would call her and apologise. But not tonight. It was still a matter of pride for him.

Down the corridor, he knocked on the door and called Max. When there was no answer, he opened the door, but the room was empty. He must have gone downstairs to the lounge to play with his video game console while he was showering. He stepped down the stairs, feeling lighter. But downstairs Max was nowhere to be seen either. He went out, calling him louder.

There was no reply. He walked to the swimming pool, but he was not there. He went round the house but there was no sign of him. His heart started racing somewhere between the swimming pool and the house. He went into the living room and up again but could not find Max's mobile phone.

A noise in the kitchen made him hope that he would be there, but he found only Manuela, hands deep in a bowl full of flour and butter. She was surprised and then alarmed.

'Have you seen Max?' he asked her as calmly as he could.

She shook her head. 'Not in the swimming pool?'

She looked puzzled when he said no, then something seemed to come to her. 'I heard the gate open and close,' she said in her broken English.

'When?' The question had come out harder than he would have liked and she looked alarmed.

He moved his hands up as a sign of peace, mumbling that he was just worried. She looked at the clock and said one hour, maybe with a shrug.

Mark stood there for a few seconds, trying to understand what it meant. Max had left the house, but to go where? He wondered if he had heard him dismiss Léa. It had been an idle threat, a spur-of-the-moment thing, but he had taken it earnestly. He had seriously misread how much his son loved her.

'What can I do, Monsieur?' said Manuela softly, shaking her hands above the bowl and wiping them on her apron. 'Do you want me to call my husband, to ask him to look for him? He just went back to Uzès.'

'Nothing. Stay here. Can you? If he comes back, please ask him to call me. Straightaway.'

He turned around not waiting for her to answer, walked to the library to grab his car keys and ran to the car. The light was fading as he joined the road to Uzès, and thoughts of his son lying injured in a ditch sent a shiver down his spine. He reasoned with himself. Max was sensible. Even if he had walked into town, he would have paid attention and been careful.

He drove slowly, looking on both sides, letting other drivers overtake him. It was quarter to nine.

Something Max had said several weeks earlier came back to him too as he drove into town.

Mark had found him crying on his bed one Sunday evening and when he had asked what was wrong, Max had said, 'I can't remember Mum's face, Dad or the sound of her voice. I'm worried she thinks I don't love her anymore.' The memory came back to him with such force that he felt like someone had punched him. Did Max's question about loving two people the same way had to do with the fact that his son had felt that Léa could take the place of his mother's in his affections? This was stupid. It had only been ten days. But as he parked his car, he knew he could not dismiss the thought.

He had to ask directions twice before he could find Léa's place. He rang her mobile number, but there was no answer. He tried Max for the umpteenth time, but it went straight to voicemail. The craziest explanations swirled in his head as he approached her house. Maybe she had abducted him or seduced him. Maybe she was not so innocent.

He finally found the house in the middle of a narrow lane. What was it with people and street lighting here? It was so dark by the house that he almost missed the bell. He pressed it. There was no sound. He took two steps back, but he could see no light inside the house. He pressed again and somewhere deep inside; he heard the rattle of a chair being pushed, steps approaching. His blood was boiling. If Max was there, and she had not called him, he would end her contract on the spot for good.

19

The night had almost fallen, and it was still warm outside in the courtyard. Twenty-eight degrees had said the ticker display at the chemist on her way home. It could not have gone down much since. Léa had not moved from her chair since getting home, her eyes fixed on the beautiful coral-coloured flowers of the hibiscus.

She sighed. She was still angry for having fallen once again into Mark Hunter's trap. He knew how to push her buttons and she had walked right into it. What did it matter that she taught Max or not? He was just another kid, another job. Yes, she knew that this was not true either. She loved that boy and felt it was her duty to protect him. What was it to Mark that she had taken him around to Arles, getting him to see some historical buildings and buy little bits and bobs so that he could practice his French? He surely knew she would do everything to protect him. His reaction had been incomprehensible. The man was incomprehensible.

She would have to tell Michel that her contract had been terminated. It would upset him. Mark Hunter was a good client, apparently. At least he did one thing well! And it could not have come at a worse time either. She needed the money to show the bank that she could afford to buy this house.

Something buzzed somewhere. Her phone, probably. She felt exhausted. Why did she always had to fight? Why could anything happen easily to her, just like it did with other people?

The bell rang, shattering the silence. She waited, hoping whoever it was would go away. But it rang again, more insistent this time. She got up heavily and went slowly through the house to the door. Mark Hunter was standing there, hands on hips, looking as angry as he had been earlier. His white shirt was half tucked in his cargo shorts, his hair wet and slightly dishevelled.

'Is he here?' It had come out as a bark rather than a question, and he regretted it immediately. Léa was looking at him, puzzled.

'Who?'

'Max. He's disappeared. I thought he'd gone to his room, but he isn't there.' He swallowed with difficulty. 'Manuela said she heard the gate, and I thought he might be with you.'

'He doesn't know where I live.' It was all she could say. 'Stay here.'

She ran back inside, put on a pair of flat pumps that were lying around by the staircase and grabbed her phone. She was back in no time. He had not moved but was tapping his foot. Was it because of fear or impatience? Léa could not tell.

'Have you got any ideas where he can be?' The accusatory tone was back, but she knew better than to respond.

'Have you called his mobile?'

'Several times. It goes straight to voicemail.'

She closed the door and passed in front of him, her shoulder brushing his. He smelled her perfume again. She started walking, and he followed her. She was wearing the same off the shoulder top and long skirt that she had had on earlier, but her hair was loose and moving around her as she walked.

'Did you hear me? Do you know where he is?' His voice was pressing hard. He was holding her responsible when it was him who had pushed his son over the brink. She felt her anger rise again. She stopped and turned around to face him just as they got to a crossroads. A street light shone a yellow light above them.

'No, I don't. Why do you think it's my fault?'

He wiped his mouth with his fingers, but she did not let him reply.

'Has he ever done a runner before?'

'Never. It's not his style. He's a quiet boy. It's unlike him. Or at least it was.'

He saw her eyes flash with anger.

'What are you saying? That this is my fault? Yes, he's changed. I'm amazed you've even noticed. He's gained in confidence, he's trying unfamiliar things. He isn't the shy little boy you want him to be anymore.'

She knew straightaway the last sentence had been a mistake. She saw him clench his jaw and thought for a second he would hit her.

'I don't think you should tell me how to raise my children.' The tone was glacial and threatening.

She turned around and started walking. She suddenly knew where Max could be.

'Where are you going?'

'You'll have to follow me if you want to know.'

She led him towards the Place aux Herbes. People were still walking about, but the cafes and restaurants were starting to wind down. On the place itself, she could not see Max but went around under the arches just in case. There was laughter and music somewhere above them, chairs being piled up and doors being slammed shut. They walked to the fountain under the trees, but Max was nowhere to be seen. She could feel Mark's tension next to her and she was started to feel worried too. Where was he?

'Let's try the Duché. I told him once that I did not live very far.'

20

Max had gone to all the places he had been with Léa, but there had been no familiar faces among the crowd. Yet he was not worried. What could happen to him here in this small town? He felt safe. And it was still warm. He would wait until morning and meet Léa at their usual spot. He only regretted not having taken something to eat. Lunch with Léa was a distant memory. He shrugged and sat on the pavement, his back against the high wall of the Duchy, trying to make himself as comfortable as he could. He was hidden behind a tree but could still make out the *mairie*[4] on the other side of the road, lit up with the French national colours.

He took out the notebook and the pen from his backpack. He had not written a word in it since Léa had given it to him. Diary were for girls. Bet Dad does not write in a diary, he thought. But what else could he do here, waiting for morning to come and no phone to keep him company?

He hesitated but opened the first page. Léa had said there was a kind of magic in writing what you wanted without fear. She had even said he could write to his Mum. It was a stupid idea. She was dead. She had laughed when he had said that and had told her the story of her requests to her late grandmother and how some of them had come true. He had thought for a minute she had probably said that to make him feel better. Yet he was

---

[4] Townhall

starting to know her. She was the real deal. If she had said that, it had to be true.

'Writing is like talking to the stars. You have the right to ask for what you want. It may not be enough to get it, but if you don't ask, you don't get,' she had told him.

When he had asked her what he should write about, she had said what first came to his head. There were so many things inside his head: his Mum, the fight with his father, what had happened the night before with Freya, and Léa. Which one to pick?

His hand hesitated on the paper, and then it happened. Anger, frustration, but also hope engulfed him. There were so many things to say that he had trouble keeping up with his thoughts. It was a curious feeling, like a liberation. Maybe she had been right, this writing thing could work after all. The fear that had been gripping his heart for so long seemed to melt away in the warm night air.

PART TWO

21

Léa led the way as they walked along the dark streets. She tried to peer into the distance, but the light was too dim for her to see. A dog barked somewhere. There was the sound of a TV audience applauding, someone talking. On the square, in front of the Duchy, she first saw nothing. The moon was casting long shadows near the high walls. The tower, lit against the inky sky, loomed above. You could barely see the stars from here.

Mark saw him first. 'He's there, behind the tree on the other side.'

He was about to walk over to Max, but she stopped him by putting her hand on his arm.

'Stay there. It's probably best if I speak to him. He's probably expecting me.'

She released his arm and hurried to the other side, calling Max softly. The boy moved beyond the shadow of the pillar and came towards her. He was smiling.

'I know you'd come for me.'

She held him tight, ruffling his hair. 'You silly boy. You scared your Dad and I to death. I had no idea you had escaped.'

She felt him tense against her.

'Is he here?'

'Of course he is. He was anxious. It's a good thing he knew where I lived. Why didn't you call me?'

'Is he very angry?' His voice was small. Gone was the grin.

'He'll be ok. Why didn't you call me?'

'My phone died when I got here. I didn't know who to ask. The café I've been to with you was closed.'

'What if I hadn't come?'

'I would've waited until tomorrow morning.' He smiled again and stood taller.

'Come on. Let's go and see your Dad.'

'I won't apologise. He's got no right to treat you the way he does. I hate him.' His voice had risen, and she wondered if his father had heard.

She put her arm around him and pulled him gently on.

Mark was waiting for them where she had left him at the top of the street. All his anger had disappeared as she had touched him, and he could still feel the imprint of her hand on his forearm. He moved towards them as they walked across the street and took his son in his arms. It was an awkward embrace and Léa could not help thinking it was about time he showed some love to his son. She stood aside and waited for them. Mark was the first to stand back but Max, probably feeling that his father would take him home, was the first to speak.

'Léa said she would cook for me.'

'That's very kind, but we should go home. It's well past your bedtime.' He had said that without conviction, and the boy jumped straight in.

'Dad please. Then I'll know where Léa lives.'

Mark looked at Léa. She nodded. Max took her arm, Mark following behind them.

The house was still cool when they got in despite Léa having left the windows opened. She looked at Max, his eyes widening at the size of the walls.

'I did say it was an ancient house I lived in.'

'Can I have a look around?' he said, shifting from one foot to another.

She saw his father about to say something and interjected that he was welcome to do so until dinner was ready.

Mark followed her to the kitchen.

'We'll have dinner outside in the courtyard,' she said, opening the door.

'What can I do?'

She turned around and looked at him. He looked a little lost in her tiny kitchen. She wondered how many times he walked into his own kitchen at home.

'Plates are in the cupboard, knives and forks are in the drawer and glasses on the shelf. There's rosé in the fridge.'

While he did this, she put together a quick salad, spread dry-cured ham, cheese and olives on a plate and cut the bread.

'Do you have a corkscrew?'

'In the lower drawer.' She gestured towards the drawer and he went outside. By the time she joined him, he was standing looking at the back wall with its little lights. It gave the place a festive air.

'Do you like it?' she said putting the dishes on the table.

He seemed to come out of his reverie and smiled to her. It was a warm smile that went up to his eyes.

'I love it! It reminds me of the lights we used to have in the garden in the summer when we were kids.'

He took a glass of wine and handed it to her. They clinked their glasses and sipped; the silence growing between them.

'Is this your house?'

She sat down, choosing the ricketiest chair before answering.

'I wish it was, but no. I'm just the caretaker until the people who own it sell it. But I love it. It's small but perfect for me. I love being able to sit outside. I couldn't do that in London.'

He was about to say something but Max came rushing in, full of excitement about the house and the size of the walls and how long ago it had been built. They let him babble, answering when prompted, letting him fill the space. She caught Mark looking at her a few times, and she returned his gaze. She was not sure she could read this man. He could be warm one minute and cold and hurtful the next. And yet, there was something about him that troubled her.

He could not help looking at her or work out his feelings towards Léa. He had been so angry with her today for taking Max out somewhere without his permission, and then for him to disappear to find her. He had been worried sick about his son, but there had been more to it than that. Looking at her in the soft light of the candles on the table and the little lights on the walls, he realised that he was just as attracted to her as his son was. He loved the way she moved, how her simple clothes hug her figure beautifully, the smile she had for Max. He was definitely a little jealous of that. She was so different from other women he knew. There was no pretence about her, no hiding her natural beauty behind make-up. He loved that she seemed to enjoy eating and drinking and did not toy with the food on her plate. There was something wholesome and open about her he found terribly attractive.

'Tell me about yourself.'

She was so lost in her thoughts that she had to ask him to repeat the question. 'What do you want to know?'

'Max said that you used to work for publishing houses in London before you moved back here. That you have two degrees. I just wonder how someone like you end up doing what you do here. It's been great for us, but I just can't help thinking it can't be that great for you.'

She looked at him. His face was half-lit by the candle on the table, his eyes shining, fixing her.

'The last ten days have been great. I loved working with Max. I really do, despite not knowing much about children or teaching!' She laughed, tilting her head back. 'I moved to London twenty years ago from Paris. I'd always wanted to live there and work in publishing. So I just booked a ticket on the Eurostar, found a place and never looked back.'

'Did you have a job?'

She shook her head, her curls changing colour in the light. 'No, but I found one quickly and became an assistant in the marketing department of a small publishing house, then I just kept going. I moved jobs a few times until I was made Head of Marketing about six years ago.'

She stopped speaking, expecting him to say something, but he did not. She wondered where Max was.

'What happened?' It was said in the most gentle voice and it touched her. She turned to him.

'I don't know. I changed, I guess. My job didn't make me happy anymore, London wasn't what it was when I moved there. It just wasn't where I wanted to be.'

'So you left?'

'I did. I know it probably sounds strange, and it hasn't been easy but it was the right thing to do.' She smiled and looked at him. 'Sometimes you have to jump into the unknown to find your way again.'

'Have you found it?'

She shrugged and nodded. 'I'm getting there.'

There were more questions he wanted to ask, but Max came back and they had dinner.

Max asked to be excused - he had put his phone on charge and wanted to take pictures of the house with Léa's permission. She smiled graciously and Mark made him promised not to put anything on social media before dismissing him.

The silence returned between them. He was the first to break it. 'I'm sorry about what I said to you earlier. I was out of line and no matter how angry I was I shouldn't have said what I said.' He stopped. She was looking at him intensely, perfectly still. He wondered if she had heard him.

'It was very wrong of me.'

She nodded. 'You need to spend more time with him. He misses you.' She stopped, wondering if she should continue.

'Freya left today so things will be easier from now on.' He looked at her, wondering what she made of that.

'I'm sorry about that.'

'No, you're not,' he said, a smile forming on his lips.

'You're right, I'm not.' She paused. 'He said you're going back to London next week. Is that true?'

He nodded. 'My mother and sister will be looking after him for the next week or so.'

'Then spend the next couple of days with him. Do something with him. Anything. That's what he wants.'

There was an intensity in her eyes that unsettled him a little.

'Where should I take him do you think?'

'If it was me, I'd take him to the Pont du Gard, the famous

Roman aqueduct south of here. Make a day of it, ask Manuela to prepare a picnic for you. You can rent canoes or swim in the river. It's a magical place. Or you could try the Arènes in Nîmes. They have gladiators and many animations at this time of year. I know he'd love it. He's so interested in history.'

He looked at the candle before looking back at Léa.

'Will you come with us?'

She shook her head softly and a dark curl fell forward. She pushed it back behind her ear in a movement that had become familiar to him.

'No. It's between you and him. I would just get in the way. You don't have to pay me for those days.'

He shook his head. 'It would be mean of me to do that given all that you've done for Max.'

She seemed to remember something. 'Oh! I forgot. I've got all this pocket money you asked Max to give me. We've only spent a hundred at most.'

'Keep it. Buy yourself something. Do whatever you need with it. I don't need it. I don't want it back.'

'That's very kind of you but…'

He smiled. 'Please.' He let the silence fall between them before adding, 'I should get Max home. It's late.'

They got up, and she declined their help to tidy up and walked them to the door. Max kissed her, and she told him she was expecting to see him first thing on Saturday morning for the market at their usual meeting spot.

'Thank you again,' he whispered as she kissed him on the cheeks.

She watched them walk up the street. So similar and yet so different.

Léa walked back to the courtyard. Instinctively she put her hand on the chair Mark had sat on. What a strange man he was. He could insult her one minute and be perfectly charming the next. She was not sure she liked that. He did not scare her, but these changes in his moods were alien to her and made her feel on edge. She sat on the chair. But was it just his moods that made her feel on edge? There was something about him that seemed to try to - what was it? - win her over? Surely not. They were like chalk and cheese. They would never work out as a couple. The thought made her get up. This was stupid. She did not fancy him. At all. And all the charm he could display would change that. This was not about her, anyway. It was about him and Max. She sighed and started collecting the plates.

But Freya was gone, and that was a good thing. For Max, she reflected. A line Mark had said about her not being unhappy about it either came back and she blushed. It was, but not for the reasons he thought. Definitely not, she told herself as she put the last of the glasses to dry on the ledge of the sink.

She went outside again, admiring her little outdoor paradise. Not everything was perfect but, like her, it was a work in progress. And for the time being, it was hers. She sat on the little bench and thought of Max. He was starting to assert himself. Not that she condoned him disappearing like he had done tonight and she would tell him so. But at least, he seemed to be showing some form of strength in facing his father and this felt healthy.

She sighed. It would be another sultry night here in town. She dimmed the lights inside the house, picked up her laptop and the remaining of her glass of wine and sat at the little table.

22

Léa stepped down from the train in N"mes around ten the next day. She recognised her Dad's shock of white hair and waved to him. They embraced, and she took his arm, happy to see him and slightly apprehensive about their meeting at the bank.

'We have twenty minutes, let's find a café,' he said, pulling her towards the Arênes. They walked up the pedestrian street that connects the train station to the old N"mes, staying in the shade. The sun was already blazing hot and Léa could feel sweat at the nape of neck despite having her hair up.

'How's your pupil doing?'

'Better and better, although yesterday he decided to runaway which didn't earn me any brownie points with his dad.'

'What happened?'

'I took him to Arles without asking his father's permission first and, unfortunately, the car I had borrowed, broke down which meant we were late home and Mark threatened to end my contract. Max did not take it well and disappeared after I left. We found him in Uzès near the Duché waiting for me. The whole thing was just silly, really.'

'Mark, hey? You're on first terms with his father already?'

'He's British Dad, you call people by their first name pretty much straight away over there.'

She noticed his amused look. Surely he did not think there was more to it than a professional relationship?

'What does he do this Mark guy?'

'He runs a hedge fund. Very rich, apparently. Well, you just need to look at the house he has rented for six weeks. It's exquisite Dad.'

'Is he paying you well at least?'

'That's why I agreed to do the job,' Léa said with a mischievous smile.

'Good. Do you think you could teach full time?'

'I could, but that's not what I want to do. And Max is just a lovely boy. It's different from teaching in a classroom, you know. It's more about developing his natural talents. He's such a gifted kid.'

She had been more talkative than she had wanted to, but it was how she felt about Max.

'You seemed to be very invested in that young boy?'

She shook her head. 'Maybe. I don't know. I feel if I can help him, I should. It's just awful to see a great kid not reach his full potential because of…' She trailed off.

'And he isn't even your kid,' her father said, shaking his head, a smile on his lips.

'Do you think I have any chance of getting the house, Dad?'

He pressed her hand in his. 'We can only try my darling, we can only try.'

The meeting at the bank was over fairly quickly. They would study the proposal and get back to her father in a few days, but it was looking good as he was guaranteeing the mortgage. Léa was feeling much happier when she got out and allowed herself to believe that she would soon own the little house. She had plans to transform it already and was not afraid of doing most of the work herself.

Her father took her to lunch, and they ate in the shade in a little restaurant he knew in the heart of the city.

'How's Mom?' asked Léa after they had finished their first course.

'Good. She just worries, you know.'

'About what?'

'You. Your brother. Her granddaughter.'

'Won't you go and visit Fréderic soon?'

'I'd like to but he keeps saying he's busy and his wife doesn't....' He looked at his plate and winced.

'She doesn't like Mum,' said Léa. Her sister-in-law had not taken kindly to her mother. There had been an instant dislike between the two of them, and the birth of her niece had not helped the matter. Léa blamed her brother too for his lack of involvement. He seemed to agree with everything his wife said, but then, he had always been one for an easy life when it came to family stuff. Being overworked was his favourite excuse, but it did not hide from their parents or Léa that he did not support them much in front of his American wife.

'You should just go,' said Léa, 'just turn up. She may not like it, but I can't believe Fréderic would not welcome you both with open arms. How long has it been since you saw them?'

'Almost a year.'

'I'll call him and ask him when he plans to come and visit.'

'That's very kind of you my love but I doubt he will anytime soon.'

The waiter had turned up with their second courses and they felt silent.

'I'll try, anyway. You never know.'

'Thank you ma chérie, to your house,' he said raising his glass to her.

23

Mark and Max had spent most of Friday in Nîmes. They had gone early to beat the heat and explore the Arênes, the Roman amphitheater right in the middle of the city. Max had ordered their tickets, and they had gone inside, walking along the corridors and up the steep steps that opened onto the arena.

Lunch had been in a restaurant that Léa had recommended before visiting the Maison Carrée and exploring Nîmes in the shade. Then they had made their way to the airport to pick up Mark's mother and sister, who were to look after Max for a week. Caroline, Mark's sister, had been her bubbly self, chatting almost all the way from the airport to the bastide while Mrs Hunter had sat in dignified silence until they had arrived. At last, as they sat under the pergola enjoying the beautiful evening before dinner, she had seemed to relax. Mark wondered if she was expecting Freya to turn up. She had not asked about his ex-girlfriend and he decided he would not volunteer the information. If she wanted to know, she would have to ask.

'Come and sit down near me, Max,' said Caroline patting the space next to her on the sofa, her fair skin on her arms and face already red from the afternoon sun. 'You seemed to have grown since I last saw you.'

Max did as he was told, slipping between his grandmother and his father. He liked his aunty Caroline. She had always been there for him, taking his side when she felt his father was going too far.

'How's Sophie?' asked Mark, 'have you heard anything from her since she left for Miami?'

'My cousin's in Miami? Whoa, lucky her!' said Max, grabbing a crostini smeared with *tapenade*.

'She is thanks to your Dad, and she sounded super excited when I spoke to her yesterday. They take such wonderful care of her there. They're wonderful, wonderful people, you know Mark? I'm so glad she can do all this stuff with their help.'

'Sophie's stronger than you think she is,' said Mrs Hunter to her daughter who was wiping a tear from the corner of her eye, 'cerebral palsy has nothing on her.'

'I think nothing can stop Sophie,' said Mark, a smile on his lips. He loved his goddaughter. Despite having cerebral palsy and spending her life in a wheelchair, she was one of these children who took everything in their stride. He had worried in the past it was all a front to show strength in front of her parents, but not anymore.

'So how's your French coming along, Max?' said Caroline, changing the subject. Talking about her daughter was always a sensitive topic for her, and Mark suspected that she saw herself as a failure as a mother. Something she overcompensated by being constantly at her daughter's side when she was at home. As she was about to turn fourteen, this would not last much longer which was why he was only too happy to pay for his goddaughter to have three weeks twice a year away from her mother and the rest of the family. He was all for her being as independent as she could.

'Super good. I've got this French teacher, she's great! You'll meet her next week, she comes to teach me here some days and then some days we go,' he hesitated looking at his father for approval, 'to Uzès and other places so that I can practice with different people.'

'Does she speak English?' said Mrs Hunter.

'She does, but we mainly speak French when we're together. She only speaks English for Dad.'

'No improvement here, then?' said Caroline, a cheeky smile on her red lips.

Mark held his palms up. 'I've never been good at languages and Léa speaks much better English that I will ever speak French.'

'Who's Léa?' asked Mrs Hunter, her right eyebrow up.

'My French teacher. You'll like her Gran! She's lovely, isn't she Dad?'

Mark nodded, smiling at Max's enthusiasm, but the look in his mother's eyes told him it was better to keep quiet.

'When will we meet her?' said Caroline, 'any chance she could come and have dinner with us tomorrow?'

'That's be so great Dad! Can I ask her? Please, Dad?'

Mark agreed silently. He already knew the answer as he had texted Léa earlier that day asking her if she would like to come and have lunch or dinner with them. Her answer had been that she could not. He did not know why and had wondered if she was still annoyed with him. Maybe if Max tried, he would have more luck.

'What are the boys doing? Why didn't you bring them with you?' Mark asked his sister.

'They're at Tim's parents, in Cambridgeshire. They love it there, some of their cousins are there too and they can run around and play in trees as much as they like. I have no idea how my mother-in-law handles all these kids on her own, but she does. To be honest, I'm rather glad they're not around, I couldn't get them out of the pool if they were!'

'Is Tim working?'

Caroline took a sip of her champagne before answering. 'He is. He has a big case coming up. The courts never stop as he likes to say! When are you going back to London?'

'Monday first thing. I don't fancy it, to be honest. I'm starting to like it here!'

'And who wouldn't? It's an absolutely gorgeous house. I wouldn't let it if it was me to be honest.'

'I'm pretty sure the amount of money the owners make in the summer enables them to pay for the upkeep all year round. An excellent investment, if you ask me.'

'Have you met them?'

'Nope, just the estate agent.'

Max came back from the living room, pouting. 'She can't come this weekend. She's at her parents, she said.'

'That's a shame,' said Caroline, 'but to be fair it's her weekend too. She's probably had enough of the two of you!'

Max looked at his father and grinned. She probably has, thought Mark. He was as disappointed as his son, but it reassured him a little that she was not in town. Maybe she was not so pissed off with him after all.

24

'Léa darling, could you come and help me?'

The call from her mother had come as Léa was helping her Dad scoop the last of the leaves that had fallen into the swimming pool during the night.

'And me who was going to ask you if you wanted to come and get some bread with me!' her father said, mischief in his eyes.

It was an old pattern between them, something that had happened again and again when Léa was growing up. A Sunday morning tradition along with Sunday lunch.

'You don't have to say yes, you know, she'll understand.'

Léa laughed softly. 'No, Dad, she won't. I better go and help her,' she said, handing him the scoop. 'Don't stay out too long.'

She kissed him and walked around the pool. The air felt fresher here in the Alpilles than in Uzès. It would not last though, the sun was already high and she could feel the sun burning her skin.

She stepped into the kitchen, which smelt of garlic and onions frying slowly in a heavy pan on the stove. Her mother was cutting courgettes, peppers and an aubergine at the large island in the middle. It was a homely family kitchen. The house had belonged to her father's parents, and Léa had fond memories of sending summer here with them. There had been no swimming pool at the time or pretty garden to play in, just a courtyard of beaten earth surrounded by tall trees and her grandfather's shed at the end. Sometimes, when they were allowed to, Léa and her brother would walk the path just behind the house and play near the old tower and chapel that overlooked the village. An old fallen tree would become a beautiful horse and a few stones set in a circle a castle.

Her grandparents had died over ten years ago and her parents had had the old house remodelled first to use as a holiday home before relocating there permanently when they had retired. It was almost on top of the hill, on two levels with pale green shutters. From the bedrooms on the first floor and the end of the garden you could see the main road down to the village of Eygalières and further away the Alpilles, the small whitish mountains with clumps of green trees, mainly pines and green oaks.

The kitchen was larger than it had been when her grandparents were still alive, but still looked very much like a country kitchen with its gleaming pans hooked just above the island and wooden cabinets.

'What can I do, Mum?'

'Can you please make the tart? I took the pastry out of the fridge a little while ago. It should be just right to roll out. I've greased the tart tin.'

Léa cleared a space on the marble top and spread some flour before putting the ball of pastry in the middle. She found the rolling pin in a drawer and started flattening the pastry.

'So how is this job with the young kid going? Is he nice?'

'He's lovely, very bright. I like him a lot.'

'Your father said he ran away though.'

Léa had hoped her father would not tell her mother. It was silly really, but she feared she would take this as a bad omen when it had just been a way for Max to assert himself.

'He did, but we found him quickly and he's fine.'

'Why did he run away?'

Léa sighed. She was not sure she wanted to explain the reasons why. Did she even herself know why? And she had wanted to escape the Hunters that weekend, not be constantly reminded of them.

'He was upset with his dad. He's a teenager, he just wanted to assert himself, I guess.'

'Are the parents nice?'

'His mother died three years ago. His father hasn't remarried. They don't get on too well.'

Her mother was silent. She had added the vegetables to the garlic and onions in the pan.

'Do you think you could teach?'

'Nope. Max is lovely and easy to work with, but I don't see myself in front of thirty teenagers.'

'So what are you going to do then once that job is over?'

Here we go again, she thought, the question she had been dreading to hear since her arrival on Friday afternoon. She was only surprised it had taken until Sunday morning for her mother to ask it.

'I want to do more writing for local businesses, maybe set up a consultancy business, something to do with web marketing would be great.'

Her mother turned to her. She could see the weariness and the worry in her face, the disappointment too.

'But what if all this doesn't work?'

'I don't know, I'm sure I'll find something.'

'Why don't you go to Paris in September? Mathilde, your aunt, has offered to let you stay with her while you look for a position. She even talked about you to one of her friends who works for a head-hunting firm who'd be happy to look at your CV.'

Léa stayed silent for a while. It was everything that she did not want, but she did not want to disappoint her mum either. How could she explain to her that this was not what she wanted without hurting her? She pulled a curl that had fallen forward as she was rolling the pastry and took a deep breath.

'I'll think about it. I just need some time at the moment, ok?'

She saw her mother's eyes welled up. Why was it that every time her career was discussed, it always ended with one of them crying?

'But what are you going to do, Léa? You can't continue living from dead-end jobs! Can't you see you can be so much more? Your father and I always believed in you. We supported you through your studies and in whatever you wanted to do. We're both terribly worried about what will happen to you if you go on like this…'

'That's not quite true, Mum. You weren't happy when I told you I was moving to London.'

Her mother's hands were wringing the tea towel she was holding. 'Yes and no, we, I was worried, that's all. You were our eldest child, we wondered what could happen but we've been happy for you, we even thought you'd get married, you know, have children. Why is it that you refuse what you can have so easily? You're gifted, intelligent, you can get any job you want and yet it's like you want to ruin your life,' she said, shaking her head in despair, wiping a tear away with her hand.

'You need to let me be. I'm not asking for more than this. I just can't contemplate going back to work 9 to 5 for a company. I just can't. And it's not a whim.'

'Why don't you see someone?'

'Like a shrink, you mean?'

'Yes, or a coach. I could ask for some recommendations for you if you wanted?'

'Mum,' she said pulling her arms around her, 'just give me some time. I know it's hard and you want us to do well, but it's only been four months since I've been back. I need some time and some space. I'm happy where I am at the moment.'

'Will you consider Mathilde's offer? Maybe you could go in September?'

Léa smiled. 'I'll consider it. Let's just not put a time limit on it just yet. And me, who thought you'd be happy to have me around!'

'I am my love, I am. I just worry, that's all. That's what parents do, you know?' she said embracing her daughter.

25

Freya opened her eyes. The bed felt like it was moving slightly. She felt nauseous. Where was she?

A form next to her moved and, for a second, she thought it was Mark. But a quick look debunked that hope. He was blond. She could vaguely remember what had happened the night before. She had gone to a party on a yacht in Cannes with her friends, had drunk a lot, and then… She could not remember precisely what had happened or how she had come to find herself in this cabin.

She wanted to get up, but her stomach heaved. She tried to look at a fixed point on the ceiling to keep the nausea at bay. Since she had arrived in Cannes at the beginning of the week, she had been determined to have fun: dancing, drinking, going out; all these things she had wanted to do with him. Mark. She winced. She kept telling herself that she was, without any doubt, better without him, freer and without his awful son, but the truth was that she missed him a little. If only he had rented a villa on the Côte d'Azur, she would not have been partying so hard. It was his fault if she was going out too much and sleeping around since she had landed here. She would never had done that if he had not rented that house in the middle of nowhere.

A tear ran down her cheek. She felt awful, and not just physically. She had believed for a minute that, if he was taking her on holiday with him, it was that he thought their relationship could last, that she would be the one he would marry. Her mother would have been so proud. Alex and his wife would have been opposed to it but even Alex could not go against Mark's decisions. Yes, she had insisted, demanded even, that he looked after her in Uzès, but she had done everything to fan the flames of passion too. And she still could not understand what had taken him away from her so quickly.

What was he doing? Had he found someone to replace her? Was someone else already in the bed they had shared in the house in Uzès? Perhaps the girl who was giving French lessons to Max? She was so far removed though from the women he was used to going out with. No, it just could not be her. She was too... It took her a while to describe her.

Natural. That was it. She was just too natural for him. No make-up, no perfect hair, no manicure. She was like the people in that area where he had rented that bloody house. Simple. Just too simple.

She sighed. What was she going to do? The holiday was almost over. She had to go back to London the next day. On Monday, she would have to withstand people's stare and her friends's questions. She would lie, but it would only last a few days before everyone would know that she was not Mark Hunter's girlfriend anymore. Another tear ran down her neck. She felt humiliated.

Light was coming through a porthole above her head. What could she do?

How could she forget! It was the weekend they were supposed to come back to London together. Mark never left his company for long. If he was still flying back at the weekend, she was still in with a chance of winning him over again once she was back in London. Her instinct told her to fight. Give up was not something she did. She would swear her friends to secrecy. He would know nothing of what had happened down here. And even if he did, it was his fault. If he had the right to sleep around, so she had too. Yet it would be better if he never knew what she had done in those last few days.

She got up and looked for her underwear. The man in the bed turned, and she stopped moving, her heart beating hard in her chest. But he did not wake up. He was young. A handsome boy, but it was not him she wanted.

On the deck, there was no-one around except a deckhand polishing the handrails. He asked her if she wanted something. His knowing smile told her he knew what was going on around here. She ignored him and sandals in hand walked down the narrow bridge leading to the quay.

Once on solid ground, she fished her mobile phone out of her handbag. Her friends were looking for her. The nausea felt a little less strong. She walked barefoot to the first opened café and ordered a coffee and a baguette with butter and jam. For once, she knew she needed to eat.

I miss you. I want you to forgive me. When can I see you?

She had nothing left to lose.

26

Refreshed by her weekend away at home and sure that Mark Hunter had left the area for London, Léa drove to the bastide singing to the radio. She felt lighter, freer and, for the first time in a long time, happy. This week she would have Max to herself, and his father had agreed that she could take him wherever she liked.

Max was waiting for her when she arrived. He took her by the hand and they went to the terrace where two women sat at the breakfast table. The younger one rose as they emerged in the sunshine.

'Léa, isn't it? So nice to meet you at last. I'm Caroline, Mark's sister,' said the younger woman, embracing her. She wore a long colourful kaftan and had perfect blow-dried blond hair. Léa noticed the same blue eyes as her brother and nephew.

'And I'm Helen Hunter,' said the older woman, extending her hand to her over the table. The voice was almost aristocratic, and Léa noticed that she did not even say she was Caroline's or Mark's mother. It was obvious.

'Please have a seat,' said Caroline, 'Max, darling, could you ask Manuela to bring more coffee and tea please?'

It had been said with a smile and a warmth that Léa was unaccustomed to and she felt it would be rude to just go away with Max who had already gone running to the kitchen.

'I'm so sorry you couldn't join us this weekend. I know Mark and Max hoped you would.'

'I had to go and see my parents, I did say to Mark…'

'Oh, I know! But my little brother isn't used to people saying no to him,' she said, giggling. 'He's so used to getting his way that he forgets that people have a life of their own sometimes.'

Léa noticed that the elderly Mrs Hunter, who had said nothing, was observing her. She wore a dress of light blue cotton with her grey hair held in a chignon, a solid gold bracelet and diamond rings around her fingers.

'Mark said you moved back from the UK recently,' she finally said, bewilderment in her voice.

'I did. I loved London, but it was time to leave. I needed a change.' The old lady did not reply, and Léa felt like if she was taking an exam.

'That's understandable,' said Caroline as if to compensate for her mother's lack of enthusiasm. 'I would happily move here from London. It's so beautiful. Are you from around here?'

'Oh no, I grew up in Paris but I used to spend part of the summer holidays at my father's parents's home not very far from here, on the other side of the Rhône when you go east, in the Alpilles.'

Manuela arrived with a tray laden with a cafetière and a jug and some additional cups and saucers. They smiled at each other as Caroline poured tea for Léa.

'Tell me what should we see around here? Mark said he went to Nîmes and the Pont du Gard, but he said you'd know better than him.'

'It depends what you want to do. The Pont du Gard is a must, but it's quite a walk which can be difficult in this heat. Nîmes is lovely with good shopping and many things to see. Arles too,' said Léa, winking at Max.

'Could you show us around?'

Léa was so startled by Mrs Hunter's question that she was stumped for words. 'We would take Max, of course,' said the elderly lady. 'He would show us his French. Wouldn't you my love?'

Léa looked at Max, expecting him to make a face, but he seemed happy enough. She went along, although not so much out of agreement as much as curiosity.

27

The door of his office closed, and Mark got up and went to the window. His office was on the twenty-fifth floor and looked out over the City of London. He could see the dome of St Paul's in between other tall buildings on a sunny day. He looked at the tiny beads of water running down the window and wished he was back in Uzès. For the first time in his life, he did not want to be here, in London, in his office. Even the latest round of negotiations on a deal that had been complex and difficult but that they were about to win, had done nothing for him and he had come back pretty much solely for that purpose.

He put his forehead on the glass. He could see the colourful dots of umbrellas in the street below, people running to avoid the rain. He closed his eyes.

Léa. She was never far from his thoughts. He could almost see her dark eyes shining over the candlelit table, both curiosity and defiance playing in them. He could not make her out, but he was intrigued. It was not just lust. It was more than that. An attraction he had not felt in years.

He wanted to know more about her, to understand how someone like her had ended up in that small town? Her story had not convinced him. Was it a burn-out? There had to be something underneath the distance she put between them, the forceful defence of her independence she seemed to impose on him. It had not escaped him that she lived on her own. Had she left someone behind? Was that the reason she was holding him at arm's length? The idea obsessed him. True, he had not endeared himself to her. He winced at the thought of what he had said to her the week before. Anger had taken over, fuelled by fear and his own dislike of people not doing as they were told. Through Max, he had learned that there was no boyfriend in France. He smiled. What was it to him? It was not like…

The thought of their hands brushing on the small table in her courtyard, the feel of her lips on his cheeks when she had kissed them goodbye came back to him. If only he was single with no kids, no serious job, no people expecting him to behave a certain way. Then maybe, just maybe, he would have tried to… Seduce her was not the right word. To…

He stopped, pushed back and opened his eyes again. This was just a stupid daydream. He did not want another dead-end relationship, and this was all that it could ever be. He had to stay well away from this one. The phone on his desk rang. The reverie was over.

The rain had stopped by the time he exited his office just after six. The porter looked to him as if to ask if he needed a taxi, but he shook his head and stepped outside. It smelled of rain and earth and he walked the short distance to the pub where he often met with his best friend Alex, who ran his own advertising agency just a few streets away in Spitalfields.

Alex was waiting for him when he walked in the Sun & Anchor, in their usual place, a corner of the bar. The publican recognised him and with a nod started filling a glass with his favourite beer.

'Looking tanned, my boy!' said Alex, slapping Mark's shoulder.

'Wait till you spend a fortnight there. The weather has been incredible. When are you coming?'

He drank a little of his beer, enjoying the bitterness, feeling his body relax slowly.

'Next week. We've booked somewhere near Avignon for a few days, and then we'll come to you if it's still good.'

'Like you need to ask. Please give my excuses to Martha for dragging you out tonight.'

'You'll do that yourself when you see her. How's Max?' said Alex. Mark saw the worry in his friend's eyes and smiled. 'Good. Better. Provence agrees with him.'

He saw the relief in Alex's shoulders. As he went for another sip of his beer, Mark said as matter-of-factly as he could, 'I got him a French teacher.'

Alex almost spluttered beer all over himself. 'What?'

He saw Mark's expression and burst out laughing. 'That was a joke, obviously.'

'Yes and no. His French teacher at school recommended it, and we were just lucky to find the perfect woman.'

Alex caught something in Mark's voice. There was a spark in him he had not seen for quite a while. 'A woman? A French woman?'

'Who speaks English better than you and me.'

'Tell me more. I'm curious now.'

'Thought you would,' said Mark teasing Alex. 'She's been great, and he seemed to have responded to her in ways that I honestly didn't think I'd see again since Sarah's death. To be honest, it's even better than that. He's just... happier.'

'Can't wait to see him,' said Alex, shaking his head. 'That's splendid news, mate. I can't tell you how worried both Martha and I were last time we saw him. Are you going to enroll him again in that school?'

Mark pulled a face. 'Don't know yet. There's a part of me that wants him to stick it out. But...'

'But?'

'But Léa thinks he needs to go to a new school.'

'Léa, hey?' said Alex, rolling his eyes.

'That's her name. The French teacher.'

'Yep, because you call many teachers by their first name. I say you're smitten with her.'

Mark smiled. 'Don't know about that either.' He thought of telling Alex about what had troubled him earlier, but he was already onto something else.

'How did it go with Freya?'

Mark frowned. 'Come on, Alex. She must have told you.

Come crying to you, even.'

'Nope. I haven't seen or heard from her. I thought she was still in the South of France, that she loved it so much down there. She had decided to stay.'

Mark finished his beer and nodded to the publican to pull two more. He finally turned to Alex. 'It's over.'

They looked at each other. Alex was the first to speak. 'Good. I think that's a good thing.'

'I'm sorry I thought you knew,' said Mark. 'It just wasn't working out and France was a disaster to be honest. A terrible idea.'

Alex slapped him on the shoulder. 'Dude, it's not about me. She may be my goddaughter, but she's a pain. She could be a lovely girl but I don't know what it is about her, she's just bad news. I'm glad you're out of her clutches!'

He drank his beer before adding. 'Martha will be over the moon when she hears. She can't stand Freya.'

28

'He wasn't always like this, you know. He was a funny boy, lively, always up for a prank. He became this serious man after he got married, but even then, he still had this joie de vivre, this joy that would just move him and everyone else forward. Then it disappeared, gradually.' Caroline paused, her eyes lost over the valley.

She had met Léa at the front door as she was about to leave and, as Léa had given her a brief summary of Max's progress, had invited for a chat and a cool drink on the terrace. Léa, who felt at ease with Caroline and suspected she felt a bit lonely stuck between her elderly mother and her young nephew, had agreed as soon as Caroline had added that her mother was resting. She still felt uneasy in front of Mrs Hunter, who seemed to be constantly testing whether or not she would be next on the list of her son's girlfriends.

'I don't think his was a happy marriage. He's never said anything but I wonder if they would have lasted much longer. It's sad to say, but I hoped at the time, when Sarah died, that he would, after a while of course, find someone and re-marry. It's funny, I don't see him as a single man.'

'I guess he has his sons,' said Léa.

Caroline nodded, but she looked unconvinced. 'I think he became too demanding of himself and then with others. I always tell him he expects too much of people. Everything has to be just so. I'm surprised he rented this place,' she said, making a gesture towards the house.

'It's a lovely home.'

'Oh yes! But he usually goes for places that are rather sanitised. This looks like a family home.'

'Maybe he's learning to relax a little,' said Léa tentatively.

'He'd better learn to do that. His kids need him to do that. He's been far too hard on Max. Did he tell you he went to see a psychotherapist with him?'

Léa looked at her, surprised. 'A psychotherapist?'

'A woman. In London. I can't remember her name, she's well known though. She was the one who told him he needed to spend more time with Max. And yet, the first thing he does is to invite Freya Abbott. Have you met her?'

Léa nodded, smiling.

'Awful, awful woman. A true gold-digger. I just can't believe he can't see that she's after his money.'

Léa was not so sure this was what it was, but did not reply.

'Have you met her?'

'She was there the first time I came here, and I saw her a few times after that.'

'What did you think?'

'I'm not sure I'm at liberty to say that in front of my employer's sister!'

'Oh please, don't worry! Anyway, she probably wouldn't speak to you. She'd see you as inferior.'

'Me and Manuela both,' said Léa, laughing.

'You see,' said Caroline who was so crossed by now red blotches had appeared on the fair skin of her face, 'this is the thing I don't understand. Mark is anything if not scrupulous in his dealings with people. He can't stand anyone with money treating other people less fortunate than them badly.' She shook her head. 'Our father instilled that in us from a very young age. He wouldn't be acting this way if Dad was still alive.'

Léa put a hand on her arm. 'Freya's gone. They had a row, and he asked her to leave.'

She heard Caroline's sharp intake of breath. 'Hallelujah! Is it true? When did that happen?'

'A few days before you came here. I thought you knew.'

'No. Although I did think something was up as she wasn't around and he looked happier at the weekend. Oh good! Oh, this is good!' she said, clapping her hands together like a child.

'And I've got a funny story to tell you.'

Léa told Caroline about what had happened in the market the day before she had met them both, and she hooted with laughter.

'I hope he never takes up with her again. He can be weak. Like a lot of men.'

'Isn't she his best friend's goddaughter or something like that?'

'Yes. Alex.' She did not elaborate and Léa wondered what it meant. Had his friend encouraged him to have an affair with his goddaughter? It sounded so farfetched to her she dismissed the idea there and then. She must have misunderstood what Caroline meant.

'Mark is so generous. He pays for my disabled daughter Sophie to have a three-week holiday twice a year every year in a centre where she can do all sorts of stuff from bungee-jumping to rock-climbing, make friends and be like every other teenager. I know it's easy to say he can do it because he's got the money, but we never asked him. It's just something he does for her because he wants to make her happy.'

Caroline wiped a tear from the corner of her eye. 'My husband earns good money and has offered to share the costs but he always says no. It's his treat, his present to his goddaughter and also to us.'

She sighed. 'I just wish he could find someone to love, you know. And be happy. I just don't think he is at the moment.'

'You can't make him. He has to find that out for himself,' said a voice behind them.

Mrs Hunter had come up quietly behind them on the terrace. Caroline got up, and Léa did the same.

'Sit down, both of you. I'm not ill, you know. Manuela will bring me a glass of lemonade soon. Such a lovely woman.'

Léa sat on the other side of the sofa and looked at the two

women. They had similar features, and she saw a bit of Mark and Max in both of them.

'What were you too talking about apart from my stupid son?'

'He isn't stupid, Mama.'

'I grant you he isn't most of the time, but it doesn't mean he can't be sometimes. Let's hope he got rid of that dreadful woman.' She shook her head. 'Freya? What first name is that to start with?'

'Mama! She is Alex's goddaughter.'

'That means nothing. I like Alex and I don't like her. But let's talk about something more pleasant. Léa, darling, Max said you took him to Arles recently. What is there to see? What should we visit?'

29

Since Luca had told Léa that he was finally at last able to take over his father's restaurant, she had seen little of him. Their growing friendship in the last few weeks had helped her tremendously; his no non-sense attitude coupled with his natural kindness soothing her in ways she had not expected. She missed all that, so on her way back from home, she stopped and rang the bell on the off-chance that he would be home at 4 p.m. He was not and so she decided to try the restaurant, a mere ten-minute walk from the house he shared with Michel. That was the beauty of living in a town like Uzès and a never ending joy to Léa: she could just walk everywhere.

He was in the kitchen when she arrived, talking to the chef. His father was nowhere to be seen. A large smile broke over his face when he saw her standing at the kitchen door.

'Have a seat in the patio, I'll be there in two minutes!'

She did as she was told and went to sit outside in the shade. You could not hear the hubbub from the street from here, only the birds in the trees on the other side of the wall.

Luca turned up a few minutes later with a pitcher of water and two tall glasses with lime in them.

'It's good to see you, darling! Where have you been?'

'Max's aunt and his grandmother are in town so I've been alternating between the bastide and taking them to see a few of the lovely sites around here.'

'It must be fun in this heat!'

'We leave early in the morning so it's bearable. We stay in the shade at the bastide in the afternoon. Mrs Hunter senior is elderly so we stay close to the house.'

'Where's the boss? Has he forgiven you for taking his kid to Arles without his permission?' said Luca, chuckling while shaking his head. 'As if you'd do anything to hurt that kid.'

'He's in London and he has, I believe. He invited me along to have dinner with his family at the weekend.'

Luca looked at her, surprised. 'Did you go?'

Léa shook her head before taking a sip of the cool water. 'Nah. I didn't think it'd be appropriate. I stayed at my parents this weekend, anyway.'

'How did that go?'

Léa sighed. 'Good, but Mum is determined to get me a proper job,' she said making brackets with her fingers. 'She has devised this plan to send me to Paris to stay with my aunt.'

Luca raised an eyebrow. 'And? You've said yes?'

'No! But...' Léa hesitated. It was always difficult to explain what she felt in front of her mum and the difficulty she had in telling her no. 'I just told her I couldn't at the moment but that I'd think about it.'

'Will you?'

'No. I don't want to go back to Paris and I know what you're going to say that I need to tell her and all that but she won't listen.'

'You don't know that. Maybe she's only telling you this because she can't see what your plans are. Which is understandable because you haven't told her.'

It stung her a bit that he spoke to her like this. He did not know her mother. 'It's not so easy...'

'Babe, I'm not criticising you but at some point, you'll have to tell her what you've told me and other people, that you want to write and that your life is here. What does it matter to you that she agrees or not? You're old enough to know what you want.'

'I've told her that but she doesn't see it that way.' She stopped, apprehensive of voicing her fears before continuing. 'I've always found it hard to stick it to her. I don't want to hurt her you see and I know that she puts so much hope in us…'

'But it isn't her life. She can't live her life by proxy through you.'

'It's a bit harsh.'

'Is it? Ask yourself that question then. Who will benefit if you get that top job in Paris, you or her? What will you gain?' he said, pointing her finger at her.

'She just wants to be proud of us.'

'So why can't she be proud of you for who you are? And not who she wants you to be?'

The words in her grandmother's letter came back to her, and she smiled. 'You're not the first person who has said that to me lately.'

'You deserve to be happy and be who you want to be Léa. No one has the right to tell you what or who you should be.'

She looked at him. He was wistful, his eyes lost on something on the wall in front of them, and she wondered if he had suffered when he had come out. It could not have been easy to say you were gay twenty years before in a small town and to parents who, probably, were quite the traditionalists. She touched his hand.

'You're right. Isn't it strange how our desire for others to be happy has to involve some sort of transfer from us?'

'It's the human spirit. The people we love doing well reflects positively on us.'

'How's the restaurant coming along? I noticed you got rid of the tablecloths?'

He burst out laughing and she joined in, happy to have lightened the mood. 'I did. Don't think Dad was too happy about it when he came to inspect the premises yesterday evening, but there isn't anything he can do. The place's mine now.'

'Has he transferred the ownership to you?' she said clapping her hands together.

'We're meeting the notary next week but it's as good as. The doctor has told him he needs to rest. It's his heart, it's fragile, a lot more than he thought it was.'

'What is he going to do?'

Luca shook his head. 'He's supposed to stay put but they have plans to visit family and friends in Italy in the autumn when he feels better. They haven't been back for fifteen years! Can you believe it?'

'It's not a peaceful job being a restaurateur.'

'No, but I have no plan to do what he did. As soon as I can, I'll appoint a deputy manager, someone I can trust to look after the restaurant now and then.'

'What does it feel like to be master of your destiny after all these years?'

He was silent for a moment, but his communicative smile was back. 'Good, fabulously good. I can at last implement the changes I want, try things you know. I'm not stupid enough to think everything will work out, but there are some things I can do to make it all more modern. As soon as I can, hopefully in the autumn, I'll have a little work done to refresh the restaurant...'

They kept talking for a while until he was called in the kitchen. The restaurant was opening in a few hours, and he needed to get the place and people ready. As she was about to leave, he grabbed her hand, and he kissed her goodbye. 'Be you Léa. Never change, you're great as you are.'

30

Sat at her desk, Freya was tapping with the tips of her long manicured fingers the armrests of her chair. We were Thursday and Mark had answered none of the three messages she had sent him since the weekend.

She had told no one about the breaking down of their relationship and was still hoping to salvage it before it became public knowledge. When she had been asked how was her holiday in Provence, she had answered with enthusiasm while staying as vague as possible.

She looked at the time on her mobile. It was just after six thirty. To call him was useless. If he had not answered any of her texts, he was not going to answer her calls. No, the only thing she could do was to see him. She switched off her computer and grabbed her Hermès handbag, the one he had given her and that she took everywhere since her return to London. It was like a memento of him. As she was moving towards reception and the lift, one of her big boss's closest collaborators stopped her. She cursed him under her breath but gave him her sweetest smile.

'Freya, sorry to bother you but I have a few questions about some of your trading. Do you have a minute?'

She pouted and looked at her Chanel watch. 'I'm sorry, I can't. I have an important appointment. Can it wait until tomorrow morning? I can be in your office first thing.'

The man crossed his arms and looked at her, a half-smile on his lips. Her little seduction was not working out.

'That's annoying because Mr Pearson asked me to get back to him as soon as possible. What is this important meeting about?'

'I'm meeting Mr Hunter from Hunter Associates. Do you know him?'

She knew straight away from the surprise on his face that she had scored a point. It was obvious he did not read the gossip columns otherwise he would have known she was Mark Hunter's girlfriend, but today she was fine with that.

'Very well, I mean, I've met him twice. I didn't know you knew him.' He hesitated before continuing, unsure of how she could have met Mark Hunter. 'Please come to my office first thing tomorrow morning. I'll be waiting for you.'

She smiled and slipped past him as quickly as she could. She did not know what he wanted and kicked herself for not having asked him what exactly he wanted to know. Mark was getting to her head. She would never had made such a schoolboy's error before their break-up. It was too late to worry about it: she would have to turn up early the next day. But now, she had a much bigger problem to solve.

When she arrived in front of the Hunter residence in Holland Park, it was close to seven thirty. It looked like no-one was home but, as she was getting out of her car to ring the bell, a woman in her fifties opened the gate. Freya recognised Mark's housekeeper and ran to her.

The woman, surprised, stared at her. She did not seem to know who she was, and she wondered if Mark had already given orders not to let her in.

'Do you remember me? I'm Freya Abbott, Ma…, Mr Hunter's girlfriend.'

The woman nodded slowly, with no warmth. 'Mr Hunter isn't home yet,' she said sternly before adding quickly, 'I don't know what time he'll be home.'

Unknowingly the woman had just given her the perfect excuse. She grabbed it with both hands.

'Oh, I know! He said he had a meeting that was likely to finish late. I wanted to surprise him. Could you let me in so that I can wait for him inside?'

The woman stared at her again, suspicion in her eyes. 'Mr Hunter doesn't want people in his house when he isn't around.'

'I know but I'm not anybody, I'm his girlfriend. I've just spent two weeks with him in France.'

'And you are going away with him tomorrow?'

Freya's heart started to beat faster. He was leaving again. Tonight was her last chance to win him over again. 'Of course! But I have a surprise for him, a present.'

The woman looked her up and down. She was obviously wondering what present Freya could be giving her boss, given that she had nothing in her hands apart from her handbag.

'Please,' she pleaded, taking the woman's hand in hers. 'It's important. I'd be eternally grateful if you could let me in.'

The woman was still hesitating. Freya forced herself to say nothing and to just look at her with the most innocent look she could fathom. It worked. The woman took her hand away from hers and opened her handbag.

'I'm opening the door for you but I can't leave you my keys. I need them to get in tomorrow.'

They walked back to the house, and the housekeeper let her in, admonishing her not to open to anyone and saying out loud that she hoped Mr Hunter would not be mad at her for letting her in.

'It'll be the complete opposite,' lied Freya, feeling no shame, 'he'll be forever grateful that you let me in. But please don't tell him. Remember, it's a secret, a surprise,' she insisted as the woman closed the imposing frosted glass and black iron door behind her.

She stayed standing without moving until she heard the gate close. It had been easier than she had hoped. She only had to wait for him now. She caressed the marble top of the ornate table that stood in the entrance hall and looked at herself in the gilded Venetian mirror. She moved to the lounge, her high heels clicking on the parquet floor as she walked around the room. She wondered what it would be like if she was the lady of this luxurious home in central London. They would welcome the crème de la crème of the finance world and leading FTSE companies, maybe even politicians or celebrities. Besides the housekeeper - which she might want to replace -, she would have various people at her disposal. A cook, maybe a chambermaid, and certainly a personal assistant. She would give him a child, it would be the guarantee that he would not abandon her without a large settlement. She would hire a nanny to take care of the baby, and she would send Max and his brother to boarding school. It would do Max some good to be away from home. Moreover she could not live with this strange boy in her house.

She walked to the kitchen who gave onto, like the lounge, a large terrace which opened onto a landscaped garden. Maybe they could move the terrace, build a basement like most London millionnaires did, with a swimming pool and a private gym. She looked towards the garden. The light was fading slowly. It was big enough for sizeable garden parties on beautiful evening nights.

She opened the fridge. There was an opened bottle of what looked like an expensive white wine. She poured herself a glass before taking a sip. The alcohol helped relieve the tension she was feeling, and she congratulated herself on her quick thinking earlier. She would have liked to call her mother to tell her what she had done, but now was not the time. During their last conversation, the weekend before, just as she had landed in London, she had told her daughter that she could not wait to meet the man who would make an honest woman of her. She was so old school, her mother. A few weeks before, she had almost made fun of her about something similar she had said, but not this time. She had seen her chance melt into thin air in Provence, but she was determined to patch things up with Mark to give her mother that wedding she was dreaming of. What she needed to do was to think of how she was going to re-light that fire in him.

She went back into the hall and looked at herself in the mirror again. She hesitated in going into Mark's bedroom. Her idea had been to offer herself to him in his bed as he came home, but she was not so sure that this was a brilliant idea. As her mother had said to her recently, she had to be less provocative. Men did not like women who tried too hard, she had told her. Freya had always thought the opposite was true, but this time, the stakes were higher than just to be in his bed. If she wanted him to marry her, she needed to show him she was not who he thought she was, that she was better than that.

She would wait for him in the lounge.

31

Freya had been waiting for almost two hours when she saw the car lights of his car lit the entrance hall. The wheels screeched on the gravel, the car door was slammed shut and his steps echoed on the porch. The key turned in the lock and she heard him cursed his housekeeper for forgetting to switch on the alarm again.

The light in the hall came up. Suddenly her little stratagem felt like a risk too far, but it was too late to go back. She swallowed the last sip of her wine and got up quietly.

He had his back to her, his eyes on his mail. He wore one of his dark blue suits that fitted him perfectly. She could see the reflection of his tanned face in the mirror, a deep vertical line crossing his forehead. For the first time, she thought him handsome, and her desire for him took her breath away.

'Hello Mark.'

He turned around briskly and glared at her. She had hoped that he would be happy to see her, that he would come to her and would ask her to forgive him for the way he had treated her in Uzès.

'What are you doing here?' His voice was cold, sharp. She got closer to him, a smile on her lips.

'I had to see you. You haven't answered my messages. You—'

'Freya, it's over between us. We said everything there was to say in Uzès.'

'Not me,' she said, tears in her eyes. 'I have things I need to tell you.'

He shook his head, his hands on his hips. There was no warmth in his eyes.

'We have got nothing to say to each other.'

'I was stupid in Uzès. I wanted to be the centre of the world, the centre of your world. I should never have spoken to Max or you the way I did, and I'm sorry.'

A tear ran on her cheek, which she wiped with a manicured fingertip. He had not moved when she looked at to him again.

'Freya, it's over. I told you from the start that it was never serious between you and me, that it was an enjoyable moment but that, at some point, we would go our separate ways. You accepted it then.'

'But you took me to Provence with you! It meant that you wanted more, that you were looking at something else for us!'

She had come closer again to him, but he took a step back.

'No, I took you to Uzès because... because I was worried about being on my own with my son. I used you and for this, I'm sorry. I shouldn't have done that. But it's over. And no, I've wanted nothing with you other than what we had.'

'I love you Mark.'

'No Freya, you don't. You love being with me for what I am, not for who I am.'

She shook her head from side to side. 'It's not true... It was true, but it isn't anymore. I realised last week that I missed you, that I needed you,' she said in a tearful voice.

He remained unmoved. She was so close to him she could feel the warmth of his body. She noticed the small lines around his eyes, the few silver strands that were showing in his dark hair. She extended her hand to him.

'Mark please, give me one more chance. I promise you it'll be the last and that if it doesn't work, I'll go away quietly, I won't make a scene, you won't see me ever again. But you'll see, I have changed, I want things to work out between us, I'll be more like... like...'

He had crossed his arms over his chest, the beginning of a smile forming on his lips. She thought for a second that she had won, that he would give her another chance.

'Like whom?'

'Like the woman that you want.'

'The woman that I want?'

He shook his head before looking at her, a thoughtful look on his face. 'The woman I want Freya is not here. It's not you, whether or not you change.'

So it was true then, he had already found a replacement for her and it had to be that provincial teacher who pretended she spoke English.

'You slept with her?'

He looked surprised.

'With whom?'

'Her. Léa is her name, isn't it? Your son's teacher,' she said with as much contempt that she could.

She knew that she needed to control herself and she could have if it had been anybody else. But that woman? She could not accept it, not her.

'You see Freya, you don't change. You're accusing me again.'

'You've just said that the woman you want is not here!' Had she got him wrong? She felt trapped, her anger getting the better of her.

'In a matter of speaking, yes. What I mean is that you aren't the woman I love and that I have no intention of starting ever again with you. It's over.'

'You won't get rid of me like that, Mark! You used me, you had me where you wanted me to be and now you are throwing me under the bus because you love someone else.'

'I've never loved you Freya and I've never made a secret of it. I'll remind you that you—'

'I was sincere! I've never used you in any way!' she said, her voice echoing in the hallway.

Although he was smiling, underneath the surface she could feel his patience wearing thin. 'Is that a sick joke?'

'I told you, I won't go away quietly,' she said grabbing her trench coat that was lying on a chair.

'I don't care about your threats Freya but I advise you to be very careful about what you do or say in the future,' he said opening the front door wide for her. 'Goodnight.'

She had barely stepped outside that he closed the door behind her. She wanted to scream, instead she angrily adjusted the belt of her trench coat. She did not know how, but she promised herself that she would make him pay for abandoning her.

32

Léa was up early on Sunday. The heat was already high despite the sun just peeking through the trees on the other side of the far wall of the garden. She made herself some tea and sat for an hour writing in her journal at the table in the courtyard. It was her favourite time of the day, when everything around her was quiet except for the birds. She felt a little jittery and knew she needed to do something physical today. Sitting around waiting for the day to pass was not an option. The borders around the paved courtyard had not been looked after since the old lady who had lived in the house before her had died at the beginning of the year. She walked around and although they were overgrown, she noticed a rosebush, a camellia and some thyme and rosemary that would be worth saving. She would dig and get rid of the weeds, and then she would go to the nursery and get some plants in the afternoon.

She went upstairs and changed into a pair of shorts made of old jeans and an old washed-out t-shirt. Downstairs, she picked up her garden tools and a pair of gloves in a clay pot by the kitchen door. It was hard work, but within an hour; she felt better. The fear in the pit of her stomach had disappeared and she could feel herself breathing more easily. She grabbed her hat as the sun was now beating down and looked at the time. Ten o'clock. Another couple of hours and she would have cleared the three borders that surrounded the courtyard.

The rhythm of digging, pulling and raking the earth soon

became a kind of trance, leaving her mind to wander. Her thoughts turned to Mark. It had been a constant since the night Max had run away and she could not help wonder why. She did not want a relationship, not after what had happened in London. It was still too raw, her mistrust of men too great. But there was something about him. She would not have gone as far as to say she was attracted to him. Sure, he was good-looking, even handsome some would have said, he also had money and all the stuff that it can bring but she had never been attracted to that. She did not need that much. Hell, she was living with very little! But there was something. Every time she was in front of him, she felt... she was not sure what she felt. Anger? Definitely a little because he seemed to be willing to buy her out every time and it just annoyed the hell out of her. And yet, here she was wondering where he was and what he was doing. She pushed him out of her thoughts. She could focus on something else, surely she could.

She had no idea what time it was when the bell rang. She had finished the borders and was digging two big pots. She took her hat off and wiped the sweat off her brow with the back of her gloved hand. She realised as she went to the door that she would never have been seen dead in such an outfit while living in London. How we change.

* * * * *

The door opened as he was about to move away. Walking down her cobbled lane, he had wondered if it had been a good idea to come; Léa would probably tell him he should not have bothered. But here she was, standing there, in frayed denim shorts and a dirty yellow t-shirt, a smear of dirt on her forehead, garden tools in one of her gloved hands. Her curls were escaping from the low bun she had tied them into at the nape of her neck and her tanned skin glistened. She looked beautiful, earthy and crossed.

'I wanted to thank you properly for the other night,' he said, handing her a large bouquet of flowers. 'I know I was... I shouldn't have said what I said. I was angry and worried, but it's no excuse. I'm sorry.'

She seemed to hesitate, but took the flowers and smelled them.

'They're beautiful.' She looked at him. 'And thank you for the apology.'

There was a silence. He could feel the heat of the sun, sweat running down his back.

'I should put them in water,' she said, almost turning away.

'Are you doing anything today?' He had said that quickly. He did not want her to close the door on him.

She stopped and made a gesture as if to say look at me. 'Gardening. The borders in the courtyard. I was planning to get some new plants later today.'

'Maybe I could buy you lunch and we could go together?'

'Where's Max?' she said, looking on both sides of the street.

'At the house with his grandma.'

She turned around, and he followed her into the house, closing the front door softly behind him. It was cool behind the thick walls and dark as all the shutters were closed. She left the garden tools outside the kitchen door that gave onto to the courtyard and grabbed a vase. He watched her unwrapped the flowers and cut their ends before putting them in water. She took them to the lounge and put them on the coffee table. She stepped back, re-arranged a stem and finally turned to him, a smile on her face.

'I'll be as quick as I can. There's water and juice in the fridge, glasses on the shelf.' She was gone before he could say anything, her jasmine scent lingering in the cool air of the room.

He stayed there, smiling to himself. His heart had been beating faster since she had opened the door. The feelings he had had before he left were coming back to him in waves. She had been distant, but he had expected her to be as he had given her no warning. But he had wanted to play it that way, to surprise her. In truth, he could not wait any longer; pictures of her had been playing on his mind since the night Max had run away. Alex had not been far off when he had said that there was more to it than just a working relationship for him. He could not deny it any longer. If anything, he wanted her more than he had done a week ago.

Léa had a shock when she saw her reflection in the bathroom's mirror. She had not noticed the smear of dirt on her forehead. What must he think of her? She undressed quickly and stepped into the shower, scrubbing hard at the dirt on her knees and under her fingernails. The cool water revived her, and she suddenly felt very hungry. Where could they go on a Sunday? There were plenty of places, but without a reservation in August, it would be a tough call. She stepped out of the shower and wrapped herself in a large towel. She heard a noise in the courtyard and saw him through the blinds. He was standing by the tree, looking at the house. She knew he could not see her and stayed a minute looking at him. There was something intensely masculine about him. Solid too. Probably the shoulders that she could see under the polo shirt and the muscles in his arms. He turned around and seemed to inspect her handy work. She could not imagine him digging his garden in his spare time. She moved to the bedroom and got her favourite dress out.

He must have heard her step down the stairs as he was back in the house when she walked into the lounge. He smiled to her.

'Where do you want to go?'

'There's a nice little place in a village not far from here. I'll call them to see if they can fit us in.'

33

The restaurant Léa had in mind managed to fit them in thanks to her mentioning Luca's name, and they were sat at a table on a terrace that opened onto a valley below. There was a light breeze, which Léa was grateful for. It had been so hot again today in Uzès. The heatwave was not going anywhere.

The table was small, and she felt his knee brushed against hers. She did not know what to make of him and was not sure why he had come to see her. Did he fancy her?

'When did you get back from London?'

'Last night.' He smiled, and she wondered if he had noticed that he had touched her leg again. 'I couldn't wait to get out.'

'What was the weather like?'

'Atrocious!' he said, laughing. 'It rained a lot. Another wet summer in England, I'm afraid.'

As they ordered, she observed him from the corner of her eye. She wanted to know more about him. He was still such a mystery to her. But she thought it safer to talk about Max. 'Max talked to me about his mother two days ago. He's worried that he's starting to lose his memory of her.'

Mark looked at her. A curl had fallen forward, and it took all of his willpower not to move it back behind her ear. 'He told me the same thing before I left. I tried to re-assure him but, obviously, I didn't do a good enough job.'

She was not sure if the jab was for her, but Léa thought it was unfair and said so. He put his palms up. 'I wasn't accusing you,

I was just making the point that I'm not very good at reassuring my own son. But I also think that what worries him is more complex than just not remembering his mother.'

'What do you mean?'

'That you've taken a place in his heart that is just as big and that he's worried that it means he doesn't love her as much as before.'

He looked at her pause, her champagne glass in mid-air. 'I hadn't thought of this.' She took a sip and looked at him straight in the eyes. 'Do you miss her, your wife, I mean?'

The answer came straight back. 'No. No, I don't.'

He saw the surprise in her eyes and for a reason he would have found difficult to explain, for the first time in three years, felt the need to talk about his late wife.

'We weren't in love when she became sick. We were heading for divorce.'

'I'm sorry I didn't want to pry. You don't need—'

'It's okay. Maybe it'll help you understand where Max and I are at.' He paused and looked away at the valley beneath them. 'I was never in love with my wife, although I probably thought I was when I met her. We met through common friends, one of them is my brother-in-law today, Caroline's husband. She was a high-flying barrister in her early thirties who wanted children. I wanted to get married to please my father. He had become ill soon before and I just wanted to make him proud of me. So I proposed, but I knew days before we got married that we were making a mistake, that there was no true love between us. At least on my part.'

'But you went through with it?' said Léa, bewildered.

He smiled, his eyes betraying the pain he was feeling. 'Yes. And it's not even like I can say I was young and didn't know what I was doing. But I just couldn't go through with ditching her at the altar or cancelling the wedding. I wanted my Dad to be happy and proud. He meant the world to me, you see. I've always wanted to be like him.'

'I'm sure he was proud of you.'

Mark cleared his throat. 'I was always a bit of a

disappointment to him. He wanted me to go into law and become a barrister and a judge, but I was never interested enough in law to put in the hours. I got my degree and went to work for a bank.'

Léa wanted to re-assure him, but the memory of her mother's words to her the weekend before were still ringing in her ears. Why do we always need to set conditions in our love for others?

'So we got married and Max came along quite quickly and I thought for a while that if Sarah had what she wanted, a baby, she would be happy and would need me less. I lost myself in work, I guess. It was fun, the company was growing. I was on top of the world when I was there. I just dreaded going home. Weekends were the worse. I guess I didn't exactly bond with Max when he was a baby.' He paused, drank some wine. 'I regret that.'

She almost put her hand on his arm. There was a sadness in him she found unsettling. He was not the assured guy, slightly cocky, she had met three weeks before. He had let her see something of his own inner world that she guessed he had not told many people about.

'You know, I don't think he minds it too much about you not being there when he was a baby. I think he's much more interested in you spending time and connecting with him today.'

He smiled. 'You always find the positive, don't you?'

'I don't see how beating yourself up about something that happened a long time ago is going to help.'

He did not reply. Léa wanted to know what happened next. 'Did your wife go back to work after Max was born?'

'Not straight away. She stayed home with him until he went to nursery, but even then, she was less than keen to go back to work. By then we were leaving almost separate lives. We went to counselling which helped for a while and Tom came along because Sarah wanted another child and I thought maybe it would save our marriage. In the end, it didn't. We had started divorce proceedings by the time she was diagnosed.'

'Did she have long?'

'Less than nine months. It was brutal. I wouldn't wish it on anyone. At the end, she did not know who the surrounding people were.'

Mark let his eyes focus back on Léa. 'Anyway, this may explain why my relationship with Max is what it is. We haven't had the best start and since Sarah died, I just haven't known how to connect with him.'

'How did he react when he learned his mother was dying?'

Mark took a deep breath. 'I don't think he knew what it meant at first. He was nine. Death meant nothing to him. Then she died, and there was a void that no one could fill for him. Although many tried. We had so many people looking after us, from my mother to our friends. But it wasn't her. It was different for Tom. He was two, just too small to know what had happened.'

'What about you? How did you feel after your wife died?'

Mark caught his breath and looked at her. No-one until now had asked him that. Could he tell her? Did he want to?

'You don't have to tell me if you don't want to,' said Léa. She could see something almost akin to fear in his eyes and wondered if she had broken the spell by asking such a personal question.

He shook his head. 'No. It's just that I've never told anyone.' He drank a little of his wine to give himself time to think. 'I felt guilty. And empty. But mostly guilty. I knew I had treated Sarah poorly all those years, even if I took care of her when she was diagnosed. It didn't make me feel better that we stayed together until she died somehow.'

He looked away again, and Léa noticed the shine in them. The memories were still raw.

'Then I think I became angry. I wanted nothing to do with someone else. I saw long-term relationships as a problem rather than something to be desired. It took me a while to see that the life I led might not have been what was best for me or my children. I guess I became rather selfish.'

Léa smiled. 'I don't think that's true.'

'Oh, it is! When I want something I go for it without thinking too much of the consequences. I didn't think about the children after Sarah died.'

'Of course you did. You did the best you could.'

'I took care of the material stuff because it was easy but I just couldn't provide them with the care and love that they needed. It's like something in me had died. I should have looked for someone for them.'

'Don't you think you have to be happy yourself before you make others happy? They wouldn't be happy with someone you didn't love. Max certainly doesn't blame you for that.'

He sighed. 'I wish he had done so, and we had it out. It would have been easier.'

'For you, but not for him. What he wants is for you to be proud of him, to be there for him. He wants your attention.'

Léa stopped before continuing, 'You know he speaks a lot about you. He's very proud of you.'

'Is he?' he said, surprised.

She nodded. 'He is. And he's been at his happiest since you did stuff together a week or so ago. He keeps telling me how great it was.' She paused. 'Do you think he misses his Mum still?'

'I don't know. I don't think he does as much now as he did when he first arrived. He has found other areas of interest and people, I guess.'

She tucked into the fish she had ordered and took a bite. 'He's a very gifted kid, very sensitive too.'

'Which is a problem.'

'Sensitivity isn't a problem, it's a force. It means that he understands and feels the world differently from you or me. It's a type of intelligence. It just needs to be managed so that he can use it wisely.'

She felt like she had said too much, but it was too late to go back.

'I may be wrong here but I would guess you know what it means first hand?'

She nodded. 'Yes, and no. We're not the same. Have you made a decision about his school?'

'Not yet. A part of me still wants him to stick with it. He's stronger and happier, I'm sure he'd have a different experience this time.'

Léa shook her head. 'I don't think so. The damage is done. He's stronger here because he's been removed from the problem.'

'It's still the perfect way for him to get into a top university.'

'Given his intelligence, he'll succeed no matter where he goes, but he needs to be in the right environment to do so. And there's the bullying.'

'Boys together—'

'Bullying isn't acceptable no matter what the environment is. You can't justify it.'

'I can't win, can I?'

'Not on this one,' she said with a smile and a shake of her head.

Mark nodded and sat back in his chair. She had done it again, telling him in no uncertain terms that he was wrong, but he did not mind.

'If you were not looking after my son and you could do anything, anything at all, what would you do?'

The question blew her away. She opened her mouth and then closed it, lost for words.

'I don't know.'

'Come on, you must have a dream, something you want to do?'

'I'd like to write novels. I know it's crazy and no one ever makes any money from it but…'

'Do it then.'

She looked at him, frowning.

'Why are you looking at me like that?'

'Because most people tell me I'm mad and that I should get a proper job.'

'It's your life. Not theirs. Not mine.' He looked at her, and the funny smile was back.

'You amaze me, you know? If you can live in another country, surely changing jobs is a piece of cake.'

'Ah! That's much more difficult,' she said teasing.

'In what way?'

'What if I have no talent? Or it's a total disaster and I fail miserably?'

'But what if it isn't, and it works out brilliantly? What's the bigger risk here?'

'It's easy for you to say. You're very successful at what you do.'

'Forget about me. What's the bigger risk to you? To kill yourself doing something you don't want to do or try something that isn't easy but will make you happy?'

He could see she was unconvinced, maybe even a little angry.

'Why are you saying that to me?'

'Because one thing I understood when my wife died is that we only have one life. There is no other. And none of us know what will happen tomorrow or the day after next. What other people think of you is irrelevant. It's what you think of yourself that is. But you know what? I think you know that already.'

She was about to say something but their waiter came back asking if they wanted desert.

'Are you happy yourself?' she asked him after they had ordered espressos.

He took his time, sipping the last of his wine. 'It's a tricky question. But right here, I am.'

He smiled, a mischievous light in his eyes. 'So are you going to write that book?'

'I've started already.'

'Promise me one thing then,' he said, looking at her straight in the eye, 'that no matter what happens, you'll keep going.'

34

The heat was intense when they walked out of the restaurant and through the village to walk back to the car. An old man in a checkered shirt sat on a chair in front of what must have been his house. He seemed to be asleep, but raised a lazy hand as they passed. The only people milling about on this scorching afternoon seemed to be tourists.

They strolled in silence, happy in each other's. They stopped on the square shaded by a few plane trees in front of an imposing Roman church. The sky was a deep blue against the ochre of the stones.

'Are you a Catholic?'

The question surprised her, but she looked at him and laughed. 'A lapsed one! I'm afraid I'm no great believer.'

'I'm not either, but I like churches. Have you been inside this one?'

She shook her head and the auburn tones in her hair made her curls almost iridescent in the sunshine. He could have stayed there looking at her forever.

'Shall we have a look?' she said.

They walked to the main door which he opened for her, her hand brushing his arm as she passed, sending shivers tingling down his spine as he followed her in. Inside, the coolness of the air enveloped them. Léa genuflected and crossed herself. She saw his quizzical look. 'Old habits die hard,' she whispered, 'I went to a Catholic school when I was a teenager.'

There were a handful of people, men and women, some praying on chairs, others, probably tourists like them, walking around the old church. They slowly made their way round, stopping at points, speaking in hushed tones. Léa bought a small candle for one euro and lit it, saying a quiet prayer for her grandmother. She missed her wisdom and wondered what she would make of the tall Englishman next to her.

They emerged in the sunshine once again, and Léa felt relieved to be out of the gloom.

'So where are we going?' he asked as they stood at the end of the village overlooking the valley. You could see the river meandering below, vines, sunflowers and clumps of houses huddled together here and there. It was almost shimmering in the heat.

'The nursery is near Nîmes. It shouldn't take long.'

'I'm in no rush,' he said, and she blushed.

It was a good thing that he was not in a hurry because they lost their way trying to get to Nîmes via tiny dusty roads. But this was when they saw it. A château. Even from the road, with its closed faded blue shutters, you could tell it had seen better days. Mark stopped the car by an imposing if a little rusted wrought-iron gate and stepped outside. A homemade sign said that it was for sale.

'I wonder what it's like inside,' Léa said as she approached the iron gate. The garden was overgrown but you could still glimpse a gravel path that snaked its way to the castle among the dry vegetation and the brambles.

There was a padlock attached to the gate that looked ancient, and when Mark looked at it, he found that it was not properly locked. They looked at each other. 'Shall we go in?' he said first, a twinkle in his eyes.

Léa was not sure what emboldened her to say yes - in other circumstances she would have been the one to steer them away from trespassing on someone else's property. Maybe it was the wine at lunchtime, or just the fact that she was with him. He pushed the gate so that she could go in and followed her, closing the gate again behind them.

The path was dusty but cool under the mature plane trees, and the vegetation was not as overgrown once you walked a little further down the path. After a brief walk, the perspective opened, and they saw the facade they had caught sight of from the road. A few low steps led to an imposing double-wing door made of solid oak with a beautiful set of large round handles. There were four large double windows on each side, the pattern being repeated on the two levels above. There were two turrets at each side. At the top of the facade stood a large pediment with a sculpted decorative macaroon in the middle and garlands. The golden colour of the walls had faded, some light blue shutters had parts missing and the decorative balconies were in a terrible shape, but there was still something grand about it. It looked like an eighteen century French château in the Provence style.

They circled a fountain with a bronze dolphin on the top set in a sand circle before walking up the steps to the main door.

'What is this place?' she heard Mark say, 'it's just amazing.' He tried the door, but the bolt did not budge. 'Damn, I'd love to have a look inside.'

'Maybe there's another door on the other side,' ventured Léa, who felt excited.

They walked around the building and were taken aback by the garden on the other side. There was another larger *pièce d'eau*, low and green with two dolphins in the middle and three cherubs on the side. On the other side of this ornamental pond, you could see what looked like a rose garden. They followed the path under the wooden beams where rosebushes and other climbers were so tightly intertwined they created a green tunnel. At the end of the garden, there was a park with tall mature trees.

'There's something white a little further,' said Mark. They walked along a gravel path until they came to a little chapel. It was crumbling at the edges, but he tried the door. It was locked. They retraced their steps, circling around the castle, and saw a tennis court on the left hand-side. It was covered with leaves and the net was down, but you could still make out the white lines. On the other side, a dry stone wall covered in places with ivy, hid a swimming pool. It was empty, and there were cracks on the bottom floor. A couple of plastic sun loungers lay at the other end near a pool house made of dry stones.

They walked back and up the double staircase that led to what must be the south side of the building, trying the French windows one by one. None of them opened but, their hands up to their eyes, they tried to glimpse inside.

'It looks like a sizeable room with parquet flooring on this side. Oh! And there's a massive chimney on the left. It's been carved into some kind of coloured marble too.' She stepped back and he could see the excitement on her face.

'How old do you think this place is?' he asked, caressing the stone balustrade.

'Not sure. Eighteen century maybe. I so wish we could have a look inside.'

'There's a number on the sign by the gate. I'll try it tomorrow.'

She looked at him, smiling. 'Don't you think they'll ask questions if we just ask to visit without following up on it?'

'Isn't that what people do when they visit houses they want to buy?'

She shrugged. 'It just feels wrong to make someone believes something that you have no intention of doing.'

He chuckled, shaking his head. 'I'm happy to take the blame for it.'

35

Léa changed back into her old shorts and t-shirt and started planting as soon as Mark left. She knew she needed to do physical work again. She felt troubled by their time together. As she put some lavender in the soft soil, she realised that it had been the first time they had been alone together. The last time, Max had been with them. It had been different this time. After the first few awkward moments as they had sat down for lunch, the conversation had seemed to flow.

She was touched that he had confided in her about his first marriage but there, digging in the late afternoon sunshine, she wondered why. Was he attracted to her? It was so far-fetched that the thought made her stand up, her heart beating faster, her hands sweating. Surely not. She was not his type. He liked thin, perfectly groomed women. She was nothing of the sort.

She went to the kitchen to drink some water, hoping the thought would just go away, but it did not. Catching a reflection of herself in the glass door, she wondered again about what he thought of her. But what did she think of him?

He was like a daydream, a chimera, something that you would like but you know you will never get. A dream. Yet his presence, the warmth of his skin when she had touched his arm, the laughter in his eyes today, all had contributed to make her want something else than just… Just what?

It was not friendship. They were not friends. He was her boss, the guy who paid her wages and whose son she taught French to. This was not exactly an equal to equal relationship. And yet, he had not tried to dominate her or tell her what to do today. If anything, he had encouraged her to follow her dreams.

But even if by the greatest twist of fate, they… She stopped herself again. If they what? Made love? Had a relationship? Even assuming that this could happen, he would not move here, so there was no future. She had made it plain she would not move back to London and, of that, she was sure.

Once finished with the planting, she went to take another shower. She felt dirty and hot and let the cool water run on her body for a long time, thoughts of him swirling in her head. How would it feel to have his body against hers, his hands on her, to kiss him? A yearning rose in her and she realised that she had envied Freya's closeness to him. She could not deny it. She would not mind being seduced by him. It was the aftermath though that worried her. There was nowhere for them to go.

Léa stayed up late in her courtyard, typing away at the story she had been weaving in her head in the last few days. It had taken her a while to settle down to write but once she was in flow, there had been no stopping her, her imagination taking her away from her worries about the house and her thoughts of Mark.

The house. Because everything tended to shut in August in France, there was nothing she could do to speed up the process, no-one would come to survey the old house until the last week of the month. She would have been happy to buy it as it was, but the bank wanted guarantees, her father had explained. What if someone just came and snapped it up before she could get it surveyed? The house itself was in need of a lot of work, but it was prime real estate right in the centre of Uzès. Her father had reasoned with her, telling her that, as there had been no visits to the house since she had been living there, there was every chance that the situation would continue. He had spoken again to his neighbours who had said they were in no rush and would love to sell the house to his daughter. So, all they could do was wait. Someone like Mark would not go through the same issues. He could just put down the asking price and buy the house cash without worrying about a surveyor inspecting it. But maybe he would not do that. He was astute. He would want to know the house was sound. Still, it had been there for 500 years so surely there could be nothing wrong with it?

36

On his way back home, Mark pondered what had made him confide in Léa what he had not even told his best friend. Maybe it was that the need to put this part of his life to bed for good. And maybe there was something about Léa too that made him drop his guard. She bewitched him again today, even more so than she had before. He could see her laughing at him as they went round the aisles of the plant nursery, laughing at his limited knowledge of plants, her brown eyes shining. She had put her hand on his arm and it had felt electric again. As he drove up to the house, he knew that he wanted her. But was he prepared to change the rest of his life for her?

'Where have you been? Max was asking after you,' said Mrs Hunter when she saw her son walked onto the terrace.

He had disappeared earlier without saying where he was going and even though he was now too old for her to check on him; she was still curious. It was not like he had any friends around here.

Mark looked at his mother, impeccable in her white linen dress, her hair perfectly coiffed in a bun as always. He had never known her looking anything but perfect. Yet she was not a snob, or looked people down. It was just the way she was. He noticed that she had a gin and tonic by her and smiled. It was almost six. He kissed her on the cheek and touched her hand.

'Where is he?'

'In the pool.'

Her eyes followed him as he sat down in an armchair next to her. He could be so difficult to read sometimes. It was not new of course, he had always been like this. And Max was so much like him. He would have hated her for saying that, but it was true.

He got up again and went to pour himself a whisky. He felt unsettled and would have liked to think about the day, about Léa too, without having to answer questions. He envied her privacy. He would have given a lot to be on his own right now. Or with her. He sat back down and looked at his mother.

'So?' she asked, a thin smile on her pink lips.

'Wouldn't you like to know Mum?' he said, a smile on his lips, his eyes crinkling.

God, she loved him, that son of hers. He could infuriate her, and yet, he was such a charmer. She could have given up, but curiosity was spurring her on. He had been gone since before lunchtime.

'Did you go and meet Freya in secret?'

He shook his head and looked down at the valley, drinking a sip of his whisky as he did so. 'No, I didn't. I told her to leave ten days ago.'

'I heard, but I wasn't sure that was true.'

'Well, it is. It's over.'

She said nothing, but she was not sure Freya would just 'go'. That woman! Since she had put her clutches - or was it talons? - into her son, she had not let go. The strange thing was she had always known that he did not love her, but she was like a magnet, something he did not seem to be able to resist and she suspected Freya knew exactly how to get back to him. This woman had more wiles on her than any other she knew. And she had known a few in her day.

Mark looked at his mother. He wondered what she thought of Léa. They had met while he had been away, and according to Caroline they had got on well. As for Caroline, she had fallen for Léa just as much as Max had, or he had for that matter. She had waxed lyrical the night before about Léa and how lovely and amazing she was. Mark knew Caroline would accept Léa

Céline Chancelier

without a doubt. But his mother? He was not so sure. Not that it bothered him.

'I went to see Léa, Max's teacher.'

Mrs Hunter did not reply. Could it be that there was something between them? Max and even her daughter Caroline raved about her and she had liked her well-enough. Polite, well-behaved but head-strong. This was not a woman who would just bent over backwards to please him. Was he capable of dealing with that?

'Lovely woman. A shame she lives here,' she said.

She saw him smile and wished he would tell her what he was thinking.

'Why?' he asked, a hint of curiosity in his eyes.

She had hooked him at last, she thought. 'Well, surely you can't have a relationship with someone who lives so far away from you.'

His blue stare bored into her, and she knew that was what it was. He would deny it but she knew.

'Who said I'm having a relationship with her?'

'Mark, I'm not born yesterday. You don't spend six hours with someone if you don't like them. But what you do with your life is your problem. I'm just pointing out the pitfalls.'

'Thank you, mother. I think I can look after myself well enough.'

He got up, and she knew that she had pissed him off. Never mind, he would calm down.

Mark walked to the edge of the garden and looked down at the swimming pool. Max was playing in the water with his fins and his snorkel, and that made him laugh. He walked down the steps and sat on the edge of the pool, dangling his feet in the water. They waved at each other while Max kept playing, diving in and out of the water.

Max had seen the potential in Léa long before he had. For all the faults he attributed to his son, he could see now that he was an excellent judge of character. Better than he was. He wished his mother had not talked about Freya. He had long forgotten

160

about her. She was like an unpleasant dream, something he was not proud of having done. He had no regrets, but he could see that it would have been better to have refrained from that relationship. Which had not been a relationship. Just sex and a few dinners. Until he had had the stupid idea of taking her here. Why? He just could not understand what his train of thought had been then. It was like in three weeks he had walked into another life. One where he suddenly saw possibilities he did not know existed.

His mother was right, a long distance relationship with Léa would not work. But who said he could not move here? The idea had poked into his head a few times since London and he could not formulate an answer. But if he wanted to be with her, then this was the only way. He could see what it would mean in terms of… In terms of what? It would not be a sacrifice to move out here with her. He would sell the house and make money, sell his company and make money and then he would be free to invent a new life here. The castle they had seen that afternoon had given him an idea that he had been mulling over while driving back. What if?

What had she said at dinner back in her courtyard? That sometimes you needed to jump and see what happens. Maybe it was time he took a risk. A genuine risk. Something that meant something. To him. Because what was his life? He was successful beyond his wildest dreams, but that was starting to feel very empty. There is only so much money one can spend and money on its own did not make him happy. It was a mean to an end, something that gave him the freedom to do whatever he liked.

For the first time in a long time, he wanted to connect. To feel. He did not want numbness anymore. As he had said to Léa, this was what he had been doing for the last three years. Everything to numb the pain or the disappointment that his marriage had been to him. He could see that all he had done since his wife's passing had been to walk away from accepting failure, hoping that alcohol, women and too much work would magically make the pain go away. It had not.

And Léa had appeared out of nowhere to show him he wanted more. With her. She was in thoughts and in his dreams and all he wanted was to make her love him. Just like he had fallen in love with her. So far he had not gone about it the best way. The thoughts of their quarrel about her taking Max to Arles made him cringe. What had that been about? A form of control over someone whom he had no control over. Because that was the thing with Léa: he had no idea what she thought of him or even if she liked him. Although today there had been glances and something - what, he did not know - that had made him feel that she liked him a little better, that he had dared to hope until now.

Max emerged in front of him, jumping out of the water, waking him up from his reverie.

'Dad could I stay at Léa's one evening?'

Mark frowned. 'Staying at Léa's? Like a sleepover, you mean?'

The boy grinned and Mark noticed that his skin was the colour of caramel. He looked happier and healthier than three weeks before.

'Yes. She said yes but asked me to ask you.'

He was curious as to why Léa had said nothing about it today. He was about to say something about that but remember in time that Max did not know he had seen Léa. Maybe she had done it on purpose because she wanted Max to ask him. Her subtle way to empower him.

'If she's happy to have you around for one night, then that's fine with me.'

'Yeah!' said Max, jumping up and down, spraying water everywhere.

Mark smiled. He would not mind sleeping at Léa's too.

37

Uzès, Sunday 9ᵗʰ August

Mum, I'm speaking to you. I wish you were here. I do, I really do. But you're not, and I've figured out that I need a new mum. It's not that I don't love you anymore. I will always love you. It's just that Tom and I can't live with Dad on his own. He is good, and getting better with me - I think you'd be impressed - but we want a mum, someone to look after us. You know what I mean. I know you do. I'm still scared I'm forgetting you but, as Léa said, we have to live in the present even after the people we love have departed.

I think Dad likes Léa. I think he likes her a lot. He won't say it, of course. But I know he spent the day with her and I have hopes that maybe, just maybe, she could become our mum. What do you think? Do you like her? I like her a lot. I feel I can talk to her. I feel she loves me. And I love her too. Not like you. It will never be like you. But she is my hope, my shining star in the sky. I know it's unlikely that Dad would agree to move down here, but maybe if they become a couple, she would move to London with us? She used to live there, you know. She knows the place. We talk about it often. She said she will come and see me in the autumn once I'm back at school. And she will speak to Dad again about enrolling me somewhere else. I will not go back to Westminster. No way. She said bullying is not okay and that no amount of telling me to get tougher, as Dad wants me to be, will make it better. You see, she is just like you! I know you would have said the same to him.

Can you answer me, please? Give me a sign, tell me you would be ok with that. I know that I will know when you say yes. I love you Mum. Always.

Max closed the notebook and put it at the bottom of his suitcase. He felt better for having asked his Mum about Léa. He could not see a future without her in his life. They needed her.

38

Léa opened the door to the second bedroom on the first floor. This was where Max would sleep. The walls were bare and there was only a bed, a night table and one of those white Ikea shelves with four boxes instead of a chest of drawers as furniture in the room. It was stark, but that was what the owners had bought and Léa, not needing the room, had added no personal touch to it.

She used it as a storage space for the stuff she had brought back from London, but was not sure what to do with. There were coats, clothes she did not wear anymore, books, her notebooks, old files and various bits and pieces from her previous life. She knew she would have to get rid of some, but somehow it still held a sentimental value, a link to the past that she could not part with.

As she was setting the large brown cardboard boxes on top of one another in a corner of the room, a couple of smaller boxes caught her attention. She did not remember them from London. On the side of them, someone - her mum? - had written "Léa's stuff" with a black marker. Her father must have picked them up with the other boxes she had left at her parents when he had helped her move to Uzès.

She took one and put it on the unmade bed. Inside there were some photo albums she had made when she was still a teenager. She sat on the bed and looked through them. A shy teenager with eighties clothes and curly hair was looking at her. There were pictures of friends, others of her brother and her by the sea during a holiday near Marseille she had a vague recollection of, photos of birthdays, of the dog they used to have. She let her finger run over that photo. She missed that mutt, a stray that her Dad had brought over one weekend when she was eight and who had become her loyal companion for the next ten years. She smiled as she remembered all the secrets she had confided in him.

In the second box, there were old vinyl records and a few notebooks. She took one out of curiosity. What did she write in those days? Angst, boyfriend trouble, stuff about her teachers or schoolmates, maybe. As she opened the notebook, an envelope fell on the floor. She picked it up. It was yellow and had her grandmother's handwriting on the front. It said only "Pour Léa". Instinctively she brought it close to her face and the faint smell of her grandmother's perfume, Arpège from Lanvin, seemed to flutter around her.

She could not remember having ever seen this letter before. Where did it come from? Had she put it with a present and Léa had forgotten to open it? She turned it around and noticed that it was sealed. She had never read it. Not wanting to destroy the envelope, she ran downstairs, her heart beating wildly, her mouth dry. She picked up a knife in a kitchen drawer and as carefully as her trembling hands allowed her; she cut the edge of the envelope. Inside there was two wafer thin pages folded in two. She took them out carefully and went to sit down in the shade outside.

My darling Léa,
    I don't know when you will read this letter.
    I've put it in one of your notebooks for you to find. You are probably asking yourself why. I don't think at the age you are now, just about to leave the nest to live your first solo adventure, you are ready for what I am about to say.
    I know I'm taking a risk because who knows, you may never again open the notebook I will leave this letter in. But somehow I know you will. Call it intuition or magic, I don't know but I know that you and I

are kindred spirits and that, even when I won't be here anymore to listen to you and guide you along as much as I can, we will be connected. I just know it.

Why am I writing you this letter from beyond my grave (I know I have only a little time left on this earth, that horrible illness is killing me no matter what the doctors and your mother say) you may ask yourself?

There are things that I want you to understand about you and life. You are a sensitive soul, far too much sometimes. This is no criticism of you, but as I have told you many times, no matter how hard it is for you to assert yourself, you need to find your own way. Don't let anyone tell you what to do. So many people do it because they want to protect you from harm or pain, but life does not work this way.

Take your Mum, for example. She means well, I know, she is my daughter, but I worry that this path she seemed to have all set up for you and that you have so brilliantly followed, is not for you. You have a creative side to you that has been there since you were a little girl. I'm not sure you are aware of it and I believe that if I was telling you this today, you would laugh and shake your those lovely curls of yours and say 'Gran, your lovely, no-one can make a living out of writing or making music or painting these days'. It may well be so and it may still be the case at the time you are reading this letter, but it does not mean you should not try.

I believe that this creative side you have will come back to haunt you and I would like you to try it when it does. I did not, as you know, pursue a creative career because when I was your age, women like me, did not have the possibility to do so. My father was dead against me going to Paris to try my luck as an actress (you're surprised, n'est-ce pas? Your old granny, an actress?). It hurt for a while, but then, I was lucky to meet your grandfather, the love of my life, and have a family. I don't regret my life. But I do regret not having tried to do something about my desire to act at least once, even in latter life. Even if it had not worked out, it would have been something.

What I am trying to tell you in my clumsy way is that we should have no regrets in life. I can see that you are about to follow one of your dreams by moving to London. I can't say I'm over the moon about it, but this is your life and you are setting yourself free (I know you will *understand what I mean).*

As for falling in love and finding the one, stop worrying! He will be there waiting for you the day you start living your life and not someone else's. You will be happy. It may take you longer than others, but I know you will.

So, whatever happens to you when I'm not around anymore, take chances on jobs, on people, on love. Have no regrets, for they only fester and destroy you from the inside. Trust yourself and your choices. Follow your star. Be happy.

But most of all be you, my beautiful, smart, generous, favourite, one and only granddaughter. My Léa.

I love you, and I will always be with you.

Your grandmother,

Augustine

She breathed deeply, trying to regain her composure. Her eyes fell on the rosebush that was growing around the kitchen door with its delicate pale pink-orangey roses. Its perfume never failed to remind her of her grandmother. She used to have one quite similar in her garden in Eygalières. When in season, she would always have a few cut flowers in a small vase on her night table. Léa got up and got her secateurs. She smelled the delicate flowers before cutting three. She would put them on Max's night table.

PART THREE

39

Father and son walked down the narrow lanes in the late afternoon sunshine. Max carried his backpack and a bouquet of pink and white flowers they had picked up that morning in Nîmes while Mark carried a bag with food for dinner carefully prepared by Manuela and wines he had chosen from a wine shop in Uzès.

'The house dates back to the 15th Century,' started Léa.

'How do you know?' asked Max.

'If you go and look in the larder, the little room that you can access from the back of the kitchen, you'll see there is a stone with the date on it. It could be an earlier building of course but, according to my next-door neighbour who's done some research, the building has been there since that date.'

Max ran into the kitchen.

'This is better than a history lesson, it's history in action,' said Mark, shaking his head, studying the house.

He looked relaxed and happy and looking at him from behind her sunglasses, Léa thought he looked handsome. She felt a brief pang of jealousy. One day, she was sure of it, he would find the woman of his life. She wished it for him.

'It's funny looking at the house, I'd swear that it was just one building with the house on that side at one point.'

'And you'd be correct. It was one house apparently until early last century. If you go in the kitchen, you'll see there is an indentation in the wall next to the stove. There was a door there before, apparently.'

'Do you know what happened?'

'Well, my next-door neighbour again,' she said as she made a gesture to show the other side of the house from the one they were looking at, 'told me that there were two brothers living in this house. The younger one got married before going to the front during the First World War leaving his young wife in the care of his older brother and his wife.'

She saw the smile on his lips. 'Don't tell me, she had an affair.'

Léa pretended to look offended. 'It's always the woman's fault with you men!'

'You're right, it takes two. They had an affair,' he said, half-laughing.

'It's a tragic story actually,' Léa said, trying to keep her countenance. 'Her husband was thought to have been killed on Western front and the older brother's wife died, possibly of the flu, in 1917. Anyway, they became lovers, and it was a bit of a shock to them when her husband walked in one day in 1919. He had been made a prisoner by the Germans but, for some unknown reason, his name had not appeared on the lists.'

'And?'

'And he didn't take it too well to find his wife and his brother together when he came back.'

'Were they married?'

'No, because they had to wait for him to be declared dead and this was a procedure that took quite some time. I read somewhere that for some families, it took up to two years for their loved ones to be declared *Mort Pour la France*, given the butchery in Northern France.'

He stayed silent. Léa went on. 'He was very upset and wanted nothing to do with either of them. So they built this wall in the garden and closed the corridors downstairs and upstairs. As I understand it, the kitchen was in the other part of the house.'

'Sad story. Could be made into a book.'

He had said that looking at her with that wry smile of his.

'It could. Who knows? Maybe one day it will,' she quipped.

'Is it still owned by the same people?'

She shook her head. 'I've never seen the people next door, but I've been told that they're not related to the people who own this part of the house.'

'It'd be nice to reunite both houses one day.'

'I think so. It would make a much nicer house, maybe have a small pool in the garden. Their courtyard is slightly larger on this side. You can see it from the bedroom window.'

'Why don't you buy them?' he said, sitting down on a chair under the tree.

She laughed softly; the curls caught in her chignon moving in the light breeze. 'Let's see,' she said, her index finger on her cheek. 'Ah yes, I don't have the money and I'm not sure the other part of the house is for sale.' She looked at the house again. 'I've made an offer on this one. We'll see.'

'What did the bank say?'

She looked at him removing her sunglasses and sat down on the other chair.

'They think I can do it. Dad will help me and, hopefully, I can find a proper job when I finish this one.'

He was about to ask her how much money she needed, but he suddenly had a much better idea. He poured them more rosé and held his glass to her. 'To your house!'

'To my house!'

Max came running back from the house. He had found the date and taken a picture. Could he send it to his friend Chris? Mark held his hands up.

'It's not me you should ask Max. This is Léa's house.'

The boy looked at her, an expectant look on his face. She could not resist saying yes. 'But no social media please. This is not my house. I don't want a line of people beating a path to the front door just to see a date inscription on the wall. Anyway, it's about time we set the table so how about you come and help me?'

As they went together into the kitchen, arms in arms, he looked at them both. Léa had been a little distant when they had turned up, as if she was a little wary of him. He had thought it was because Max was going to stay the night, but looking at them both; he knew this was not the case. There was no awkwardness between them. It was like his son had known her all his life. He had said something along those lines that morning when they went for their swim. He had not elaborated about it, but Mark had understood that she felt like a mother to him. Maybe even more than a mother.

He sighed softly. The heat was coming down, but it was still very warm. He could feel the sun on his hand, his mind wandering. Léa came back with a tablecloth and some plates she put on a chair, her dress around her chest tightening up as she did so. He removed the glasses and bottle from the table so she could lay the cloth and plates. Max came back with cutlery and napkins and applied himself to the task. When was the last time he had seen him do that? His boys were far too molly-coddled for their own good. He would enact some changes when they went home.

Home. Watching Léa move back to the kitchen, followed closely by his son, he wondered about it. What she had said to him about the need to take a chance on the unknown had come back into his head again and again. He felt trapped between duty and the need to throw caution to the wind. It was easy here tonight to just think 'What the hell, we'll move here and it'll be all right!' but he knew life was not as simple. He also suspected that moving here would have to involve Léa in one way or another. She came back and he could not help but notice the shape of her body under the soft material of her dress, the golden colour of her skin on her arms and neck, the long eyelashes.

'Can I help at all?' he said, not wishing to daydream any longer.

'There are some prawns to grill. Do you think you could light the barbecue?'

He moved to the barbecue, turned on the gas and went to the kitchen. The large prawns he had brought earlier were already marinating with a little oil and dried herbs in a dish, a set of tongs and a long fork by their side. Max had disappeared again. The narrowness of the kitchen meant that they bumped into each other, and he felt her hand brushed against his arm. She turned her back to him and all he could see was the nape of her neck, the top of her shoulders and back under the thin straps of her dress. The jasmine scent she wore seemed to envelope him, and it took all his will not to turn her around and kiss her. He took the dish and got out of the kitchen, not sure how long he could keep a hold on himself.

Dinner was one of the best moments of his life Max could remember. Where there had been some awkwardness between Léa and his Dad when they had had dinner the day he had disappeared - he had observed them from the lounge - but there was none tonight. They talked, and they laughed, and it was not just him trying to keep the conversation going.

He felt like maybe, just maybe, he could start hoping that something would develop between the two of them. As he had said to his father, though he was not sure he had understood, he loved Léa like he had loved his Mum. He could not explain why and had felt guilty at first but both his father and aunt Caroline had said it was perfectly fine to love two people the same so he had stopped worrying. What was the point of worrying, anyway? It was not like his Mum would ever come back. He was still unhappy with the fact that, sometimes; he was forgetting what her face had looked like but Léa had said that it was normal, that it was a trick of the mind, that it did not mean we did not love people anymore; they just stayed in our hearts.

He looked at her, in her pretty summer dress, and wondered what it would be like to have her as his mum. It would be different and she would have to be stricter than she was, but that did not worry him. He felt she was and would stay on his side. She had been the first adult to say out loud that bullying at school was not right, and she had promised to speak to his father about it. He believed her. He had to. She was his lifeline to something better. Would Tom like Léa? Tom was little more than a baby, but he would like her. He was sure of it.

He looked at his Dad. Since Freya - even before Freya had left - he had been more open. Since that night he had slept in his room, they had gone for a swim together every morning and that was where he felt he could speak to him the best. He had listened when he had talked about loving two people the same and he listened to him when he spoke of Léa, which was fine with him because he enjoyed talking about Léa.

He looked at them again. They were talking about something, lost in their conversation, and he moved quietly away from the table. He looked back at them again from inside the house. They had not even noticed he had left.

Mark had noticed him leaving the table but pretended not to. At that moment, he would have given everything he owned to just spend the rest of the night with Léa in this small enchanted courtyard. The smell of jasmine and rosemary was in the air. The night had fallen, leaving them with just the soft lights of the candles on the table and on the ledge of the borders and the little lights on the wall. The tree was shading them from whoever could have been looking at them from another house. The cicadas had gone quiet and there seemed to be no other sounds than the sound of their voices. It felt like being alone in the world, cocooned in this little part of paradise.

The twisting of that curl between her long fingers kept distracting him. He wondered if she was nervous. He wanted to take her hand and kiss her fingers. The wine made him feel mellower, and he felt at ease with her. He moved his chair a little closer to hers. Their hands almost touched. He could smell her perfume. The colour of her skin was hypnotic in the warm light of the candle. He clinked her glass, thanking her for a lovely evening.

Léa had seen Max disappearing too, but she was too enraptured by her conversation with Mark. Crazy thoughts were going through her mind. She had felt so alive when he had been in the kitchen with her earlier. She had felt his breath on her neck, had waited for him to touch her. But he had not, and she had wondered when she had walked into the courtyard afterwards if she had dreamt the whole thing. There was a physicality about him that just stirred something in her. She noticed the little things, the lines around his eyes, the deep furrow in the middle of his brow when he focused on something, the shape of his hands, large with long fingers, the hair on his arms, the shape of his shoulders under his shirt. He poured the last of the wine in their glasses and she almost protested - she had drank a lot more than she had done in a long while - but then why not? She played with a curl which had fallen from the clasp at the back at her head.

She hoped the evening was not at an end yet. She wanted it to last and last. His voice low and warm resonated in her, making her feel something she had not felt in a long time. A longing. A need.

Max shouted from the lounge he was going to bed and broke the spell. They smiled at each other and he excused himself and went to him. She stayed at the table until she heard them move upstairs and then took the remnants of dinner back to the kitchen. She felt dizzy and admonished herself for even daring to think what she had thought just a few minutes earlier. It was stupid. It was just attraction, lust, the heat. She was nothing to him. A summer fling.

Mark came back down and walked into the kitchen as she was washing the dishes. He came behind her, untying the apron she was wearing, sending a shiver down her spine.

'Please stop. Come outside. It's such a beautiful night,' he whispered in her ear. She dried her hands and followed him in the courtyard. She had switched the lights off in the lounge and only the twinkly little lights on the walls and the verbena candles lit the garden. It looked magical. And just for one night, it truly felt like hers.

'It's incredible how many stars you can see here. Look, there's the North Star.'

'Which one is it?' No one had never explained to her which was which. All she could see was that some were brighter than others.

He stepped behind her and put a hand on her waist and his other hand up pointing at the sky. 'If you follow my hand, you should see a very bright star. That's the North Star.'

She followed his hand, tilting her head back, peering into the night sky. She could smell the woody scent of him around her. His hand pulled her closer against him. 'Can you see it?'

'I think so. I'm not sure.' Léa was not so much focusing on the star as the feel of his hand on her waist and his breath close to her ear. She could feel the hairs on her neck rising.

'Lean back further into me. I'm holding you, you won't fall.'

She did as she was told and his hand slid across her waist, his arm holding her tight against him.

'And now?'

'Yes, I can see it.' There was a silence before she continued. 'What else can you see?'

'Here. There is the Great Bear. Follow my hand.'

He pointed to several stars, but she could not make up the pattern and started giggling, moving away from him. As she turned to him, he caught her hand. They looked at each other, and he pulled her closer. He hesitated before his lips found hers. She let go and kissed him back, leaning in into him.

He could feel her tongue teasing and exploring. His hands went to her face before going back down her back. He had lost track of where he was. The world could have been crashing around them, he would not have known.

They moved back a little to catch their breath. 'I think I'm falling in love with you,' he whispered before kissing her again, holding her tight against him.

'It's getting late…'

'You don't want me to stay,' he said, kissing the tip of her nose.

'Not tonight,' she said, making a sign towards the first floor of the house.

He smiled. 'I think you'll find that's what he has been hoping would happen all along.'

She shook her head and curls fell down from the loose chignon that held them. She grabbed a pin and pinned them back before taking his hand and leading him back through the house and into the small corridor. The house was in semi-darkness and eerily silent. He let go of her hand and pushed her gently against the wall. She did not resist, and it was her who moved to kiss him with a long, seductive kiss. She was not sure now whether she wanted him to leave. His hands burned her skin through the flimsy material of her dress. She whimpered when they moved her skirt up slowly, finding her skin. She could hear his breathing becoming shorter, heavier, his hands getting higher on her thighs, his body tensing against hers.

She was tempted to let go of her defences and lead him upstairs, but she pushed him tenderly away from her. He did not resist. His hands came up next to her head on the wall as she smoothed her dress down.

'I'm sorry. I can't do this,' she breathed.

He kissed her forehead and smiled to her. 'It's me who should say sorry. I got carried away.'

He pulled back, and Léa opened the front door for him. He stepped out, kissed her one last time before moving away.

40

Mark was up with the larks. He had not slept well, his head full of her, her lips, the softness of her skin under his fingertips. He knew he needed to get rid of this energy or he could not deal with anyone. He got down quietly and let himself out of the house. Day was just breaking over the horizon and he stopped at the top of the stairs going down to the swimming pool. The sky had that dusty pink colour and bathed the valley in a soft glow. There was a promise in this beautiful day.

He dived and felt the coolness of the water against his skin. The fears and questions that had gone round his head all night faded away. He powered through, trying to focus on the movement until his muscles ached, before turning around and laying on his back looking at the lightening sky. Max would be there any minute now, he thought, until he remembered that he was at Léa's. An idea took shape in his mind, and he was out of the water in a flash.

He left fifteen minutes later with a bag of brioches and croissants that Manuela had just brought to the house. He opened the windows of the car and found himself humming a song that was playing on the radio. He wondered how long it had been since he had done that. Traffic in Uzès was light, and he found himself in front of Léa's door just after eight. He rang the bell, feeling like a teenager on a first date.

Max opened the door, and he heard Léa's shout, 'Who is it Max?'

'My Dad!' his son shouted back, a beaming grin on his face, kissing his father on the cheek before grabbing the pastries. 'He brought breakfast.'

Léa's heart had skipped a beat. She was still in her bedclothes, a flimsy camisole and a pair of light shorts. They had just gotten up, and she had set the table in the garden for breakfast while Max was having a shower. She had a foot on the stairs when Max came back in, his father following behind. He smiled and said '*bonjour*'.

'Max, can you boil the kettle in the kitchen, please? I'll be right back.' She flew more than she walked upstairs, grabbing her clothes that laid on the bed and closed the door of the bathroom quietly. Her heart was racing. She had not slept well, torn between the desire she felt for him and her reason telling her that there was no future for that relationship. What was she to him? A light summer romance like you read in those sentimental novels. He would forget her as soon as he would be back in London.

She could not help but look out the window. Mark had his back to her, talking to his son. Max had looked delighted that morning and seemed to be even more excited. She could not hear what he said, but she saw his father embrace him and ruffle his hair and that made her happy. At last, they had crossed the divide between them. She felt a little envious of their closeness; she would never have this, a child of her own to love and to hold.

Max went in the kitchen and Mark turned around and looked up. He was sure she had been at the window observing them. She had looked so beautiful as he had come in, her hair wild and the curves of her body showing under the light garments she was wearing. Yet had he seen a fear in her eyes?

'Max, go and get your stuff ready while I help Léa clean up,' he said. 'And please make sure the room is tidied up.' He got a 'Yes Dad' which surprised him. He went in the kitchen with the plates and put them on the counter. Léa was washing the cups in the sink.

'Léa,' he whispered, pulling her to him. 'What's going on?'

'Nothing,' she said in a quiet voice, drying her hands on her apron. He turned her around, his hands around her waist. 'What's wrong?'

She shook her head and smiled. 'Nothing! I just didn't expect to see you this morning.'

'I couldn't wait to see you.'

She wanted to say that she felt the same, but it felt contrite and she kept silent. He bent to kiss her and she let him, the smell of him enveloping her. She was lost to him for a few seconds before remembering Max.

'Max...' but he did not let her finish, kissing her more fully as he pulled her closer to him. The warmth of his body against hers finally broke through her defences and her hands found his neck, then his hair.

'Léa, Léa, Léa,' he said as he kissed her neck, 'I thought you'd never kiss me.'

She looked at him, a smile on her lips. 'There's Max, it's complicated.'

As if on cue, Max was coming down the stairs. They moved away from each other, their fingers holding until the last minute.

'I'm ready!' Max shouted from the living room.

'Ok,' they replied in unison.

They took Max to the Haribo Museum just outside Uzès because Léa had promised she would. While they looked at sweets in the shop, Mark made a call. When he joined them again, he had a twinkle in his eye but said nothing until they left him at the bastide after lunch.

'We have an appointment to visit the castle at 2pm.'

A Volvo from another age but in perfect condition was parked by the gate when they arrived and an elderly man got out as they parked.

'He must be the owner,' said Mark as he parked his car on the other side of the gate.

'What's his name?' she asked, undoing her seatbelt.

'I'll let you ask him that. Too difficult for me to say without looking like a fool.'

'Chicken,' she said as she exited the car.

'Careful what you say Ms Pasquier,' he replied a wry smile on his face.

'*Madame Hunter?*' said the old man as he moved towards them, extending his hand to Léa, '*Monsieur de Daujac, le propriétaire.*'

Léa was about to say something, but Mark interjected. '*Bonjour* and thank you to let us see the place so quickly.'

'Ah! We have had little interest unfortunately in our family home so one has to follow every lead. Shall we?' he said, opening the gate. 'I need to change this padlock, it's useless.'

Mark and Léa smiled at each other, and he took her hand as they followed their host down the path. He was wearing formal grey trousers, a long sleeve shirt with a yellow tie, a blue cardigan and his white hair was neatly combed. He was rather sprightly for an elderly gentleman and pointed out to them different variety of trees. 'This cedar was planted by the Queen Mother herself when she came to stay in the early sixties. She knew my father from his time as an officer when he worked for De Gaulle in London in 1940 and had promised she would come and see him in his castle one day. She kept her promise. Wonderful, wonderful times,' he said, shaking his head.

He opened the front door with a large key and Mark helped him push the heavy wood panel. They stepped in what had been the lobby. The floor was made of black-and-white marble tiles that formed a diamond pattern. An elegant stone staircase went up to the first floor on the right-hand side while double doors opened onto rooms.

'It was built at the beginning of the eighteenth century on the ruins of a previous older place forte by one of my ancestors. You can still see some vestige of that in the cave. I'll show you later. Let's start with the library,' he said, moving to the first set of double doors on their right.

The room they entered had shelves on all sides, even between the windows with books in them and a beautiful parquet floor. It smelled a little musty, but Léa could not resist having a look at the old volumes lined up. She ran her finger on the spines before taking out an old edition of 'Phèdre' by seventeenth century playwright Jean Racine.

'Do you know that he spent some time in Uzès dear old Racine?' asked Monsieur de Daujac who seemed to have guessed which book she had taken from the shelf.

Léa nodded. 'He was quite young, I believe.' She wanted to say that she had taken Max to see the Pavillon Racine near the Cathedral Saint-Théodorit, but she refrained, letting their host talk.

'He was only twenty-two but could already put together wonderful sentences like this one he wrote about Uzès to his friend Monsieur Vitart, 'Et nos nuits sont plus belles que vos jours.[5]' He shook his head, smiling to himself, lost in his thoughts. 'I'm selling them too if you're interested. I can't take them with me unfortunately,' he sighed, making a gesture that encompassed all the books.

'Did you live here?' Mark asked as they walked into another sizeable room, bare of all furniture.

'Until about six months ago. My wife died and I just could not bear to live here anymore. We should have moved out a long time ago, but it was just too hard to move away from what had been our home for most of our lives.'

'Where do you live now?'

'In a care home in Uzès. Suits me fine to tell you the truth. I have my own room and I can play cards with the other old men,' he said smiling, his eyes shining.

'You don't have any children?' asked Léa.

'I had a son, but he died in a car crash almost thirty years ago.'

'I'm so sorry…'

'Please don't,' he said, his eyes lost on something outside the window. 'It was a long time ago. The saddest thing to me apart from my son's death is that we did not get to have any grandchildren. I would have loved to see little children play in the park, but it wasn't meant to be.'

They had moved to one of the rooms on the other side of the

---

[5] And our nights are more beautiful than your days.

castle, one that gave onto the park with the large French windows. A few painting still hung on the walls: tall men in military apparel from different periods, a smaller portrait of a young girl smiling, holding a small dog. A vase with delicately painted flowers was set on the large black marble fireplace, which stood on one side. A couple of Louis XV armchairs covered in a pale white and blue fabric showing little cherubs and a painted coffee table were set by the set of French windows in the middle. He saw their surprise and smiled.

'Sometimes I come during the day and sit here with a book. This is why I haven't given the key to an estate agent, you see. They wouldn't let me do that. But I can't see the harm in doing so.'

Mark took Léa's hand and pressed it in his. 'You did a marvellous job of keeping this place in such excellent condition,' he said as they moved to the other side of the entrance hall and into what look like a dining room.

'I tried. I was lucky to have inherited a good deal of money from my father and a flourishing estate. We also have vines. You must have passed them. It's the ones just before the wall of the property. I still have someone who looks after them and makes wine using the property name, so I get an income from that. It helps to pay for the care home.'

'Would you sell them? The vines, I mean,' said Mark.

The old man turned around to study him. 'I would. Would you be interested? You don't look like a winemaker yourself if I may say so.'

'I'm not. I work in finance, but winemaking has always interested me.'

'It's difficult, you know,' said the old man shaking his head.

'What wine does your man produce?'

'All three: white, rosé and red.'

'So it's fairly big in terms of hectares then?'

The old man nodded before replying. 'It started with my grandfather at the end of the nineteenth century who bought some vines plots and thought vines would grow well on them and it went on from there. We have just over sixty hectares nowadays.'

Mark whistled. 'You must derive a solid income from that.'

'Yes and no. You have the good years, and you have the bad years. It's been better though since rosé has taken off as a summer drink. My tenant has been telling me that I should only produce rosé but I've convinced him to keep the reds and whites. It's just that they'd need more attention than he's giving them. He has his own vineyards you see so...' His voice trailed off and he made a gesture with his hand. 'I should really look into it more but I'm too old now and, since my wife died, I just haven't had the same stamina.'

Mark did not insist, but this was getting better and better. There was something to be done with this place. There was history, fifteen hectares of park and sixty of vines that had to produce a fairly decent wine to generate an income that paid for their host's care.

The rooms and bathrooms on the first and second floor needed a lot of work. Most had antique wallpaper that was peeling off the walls. Some flooring was missing too on the second floor, and it was clear in places that the roof was not waterproof. Yet there was a charm, a kind of magic to this place, thought Léa, that made you want to roll up your sleeves and put it back to its former glory.

It was a good two hours later when they left their host again, who had let them roam around the castle and the gardens. He had even given them the key to the little chapel that was in relatively good condition inside with its white walls, altar and wooden chairs.

'So what did you think? Would you be interested?' he asked, as he met them at the gate and Mark handed him the key to the chapel.

'Very much so. I'll get back in touch with you shortly. Have you had a lot of interest?'

The old man shook his head. 'Not really. I guess I'll have to let an estate agent handle it at some point.'

'Could you wait a little?'

The old man smiled to Mark, a glimmer of hope in his watery

blue eyes. 'Of course! There is no rush. Look at me, I'm not going anywhere.'

They shook hands before he continued. 'The *notaire* can also give you all the information you need,' he said, handing Mark a card. 'He's based in Uzès and has been my notary for many years. Great chap. See you soon then!' he said, getting into his car. Léa wondered if it would start, but it did and they waved him goodbye as he left.

'Why did you say you were interested?' Léa said as she sat in the car.

'Because I am. Damn! I forgot to ask him where this guy who looks after his vines is based.'

'The notary can probably tell you.'

'Nah, I'll call him tomorrow. He's a lovely old man. Sad story, though.'

Léa smiled. 'I'm not sure he's ready to sell.'

Mark looked at her. 'You may be right there. Or rather, I think he wants to sell to the right person, but I'm not sure they exist.'

'So why are you interested?'

He smiled as he drove, his eyes fixed on the road. 'I fancy myself as king of the castle and winemaker,' he joked.

'While working in London?' she said, a note of incredulity in her voice.

He made a face but did not reply. 'I don't know yet. It's an idea I have. I need to give it some thought, but who said I want to stay in London?'

She did not reply. She tried to imagine him here in Provence. She just could not see him giving up his important job or his exciting social life for a quiet backwater like Uzès.

41

Uzès, Wednesday 12th August

Mum,

You won't believe it! My dream has come true. You answered me; I knew you would! Léa was right. Writing creates magic! The stars have spoken back. I'm so excited I wish I could speak to someone, tell them how wonderful things are. But it's ok. I will keep it in.

I saw Dad and Léa kissed last night in the courtyard. I had crept into Léa's room because I could see that they were happy together. I didn't stay after that. All I wanted to know was that there was something between them, you know? I could feel it, but I just wanted to be sure.

I can't help but wonder what it means. I wish I could have asked Dad today if it means that we will move here. Surely they can't stay apart if they are in love, right? And I know Léa has said she won't move to London. Bad memories for her, she said. And I want to move here. I know I could follow at the local school and be ok. It couldn't be worse there that it was in London. And I know some boys now.

It was funny this morning though, as they pretended nothing had happened. I let them. They went away this afternoon but didn't say where they went. That's cool. I know Granny was curious. She has been curious to know what has been going on between Dad and Léa ever since he came back from London and disappeared on Sunday. But I won't tell her. That's their secret and mine too. I don't think Dad would be too pleased if I said I had spied on him.

It's just so annoying though to have to wait and not know what's going to happen. We're going back to school in two weeks and I just want to know that I won't be going back to the same school. But I guess until they say something I can't ask.

But I'm so happy, Mum. It's like the best news this year. I know I have to trust the process. That's what Léa said to me the other day when I asked her if she had talked to Dad about changing schools. She said she had and that we both had to trust him to make the right decision. He trusts her so I think she's right, he will do it. And then if we move here, it won't matter anymore.

I'm so excited I don't think I'll be able to sleep tonight. You'd be proud of me. I left them after dinner and got home on my own with Manuela's husband, who was waiting for me at a pre-arranged spot. Dad hasn't come back yet. That's cool. Fingers crossed that this means they'll be some news tomorrow about our future. But it's looking good, I think.

Love you Mum and thank you again for making it happen!

PS: Do you remember when I told you I couldn't remember things about you anymore? Well, I have finally remembered your perfume! Léa had put cut roses in my room, ones from the rosebush that grow in her courtyard. Their smell reminded me of you, of that scarf you gave me before you went into hospital. She let me keep the roses and I've put them in my room at the bastide. Every time I smell them, it's like you're here with me again. I so wish I could bottle it.

42

Léa felt excited and kept looking around to see if she could see Mark. It was almost seven, and Uzès was busy with people enjoying the evening. The air was a little less hot and there was a light breeze playing in the leaves of the plane trees on the place. The sky was still deep blue against the golden colour of the townhouses.

She saw him before he saw her, Max walking just in front of him. She looked at them, father and son. Maybe it was the sun, or that they were both tanned, but they looked even more alike than when she had first met them. Max was still gangly, but he seemed to have grown taller. They both had the same walk, the same way of moving, a similarity in their features too. She saw people, women mostly, turned around as they moved towards her. She hugged Max before Mark kissed her on the cheek, holding her close to him. She could feel the warmth of his hand on her waist and wished they could lose the crowds, but there was no escaping Max's excitement of being out with them. They went around the artisan stalls on the square, not saying much to each other, Max babbling away in front of them.

She had booked a table at Luca's trattoria. They embraced, and he clapped Max on the shoulder as if he was an old friend. He looked immaculate in a light blue linen shirt and dark blue chinos. She wondered how he could look so cool in this heat. She introduced Mark to him and he winked at her as he took them through the restaurant and into the small courtyard at the back. They were sat in a corner with the climbing vine behind them. There was a large candle in a glass jar on the table and a small vase of green and white flowers. Luca brought a coke for Max - his favourite, the one with no sugar - and two glasses of champagne.

'On the house!' he said before disappearing again. They clinked their glasses and she could feel Mark's knee against hers. She felt happier than she had been in a long time. She reflected as she took a sip of her glass that it almost felt like a small family going to dinner together.

Dinner was a raucous affair, with Luca telling them to trust him with the dishes. Even though he was not in the kitchen, many of the small Italian dishes he brought to their table had been devised or updated by him, he explained. He looked in his element tonight, managing the restaurant and the staff with an assurance she only knew him to have in the kitchen.

When Max got up to go to the bathroom, Mark took her hand and kissed it lightly. She looked so beautiful tonight. The evening light played in her hair, her skin looked like velvet, and there was a light in her eyes he had not seen before.

'I wish it could only be you and me here tonight,' he whispered in her ear.

She shook her head slowly, and that damn curl fell forward. He could not resist pulling it back behind her ear.

'Me too, but Max's happiness tonight is so lovely to see. I'm so proud of him.'

'He's grown and in more ways that one.'

'What will you do about his school? He's worried sick of going back, even though I'm sure his experience would be different. He's so much more confident than he was. He just can't get over the bullying.'

'I'm not planning to enrol him back there. I have other plans for him.'

She wondered what that meant. Was there a link with the château he seemed to think of buying?

Max was coming back, but Mark noticed the look of surprise in her eyes. He could not wait to tell her about his plans. He was sure now that this was the thing to do for both his sons and for him too.

Luca came back with lots of small desserts and Max polished off pretty much all of them on his own, to Luca's delight.

'You've got a lovely place, and the food was stellar,' Mark told Luca as he brought them coffee.

'Come for a tasting then if you're free Sunday evening. I'm updating the menu and I'd love to know what globe-trotters like you two think. I know that Léa loves my cooking, but it'd be great to see what you think.'

Mark was only too happy to agree to that. He had every intention of enjoying the rest of his holiday and start building relationships with the locals. Luca was his kind of man too: affable, well-spoken and accomplished. It fitted with an idea he had had about that dilapidated castle.

When they left the restaurant, night had fallen, and Mark told Max he was taking him home. He expected him to sulk a little, but the answer he got surprised him.

'Don't worry about me, Dad. I'm meeting Manuela's husband at 10pm at the café where Léa usually picks me up in the morning. He's going to pick up Manuela at the house so he's offered to take me back home,' he said, a big smile on his face.

'Are you sure?' was all Mark could say. He was about to ask where was the café, but he guessed his son had a better idea of where it was than him. He had been crisscrossing Uzès with Léa for close to four weeks now. The boy nodded.

'Is your phone charged?' Léa asked. 'If there's anything you call...' She was about to say 'me' but Max answered first.

'I know where you live so I can come to you. But it's ok, I know Mateo will wait for me.' He kissed her and embraced his Dad and was gone.

Léa felt a shiver go through her. It was the two of them now. He took her hand. 'Do you know where this café is?'

She nodded, grabbing the chance to have more time to make up her mind. 'Shall we follow him? I'm sure he'll be ok but...'

He smiled and bent to kiss her softly on the lips. The feeling of his lips on hers again reignited the desire she had felt the night before. Suddenly she was not so sure she wanted to follow Max. She kissed him back more fully as he pulled her closer to him.

'Let's do that,' he whispered softly. 'We have all night.'

They could not see Max among the people walking around, and Léa took some less crowded back streets. They walked hand in hand in the soft yellow lights of the medieval streets without speaking, just happy to be in each other's presence. There were so many things they needed to tell each other but there would be time he thought as they emerged near the Duché. As they approached the café, they stayed at a safe distance, not wanting to make Max feel like he was being watched. Mark was delighted that his son seemed to stand on his own two feet at last and starting to become independent. It was not a moment too soon, even though he knew this had little to do with him and everything to do with Léa. And it was one more reason they - he - had to make some life changes.

They retraced their steps back slowly. It was him who broke the silence.

'What do you want to do?'

She looked at him alarmed and gripped his hand. 'What do you mean?'

He pulled her to him, embracing her. 'Léa, I'm not going to force you to do anything. If you want me to go home, that's fine.' He pulled a strand of her hair off her face and kissed her forehead.

'I want you to come home with me,' she whispered before kissing him. And it was true. She had no idea if she was ready for this relationship, but she knew she wanted him. There was no more time for fears or inadequacy, only time for the here and now and him. She was a little afraid too that if she said no, there would be no more chances. And she could not bear losing him even though she did not know where this would lead. All she knew was that she had to step over the threshold. Take a chance, as her grandmother used to say.

He closed the door softly behind them. The little lights from the garden shone a warm, soft light in the lounge that reflected off the mirror in the corridor. He could see her eyes shining in the darkness and pulled her tenderly to him. He could feel her heart beating fast against his chest as he held her tight.

'I've fallen in love with you, Léa Pasquier,' he said in a breath. 'You're so beautiful tonight.'

He kissed her by little touches until he felt her hands go up his back and on his neck. There was a hunger in her he had not felt before that drove him wild. All the desire he had felt when they kissed in the courtyard was coming back, and it took all his willpower not to carry her upstairs. He knew instinctively that he needed to take his time with Léa. She was not one of his conquests, but the woman he loved.

The zip of her dress went down a little, revealing the swell of her breasts.

'Tell me if you want me to go,' he whispered as he kissed her neck. She moaned when his hands reached the back of her legs under her dress, the tips of his fingers stroking her skin. He aroused an ache. A yearning.

'Come,' she said, taking his hand and leading him up the narrow stone steps and into her bedroom. The shutters had been half pulled and the light coming from the courtyard bathed the room in a golden glow.

He unzipped her dress fully which fell on the floor while she undid the buttons of his shirt, taking her time, running her hands over his chest, his shoulders, feeling his skin warm under her fingertips, the palms of her hands. He groaned as she undid the zip of his cargo shorts, her fingers sliding and pushing the heavy fabric down, feeling the desire in him. He sat on the bed and pulled her against him, burying his head in her chest, holding her tight, so tight she felt she could not breathe. She kissed his hair. It smelled of cedar-wood and expensive soap. His hands rolled her knickers down and he lowered her slowly on the bed, taking her in, letting his fingers run on her skin, teasing her until she felt like her skin was alive, like every single part of her body was alight.

'I want you,' he whispered in her ear.

He kissed her and let his lips lightly travel down her body. Her skin was warm and smelled of jasmine and sunshine, of sex too. It was intoxicating.

She felt his hands caressing her, his mouth lightly sucking at her breasts, his tongue exploring each curve of her body. He seemed to take his time. The light outside made shadows across them, falling in pools on his back. Time felt like at a standstill. He kept kissing her, caressing her, arousing her. She could feel desire rising and something akin to shame at the same time. She had never found it easy to let loose in those circumstances. She knew she could ask him to stop, but she just did not want to.

He was kneeling at the bottom of the bed, playing with her feet, kissing and licking the inside of her thighs, stroking and teasing her, relentlessly. She could feel his breath and his hand sometimes touching her. She tried not to make any noise but she could feel anticipation and pleasure mounting in her in equal measure and she bit her lip and gasped when he kissed the top of her thighs and then the hollow between her hip and belly.

It was as if he sensed that she was ready. She gasped and almost screamed when she felt his tongue, warm and wet, his hands opening her wider. She tried to wriggle free, but he was holding her tight. Her hands grabbed at the sheet, pulling it. She wanted to scream as he teased her again and again, but remembered in time the windows were opened. The combination of having to keep quiet and him taking her so close to release every time increased to the point where she was not sure where she was anymore. She could hear herself panting, her back arching, wanting him more, wanting more.

He stopped and moved back next to her, his naked body all lines and shadows. Léa instinctively wrapped herself around him. She could feel his skin dewy with perspiration against hers, his breath short and heavy on her neck, his voice saying words she did not understand. It was dirty, sexy, raw love, and she knew there and then that she had to let go. There was nothing to be afraid of anymore. Waves of pleasure rose in her again as she let go, giving and taking as much as he did, begging him not to stop softly, losing herself in him as he was in her. She came in a muffled scream just before him, exhausted, happy, madly in love. They did not talk, but he held her close, his face in her hair, rocking her gently.

He fell asleep and she must have dosed off a while. Something was buzzing somewhere. She thought it might be her phone, but hers was downstairs in her handbag that she had dropped in the corridor.

'Mark,' she called softly.

A moan came out. She looked at him, sprawled on his back, oblivious to the world, and smiled to herself. She had never felt so sexy after making love to someone. She touched his arm with her fingertips, feeling its warmth. The buzzing sound started again somewhere, and she pushed him a little, kissing him on the cheek.

'Mark, your phone is ringing.'

'I don't care,' came the reply before he turned around and embraced her. He kissed her neck before reaching for her mouth. A sexy kiss that aroused them both. They looked at each other, smiling, ready to start again.

The buzzing came back, insistent. He swore and sat on the bed, looking for his clothes. He stood up looking at the screen and she surreptitiously looked at his shoulders, letting her gaze go down his lower back, his hips, his buttocks, his long legs.

'Shit.'

'What is it?' she whispered as he moved to pick up his clothes and put them back on.

'Work.'

He sat on the bed next to her as he put his shirt on and she kneeled next to him. His arm snaked around her and he kissed her deeply. 'I just so wished I could stay with you but I've got to go. I may have to go back to London in the morning. Markets in Asia are crashing.'

He kissed her again, pulling her closer, one hand resting on the small of her back, the other on her belly. He smiled in the darkness.

'But I'll be back,' he said, kissing her again.

'How long will you be away?'

'Don't know yet. A day or two. Hopefully not any longer.' He looked at her, longing to take her back to bed. 'I've got to go,' he said, kissing her lightly before getting up.

She put on her bathrobe and followed him downstairs to the front door. He bent to kiss her but she could see his mind was already somewhere else, racing ahead to meet challenges that were out of her reach. Léa opened the front door for him. He stepped out, waving at her. She watched him go down the street and disappear at the end of the lane.

The bedroom felt empty when she went back to bed. But she felt happy. She was not sure what was ahead, but something had finally let go inside her. A dam she had been building for as long as she could remember had broken. Love had finally come in.

Léa picked the pillow he had slept on and embraced it, feeling the coolness of it against her naked body, burying her head in it, breathing him in.

43

Léa rushed to her computer when she got home. Her head was buzzing with the gossip she had gleaned from Mrs Hunter. Once Max had got out of the table, she had confided in Léa that she was worried about her son. It was not the first time she had said something like that, but she had seemed more wistful this time.

'I worry about him, you know. Since the death of his wife, he seemed to have become more single-minded. All he seems to do is work. Even here. He has spent hours in the library, checking God knows what. And then there are the women. All of them gold-diggers, if you ask me. Freya was the worse, and I do hope it's over between them. I don't know what hold she had on him, but she has something. And she's awful with Max. And Tom, of course. But Max has become her, her... how do you call it in French?'

'Bouc-émissaire?'

'That's it,' she had said with a heavy sigh. 'He said it's over but they work and play in the same circles so he's bound to meet her again.'

Léa had felt sick at that point. Had he gone back to London not because of a work problem but because Freya had said or pulled him back? No, that could not be true. There was the night before. And the last two days had been magical. Surely that meant something to him too. Didn't it? Or was it all just a front? Maybe he had been emailing and talking to Freya on the phone in his makeshift office. What did she know about him, after all?

She checked her phone for the umpteenth time that day, but there was still no word from him. There was indeed something going on with the markets, something to do with Chinese economy, but that was just gobbledygook to her. She thought of calling her brother in New York and asking him, but he would surely ask her why she was interested.. She tried to calm down by going for a run, but the fear was still in the pit of her stomach when she came home.

She took a long shower, put on a cotton dress and went to sit in the courtyard with her notebook and a glass of white wine. It was the third today; she thought. Stress was getting to her.

Mark had left the house early in the morning. The private plane his personal assistant in his Hong Kong office had ordered had landed just as he had arrived at the small airport near Nîmes. He was in London by 7 a.m. and at his office before 8. He had thought of sending Léa a text when as he made the call to fly back to London and again in the car that had taken him to the airport but that had proven impossible. His phone had rung almost continuously and decisions that would affect his clients had to be made.

He got to his home in Holland Park at around midnight. He was exhausted and knew he would probably only sleep a couple of hours at most. The Asian markets were opening in exactly three hours. He sunk into the sofa, a glass of whisky on the low table next to him, his phone in his hands. There were messages he needed to respond to, but all he could think about was Léa. She had been at the back of his mind all day, like a dream floating around his subconscious. He needed to hear her voice. He dialled the number, realising too late that it was 1 a.m. in France. She picked up the phone almost immediately.

'Mark?'

'Sorry to call you so late, I just didn't have the time to call you before now.' He felt like he was making excuses when there had been no other way. She did not reply, and he wondered if she had hung up.

'Are you there?'

'What happened? You said something about financial markets last night...'

'There was a serious hiccup when the Chinese markets opened. We needed to move fast to protect our investors. I had to come back.'

She could hear the strain and the tiredness in his voice. 'Is it terrible?'

'We've protected ourselves from some major problems but we need to monitor what will happen when the Asian markets opened in...' He looked at his watch before continuing, 'less than three hours.'

'You should go to sleep then.'

'I should, but I wanted to hear your voice.'

She felt insecure and was not sure what to make of this. What if he had spent the evening with Freya?

'I can't get you out of my head. I've replayed last night in my head so many times. I wish...' He sighed. 'I wish you were here. I need you.'

She felt her heart tighten in her chest. She could hear him breathe, and it took her back to the night before. She felt the yearning coming back.

'What are you doing?'

'I was in bed reading. I couldn't sleep. I was wondering where you were.'

He shut his eyes, trying to imagine her in her room. He exhaled. 'What are you wearing?'

'No, your turn. Where are you?' Her voice was firm, which surprised him. He opened his eyes and looked around him.

'In my house, in the lounge. All I've managed to do is remove my tie. I still have my jacket on.'

There was a silence.

'What are you wearing?'

'Why do you need to know?' She felt herself on the defensive without knowing why.

'Humour me please. You can even lie to me if you want.'

'A t-shirt.' She wanted to add I'm not lying, but it felt wrong. Maybe she was reading him all wrong. Maybe he had had an awful day, and Freya had not been involved.

'Are you asleep?'

'No, I'm just trying to picture you. I want to remember what your skin feels like, what we would do if I hadn't had to come back here.'

'Sleeping probably,' she replied.

'Very funny. Next time I see you, I'm not going anywhere.'

She could not help but wonder if he had said that to Freya too.

'It's late. We should go to bed.' She let the silence hang. 'I reckon you're asleep.'

'Pretty close. Talk to me until I fall asleep.'

'Maybe you should be in bed then.'

'The sofa is very comfortable,' he said, lying down.

Léa heard him fall asleep and cut the connection, putting the phone down next to her. She sat on the bed in the dark for a long time. Mark's voice and lighthearted talk had not removed the fear she felt. She thought of the night before, of the love and lust she had felt then. It felt like light years away. She felt stupid for having fallen for his oh-so-easy banter about the stars.

She laid down on the bed. There was no breeze again tonight, and everything felt so still. She looked at the sky outside; it was pitch black. She had fallen for him. She knew that. Maybe it was loneliness. She had left someone back in London and had come here with nothing, trying to rebuild her life. But like everyone else, she wanted someone to love her and touch her and make love to her. She had pretended that she was strong and did not need a man, but he had seen through her. For someone like him, it must have like picking a low-hanging fruit. Easy. A little romance while in Provence. She felt sad and dirty. Naive, too. Tears burnt her eyes and when they came, she let them fall hoping that they would release her from his grip, from this pain.

* * * * *

Mark was still lying on the sofa when the alarm on his phone rang at 2.55am. On the screen, the last call was showing: Léa. He had fallen asleep talking to her. He felt guilty but happy that he had talked to her. She had not chased him yesterday, and he was grateful. The day had been long, and he had had to focus hard. Hopefully things would be easier today. He needed to think about what he could get her to make up for letting her down. An idea that had formed in his head in the courtyard two days before came back to him. He made a mental note to call his lawyer during the day.

There were no urgent messages, nothing that needed his attention right away. He hesitated for a minute. It was 4am in Uzès, but what the heck, life had to be lived dangerously. The text went, and he hoped she would call him before he had to leave the house.

He took a long shower, letting the water run on his body, alternating between hot and cold. Visions of Léa danced in front of him and caught his breath away. He wanted her, but this was different from the women he had been with since his wife had died. He saw himself living with her, protecting her, pushing her to achieve more. She could be so much more. He would help her. They would buy a house near Uzès, enrol Tom and Max in a French school. He was not sure what he would do yet, but it did not matter. They would have more money than they needed in the bank, regardless of him selling the hedge fund. Family and friends would advise him not to, but that had never stopped him from doing anything and it would not to stop him now.

He looked at the rows of suits in his dressing room. The pairs of polished shoes. The white shirts. Suddenly all this did not seem as important as it had before. He could happily let all that go. Not wear a suit or a tie, not manage a few hundred people across several continents. It was time to get out of the game.

A picture of his younger son Tom caught his attention as he was putting on his tie. It was high time he met Léa too. He wondered what he would make of her and she of him. He was so different from Max. Ebullient, funny, sharp-witted. And he had been as his widow's parents for far too long. He had indulged them for long enough. Life would be very different.

He checked his phone as he made his way to the kitchen.

Messages were coming through, the markets seemed to have settled down a little. It was 3.45am. He called Hong-Kong as he poured himself a cup of coffee. This was another drug he would have to do without. Just espressos. He smiled as he spoke to one of his analysts.

* * * * *

Half-asleep, Léa heard the buzz of her phone. She knew before she looked at it, it would be from him. She willed herself not to look at it, but curiosity became too great, and she tapped on the screen.

Can't stop thinking of you. Hoping everything'll be sorted today. Should be back in town tomorrow evening. Call me. Mxx

She looked at the time. Too early to get up. She let the phone down and laid on the bed, trying to make sense of the message and her feelings. What game was he playing at? Had she been wrong last night? Did he really care for her? Had Mrs Hunter's fears had influenced her? She wished his sister Caroline was still in town. Her no-nonsense approach would have been very welcome now. She had her number, but what could she say to her? That she did not trust her brother?

She read the message again, her fingers hovering over the call button. But she fought the urge. A friend had once told her it was better to make yourself scarce with men sometimes. It was time for him to show he wanted her. She had been far too easily accessible in the last few weeks. That resolution made, she switched her phone off and went back to sleep.

Mark called Léa as she was about to meet Max at their usual corner. Her heart jumped when she saw his name on her phone, and she hesitated. But a need to hear his voice proved stronger than her second thoughts. Her skin tingled as she heard him say hello.

'Did you get my message?'

'I did. I just got up late and needed to get ready to meet with

Max.'

There was a silence, and she could hear him breathe. The sound unsettled her, taking her back to two nights before. She wanted to tell him she missed him terribly but a niggling fear at the back of her mind kept rearing its head making her wonder about the reality of their budding relationship.

'I can't stop thinking about you,' he said, and she wondered if he was on his own or surrounded by people.

'Where are you?'

She heard him gasp and chuckle. 'In my office, why?'

'I just wondered that's all.'

'I'm on my own if that's what's worrying you.'

There was a silence. 'Léa what's wrong?'

She almost told him there and then what his mother had said the day before but, as she walked up the street in the sunshine, she felt she could not. It was stupid. He had chucked Freya out weeks ago. He had told her himself.

'Nothing. I just miss you. It was just all so sudden, you know. You going away when…'

She heard a door open and someone spoke to him.

'I've got to go. I call you back later.'

He hung up before she could reply, and she looked at her phone as she walked up the street. In the distance, she saw Max waiting for her, munching happily on a pain au chocolat.

She could ask Max about his father's life in London, but she felt wary of making him believe that there was something between them. What if it did not work out, and they went their separate ways? Once again Max would be left disappointed and she could not bring herself to do this to him. She loved him too much; she thought as she watched him read to her in French from a newspaper.

44

It was just after 6 p.m. when Mark exited the car park below his office. The streets were slick with rain and people hurrying to catch their trains and buses home, but he felt happy. A situation that had looked critical the day before was now under control and could be managed without him. He was going back to Léa tomorrow. He thought of calling her to tell her, but the traffic was heavy as he got on the motorway and he needed to focus. He also wanted some time to think, something he did best when he was driving. So many things had happened in the last couple of weeks and he was about to make a momentous decision while not having all the facts. Yet he felt excited, like a child on Christmas morning. Something new had happened, a new direction had come to light which he had not expected. For the first time in his life, he felt emotionally connected to someone. Someone he was about to make one of the biggest decisions of his life for when their relationship was still only in its infancy. But he knew she was the one. She had shifted this cloud that had been hanging over his head for a very long time. This self-loathing of late seemed to have vanished. He smiled to himself as he remembered kissing Léa. It had not felt cheap like it had before. He had wanted her, but it had been more than just a physical urge this time. He wanted to be with her, to care for her, to protect her, to see her grow into herself. She could be so much more than she saw herself as and he had every intention to help her achieve her ambitions. As for him, he had succeeded beyond his wildest dreams, but the time had come to move on. Success meant nothing if it was without her in his life. He smiled to himself as he sped up. Life was good.

Tom came running down the path from the manor house his ex-parents-in-law called home, in a picturesque village on the edge of the Cotswolds. He scooped his son in his arms and kissed him. He smelled of soap and he noticed his hair was a little wet. He saw his widow's parents at the front door. She looked sad, and he looked resentful. Nothing new here. There had been some harsh words spoken and actions taken on both sides. He extended his hand, and she took it, but he refused.

'Why could you not leave him with us until the end of the holidays?'

'He has to spend some time with his brother and with me too, Edward.'

'I put all his stuff in the suitcase,' said his wife in a small teary voice.

She always tried to smooth things over, aware that between the two men, resentment was high and could blow up at any time. Mark had threatened many times not to let Tom stay with them anymore and having already lost Max, she could not bear to lose her other grandchild to a feud she did not want anymore. Mark pitied her more than he respected her for it. She had been complicit with her husband in trying to wrench his children away from him after his wife's death, and he could not forgive her or him for that.

'How's Max?', she continued trying hard to regain her composure.

'Very well.' He should have stopped there but could not help adding, 'France has been very good to him. His French is coming along nicely.' She nodded, her eyes glistening.

'Come on Tom, let's go.'

'You're not staying for dinner?' she asked.

Her husband glared at her, a look of horror on his face, and Mark shook his head. 'I need to get home. It'll take another hour and Tom needs to be in bed soon. Has he had dinner?' She bowed her head in silence.

Mark grabbed the suitcase and Edward a box. It was overflowing with toys and books, and he felt a wave of resentment come over him. As always, they had tried to kill their grandson with kindness and presents and he wondered if this would backfire, just as it had with Max once Tom would be a little older. He breathed deeply. There was no point arguing when they would all soon be in France. Their influence would wane then.

They got home just after nine, and Mark carried his sleeping son to his bed. As he pulled the duvet over him, he wondered how he would take the changes he had in mind. He was so different from Max. Bubbling, constantly on the move, always ready to climb and jump and fall, he did not have the reflective side Max had always had even as a small five-year-old child. He kissed him, leaving the night lamp on, and closed the door softly.

Downstairs, he poured himself a whisky, sat at the kitchen counter and dialled Léa's number.

'Are you only getting home?'

'I went to pick up my son Tom from his maternal grandparents,' he said, swirling the ice around in his glass.

She could not help but wonder why he had not told her this. Was this true? She shut her eyes. She did not want to question everything he did but felt at a loss to understand parts of his life she did not know.

'You sound tired.'

'I'm exhausted but I'm coming back to Uzès tomorrow.'

Her heart flipped in her chest. 'Are you? When?'

'We'll land sometimes in the afternoon. I'll have to take Tom to the house first, but I'll come to you straight after.'

'Max said your friend Alex and his wife are arriving at the bastide tomorrow. He asked Luca on your behalf to organise a dinner.'

Mark winced. In the mayhem of the last couple of days and his desire to see Léa, he had forgotten about Alex's call. She sounded as disappointed as he was, and he tried to sound cheerful.

'I'd forgotten about that.'

There was a silence, and he tried to imagine where she was. 'I miss you.'

She heard his breath caught in his mouth. 'Me too, Mark.'

'Where are you?'

'In the courtyard. It has been so hot again today.'

'It's been raining cats and dogs here.'

'Summer in London and all that.'

'I want you.'

He had said it without thinking. It was just the sound of her voice that made him yearn for her, the feeling of her skin under his fingers, the warmth of her body. He heard the shallowness of her breathing over the phone, but she did not reply. He smiled to himself. The shyness was still there, and he loved it. He could not wait to show her she did not need to be like that around him.

Léa hung up and stayed in the courtyard, looking at the night sky, trying to remember what Mark had said about the stars. She felt both madly attracted to him and yet apprehensive. Not that she did not believe him, but the thought of Freya or maybe someone else being with him did not go away. Impostor syndrome. It had plagued her all her adult life. How could someone like her could tame someone like him? He was successful, used to getting his own way with work, people, women. She had seen it with her own eyes. Who was she to believe that she could change this? And yet, she had also seen another side to him. A softer, more fragile side. But it had been so fleeting that, here as darkness fell, she wondered if she had not dreamt it. And what about the fact that they lived in different places, different lives? He could no more move here that she could move back to London. This love story, if it was what it was, seemed to be doomed from the start.

A silent tear rolled down her cheek. How could she be so stupid as to fall in love with someone she could not have? He could say all the things, he could tell her he wanted her and missed her and maybe it was true, but he did not understand what turmoil he was creating in her. She needed him, his hands on her skin, his lips on her lips. The memory of that night was still fresh in her mind, and it hurt. It hurt her to think this was all but an illusion. She wiped away the tears trying to get a grip on herself, but she could not do that anymore that she could forget him. It was like he had left an imprint on her, her skin, her heart.

45

Freya fell backwards on the bed of the hotel room. She was so pleased with her find. A last-minute cancellation that had enabled her to nab a pretty room in the only five-star hotel in Uzès. Luck was on her side.

Since her last exchange with Mark, over a week ago, she had carefully planned what she would tell him.

But first, she had to find an address. By chance, the night she had got into his place in Holland Park, she had found the name of the recruitment agency that had sent Léa to him. She rang the number she had saved to her phone. A voice with a strong French southern accent answered almost immediately.

'Allo?'

'Hello, I'm Monsieur Hunter's assistant,' she said in hesitant French, trying not to stumble on the words she was reading from the Google translation she had done the night before. 'I need Madame Pasquier's address.'

'Yeah, wait a second, I'll find it for you.'

There was a silence and the rustling sound of papers moved around.

'Why do you want Léa's address?' asked the man.

'I have to send her some documents to fill in. It's for Mr Hunter's son's school.'

There was another silence, and she wondered if he had understood what she had said.

'Listen, just send them to me here and I'll give them to her.'

'I can't. I have been instructed to send them to her only. Confidential information, you see.'

The man grumbled, then seemed to find what he was looking for.

'Do you have a piece of paper?'

She asked him to repeat and then spell the street name for her. While he did that, she looked up the street on the map she had picked up at reception.

Once she had hung up, she put the photos in a brown envelope and wrote Léa's name on it. She would take them to her later if he still refused to see her.

It was time at last to put the other side of her plan in motion.

Mark I need to see you. It's important.

She waited half-an-hour, but he did not reply.

Mark what I need to tell you is important. If you refuse to see me, I'll tell everyone what you've done to me.

> *And what have I done to you exactly?*

I'll tell you face-to-face.

> *Can't do. Don't have the time at the moment.*

I'm in Uzès.

Sat in the VIP lounge of Biggin Hill airport, southwest of London, he wondered what she wanted and what this half-hidden threat meant. Since her intrusion into his house, he had not heard from her. All his thoughts had been taken by Léa, so much so he had forgotten all about Freya. It was like she belonged to a previous life, a life that he did not know anymore and could not understand.

His youngest song was listening to a pretty air hostess telling him a story. He was laughing, joyously free from worries, and

Mark envied his innocence.

I'm in London.

Freya's heart flipped when she read the message. She had not expected him to still be in London. There had been that minor crisis on the markets in Asia earlier that week, and he must have needed to come back. But nothing prevented him to be back in Uzès for the weekend. We were early afternoon on Friday; at worst, he would be back here the next day. She had nothing to lose.

I need to see you. It's important.

Why?

I have to see you.

'Mr Hunter? Your flight is ready.'

Mark was so lost in his thoughts that he barely heard what the steward had just said.

'Daddy, daddy, we have to go to the plane!'

He looked at his son and smiled before picking him up.

'Yes, let's go buddy. Let's fly.'

In the car that was taking them from the lounge to the plane, his phone seemed to burn in the inside pocket of his jacket. He kept wondering what Freya wanted. Money? They were not married or even engaged, and he had never made that promise to her. Was she going to do something against her son, accused him of something? She had better not even try. He would destroy her career if she did. But no, he could not see what threat she could have on him. It did not matter anyhow because he had taken his decision that morning. The estate agent he had summoned had confirmed that his house would sell easily. Even then, he did not need this sale to move to Uzès. Maybe they would keep the house so that they could come and spend a few days in London whenever they wanted.

As they were getting on the plane, he decided not to answer Freya's last text. The next sixty minutes would give him the time to craft the perfect answer to her threat.

* * * * *

Freya waited for an hour, but no reply came through. She was pacing back and forth in the room, her phone in her hand, both angry at him and herself. She should not have been so direct in her threats. She knew it well; it was a side of her character that he had never liked. He did not like demands that were threats in disguise. Every time she had been too forceful in her requests, he had given her the cold shoulder. No one threatened Mark Hunter.

Well, she would be the one to do it. He did not want to answer her, and she would show him that he should have. But first, she needed to kill this romance between him and the French girl in the bud. That sentence he had said the night she had confronted him at his house had been going round and round in her head. Without being fully aware of it, it had stoked her vengeance. She would not leave her place to this woman. He may not love her, but he would have to look after her. She took the brown envelope and shoved it into her handbag before going out.

46

Léa heard the bell and tried to dry her tears quickly. When she opened the door, Max was in front of her with an enormous bouquet of pale pink roses. She saw the worry in his eyes.

'Why are you crying? What's the matter? Is it my Dad? Has he said he isn't coming?'

She shook her head as she let him in.

'It's nothing. Something stupid. It has nothing to do with your Dad.'

She had forgotten that she had left the pictures on the coffee table, and it was the first thing Max saw as he handed her the flowers. He grabbed them, a dumbstruck look on his face. They showed his father and Freya together, smiling.

'Where did you get those?'

'The envelope was in my mailbox when I got home from the bastide earlier.'

Max was checking the photos carefully. He took them to the courtyard. 'They're not new. I took this one at the bastide the night we arrived. And this one, it's in our house in London. And look at how they're dressed, it can't be recent.'

He raised his eyes to her and saw she was observing him.

'You know?'

'I know what?'

She hesitated. Was she mistaken? An enormous smile was lightening up his face.

'For you and my Dad? Yes. I saw you kiss the night I came to sleep at your house.'

Mark's words came back to Léa. He had told her that his son had been hoping for this all along, that he was sure he even dreamt of it. She hid her face in her hands. How had she been so blind not to see that Max knew? She was seeing him almost every day. She had naively believed they had hidden it well enough for him not to guess.

'I'm sorry… I don't want to take your Mum's place. It all happened so quickly… Only days ago we were fighting each other…'

'She isn't here anymore, my mum. I'll always love her, but she can't look after me anymore.'

She took him in her arms.

'Who took you to Uzès?'

'Alex, my godfather, Dad's best friend. He and his wife turned up just after you left. You'll love Alex, everybody does. He's so cool. Dad did tell you we're all having dinner together?'

She nodded before kissing him on the cheek.

'You know that it's possible that it may not work between your Dad and I, right? There are so many difficulties to overcome. Maybe we won't succeed.'

'What difficulties?'

'We don't live in the same country to start with.'

'I know you don't want to go back to London but we can come and live here. I'm sure I could manage at the high school in town.'

She smiled while rocking him gently.

'I know you would but I'm not sure your Dad could live here or even that he's going to agree to send you to a local school given that he wants you to attend Oxford or Cambridge.'

'That's what he wants but me, I don't know what I want yet,' Max said with a shrug. It was an improvement on the 'I-don't-want-to-go-to-Cambridge' that she had heard him say so many times.

He moved away from her and let the photos fell on the table.

'You can put them in the bin. They're fake. I'm sure Dad will tell you the same.'

He was so sure of himself that she knew she believed him. There was a strength in his voice which left no place for doubt.

The bell rang again.

'You're waiting for someone?'

'Your Dad said he would come and pick me up for dinner,' she said with a smile.

She stopped and put the photos back in the envelope before giving them to him. 'We don't tell him.'

Max put his index finger on his lips before taking the envelope. 'I'll put them in the bin.'

As he did so, he could not help but wonder who could have send these doctored photos to Léa. Freya? She was supposed to be back in London. Yet who else could it be? He prayed silently that she was not back in Uzès. Everything he had hoped for was coming together so beautifully. He would not let her ruin everything. A word from his grandmother about Freya came back to him as he pushed the envelope far into the bin. She could cast a spell on his father, she had said and was capable of everything to get him. He would have to be vigilant.

He heard his father's voice and waited a few minutes before going out of the kitchen.

* * * * *

When he had arrived at the bastide, Mark had barely taken the time to say hello to Alex and his wife Martha leaving Tom in Manuela's care before jumping in the car again to go and pick Léa up. He had organised this dinner at Luca's restaurant but could not wait any longer before seeing her. He had not replied to Freya and only remembered that she was in Uzès as he parked his car. He was not scared of her. It was an empty threat, just the words of a jilted woman.

When Léa opened the door, she was as beautiful as she was in his dreams. Her eyes shone, her hair up in a loose bun showed her slender neck and the thin straps of her dress revealed her golden shoulders. He kissed her before she had the time to close the door.

'I missed you.'

'Me too. Your son is here,' she whispered.

'I hope he bought the flowers I asked him to buy,' he said before kissing her again.

Her perfume bewitched him. He would have liked to have her to himself, but Max was already coming out of the kitchen.

'They're gorgeous. He chose very well,' she said, moving away from him while smoothing her dress. 'He just arrived and I haven't had the time to put them in water.'

She exchanged a look with Max, who smiled to her. She was embarrassed, but he was on cloud nine. It was all he wanted to see.

'Where's Tom?' she asked from the kitchen.

'At the bastide. Manuela will look after him tonight.'

Max was looking at his father. He was dying to ask him if he had heard from Freya, but he did not dare. Léa had asked him not to say anything, but the idea that this woman could be in town worried him. Would his father have been able to lie to Léa if he had taken up again with Freya? He looked at him closely as he was talking to her. He had the deep line on his the middle of his forehead, which usually meant that something worried him. It was obvious though that he was smitten with Léa. He tried to remember if he had ever had that look with Freya, but nothing came. All he could see was his father pushing her away the night she had tried in vain to seduce him on the terrace. No, it had never been the same.

* * * * *

Léa felt nervous, febrile almost. She was so happy to see Mark again, and if they had been on their own, she would have felt freer, no doubt. But Max was here, and even if he knew about them, she felt ill at ease. It was one thing to care for him as his teacher, but being his mother now that she was his dad's girlfriend felt wrong. What was the difference between her and Freya after all? It was even worse in her case because, not only was he paying her for her services, but she was also very far from earning what Freya was earning.

And yet when he had told her he knew, Max had looked happy, happier than she had ever seen him. It was almost like he was already seeing himself living in Uzès, going to school here, making friends. But going to school here did not mean that he would not be bullied here either. Harassment happened in France too and, if his father was to move here, he would be a choice target given his difference and his father's income.

She had gone up to finish getting ready and could not help observe them through the bathroom window as they talked in the courtyard. They were laughing and jostling and looked comfortable with each other. Maybe her fears were unfounded. Max was not the shy teenager he had been only a few weeks before. He was now standing tall, looked people straight in the eyes when he talked to them, and seemed to have understood that he should not fear confrontation with others. The ease with which he had made progress in French had encouraged him to believe in himself, and the kindness of the surrounding people had done the rest. As for her, she had only been a guide. She was proud of it, but his devotion to her worried her. It was a positive thing that he had finally come out of mourning his mother, but she could not replace her. Even less so when neither his father nor she knew if this holiday romance would last.

Holiday romance was maybe simplistic. She loved Mark. She understood that underneath the sometimes provocative attitude was a man who, like her, had been wounded by life many times. But was she ready to have a long-term relationship? The injury caused by her ex-partner's treason was far from being healed, even if she did not think of William as often as she had done in the past. She had accepted that they were not made for each other and even suspected that she had always known. But was she made for Mark Hunter and him for her? Was he the one? She still remembered the sentence her grandma had told her after her first big heartbreak.

'When the right person comes along, you will know,' she had said in that soft singing voice of hers.

But did we ever know?

* * *

* * * * *

Léa seemed a little distant since he had arrived. He would have liked to be alone with her and talk about his plans, the decisions he had made. But Max was there and although he suspected his son of having known about his feelings for Léa for a while, possibly before he knew, he did not want to embarrass Léa.

But Max would be happy with the decision he had made. What had still been that morning a rough outline, a daydream even, was now on tracks to happen. He had thought long and hard during the flight, with Tom asleep curled on his lap about what he wanted for his children and for himself. Max was right, London had become toxic. It was time to find a healthier way of life. He was tired of running after time. The last two crazy long days had been a case in point which had reminded him he did not want this constant mad rush in his life. And living between London and Uzès would not be satisfactory either. It would satisfy no one, including himself. He did not want to live on his own in his large London house which had too many memories from another life. Time had come for his sons and for him to start anew.

There would be many people telling him he was making a colossal mistake. He could almost hear his mother already. She had guessed something was on and had already tried to dissuade him twice by pointing out all the problems he would face. She had even hinted that he would be incapable of living in a small town like Uzès. But what did she know? Alone, he would probably have thought twice about it, but with Léa, it was not only possible but desirable. And then, he had achieved everything he had wanted in London: success, glory even, women, luxury, money had all been his. And none of it on its own or combined made him happy. He was, without a doubt, about to turn a page, but he felt ready for it. Every time he looked at her, he felt a little closer to this portentous change, this fresh life. For the first time in a very long time, he felt excited by the future and its possibilities. Tonight he would talk to Léa, and tomorrow he would tell his sons that their lives would change forever.

47

They left Léa's house arm in arm in the heat of a beautiful August night. There was a promise in the gorgeous light that bathed the stones on the townhouses in gold against the deep blue of the sky. The night market that took place on Friday nights was in full swing and they stopped to look at some stalls. Max was walking in front of them, and Mark took Léa's hand before embracing her. He was half-expecting her to move away, but she got closer to him.

'There are so many things I want to tell you,' he whispered in her ear.

'He knows,' she replied, nodding towards Max.

Mark laughed softly. 'I'm not surprised. In his head, he's already here. He doesn't want to go back to the school he was in last year. He doesn't even want to go back to London. He told me before I left for London that you had shown him the high school.'

'I didn't do it on purpose, we were walking by...'

He stopped and kissed her. They were in the middle of the street, people walking on either side of them.

'What worries you?'

She shook her head, and a curl fell over her cheek.

'Nothing,' she said, smiling with her eyes for the first time that night. 'I'm worrying about nothing.'

Max was far in front of them, rummaging between the stalls. Since he had arrived in Uzès four weeks before, he had been buying little trinkets that he had carefully arranged on a shelf in his room at the bastide. Every single one of them represented a little victory over his shyness, and he loved these objects fiercely. Tonight, he had found a small bottle made of cobalt blue glass and had chatted with the seller while waiting for Léa and his father to join him. The man had congratulated him on his French and told him that his parents should be proud of him. Max had not contradicted him, but the words 'parents' had made him happy. He wondered, not for the first time, if Léa would agree to him calling her 'Mum' when he saw them arrived hand in hand.

* * * * *

Freya had put on a long bohemian red dress with a large belt and some flat sandals. She had learnt that this town and its surroundings were not made for high heels. She also wanted to show Mark that she could be like them, the locals. She was not proud of what she was about to do that night, and she also knew that she was playing her last card. She had to do everything to show him she cared. She felt desperate for him to love her again. So much so, that in the taxi that was taking her to the bastide, she felt jittery. She had to succeed. She just had to.

At the bastide, she was about to send the taxi back when she noticed that Mark's car which he always parked in the same spot was not there. She rang the bell in a panic. She had been so sure that he would be at home that she had not thought for one minute that he could have gone out. She felt vindicated and terrified at the same time that her idea that he had a lover around here was true. Anger rose in her and she had to try hard not to bark at Manuela when she opened the front door, a young boy in her arms. She recognised Tom but dismissed him straight away.

'I'm looking for Mark,' she said in a tone that did not hide her anger.

She knew Manuela spoke a little English, and she was in no mood to attempt to speak to her in French.

'Mr Hunter is not here. He went out.'

'Where?' She had almost shouted the word and Tom opened his eyes wider. She could see he was about to cry. Manuela frowned.

'I'm asking you where is Mr Hunter. I need to see him. It's urgent.'

'Tomorrow?' said Manuela.

'Not tomorrow, now, today! Where is he?'

Despite her anger, Manuela was still hesitating and the little boy started to cry which only upped Freya's anger.

'Oh, shut up, you fool!' she told the little boy whose sobs were getting louder. 'The sooner you tell me, the sooner I'll be gone,' she said to Manuela in a threatening voice.

'I don't know the name of the place. It's in Uzès. Rue Froment. An Italian restaurant, I believe.'

Freya turned around without a word to Manuela, who was rocking the little boy in her arms. She ran to the taxi, ordering him to go back to Uzès.

* * * * *

Inside the restaurant, Luca had privatised the little courtyard at the back and laid out the table for six. Mrs Hunter and a couple that Léa did not know were waiting for them around a coffee table where Luca had laid out little plates of food and was serving champagne.

'Léa, here's Alex, my best friend and his wife, Martha.'

Alex was a jovial man with fine sandy hair that he kept up with his sunglasses. He was sporting a three-day beard and looked straight out of the rich counties just outside of London. He worked in advertising and, like his best friend, you just knew by looking at him that he was a highly successful man. Yet that was where the similarities ended. There was something more relaxed about Alex than Mark, less tension. His wife, Martha, introduced herself as an American from New York who worked as a freelance journalist for fashion magazines. She had dark curly hair and wore a chic colourful kaftan with big chunky translucent bracelets. They formed a singular couple, him a large man sounding very British and her, tall and slim with a strong New York accent.

Alex took her aside while Mark was speaking to his mother. 'I've heard a lot about you, you know?' he told her, a glint of amusement in his eyes. 'I've been told you used to live in London?'

'For twenty years.'

'What do you find in him?' Alex said, nodding to Mark. 'He has got no charm, you know. Just a finance boy if you ask me,' he said a twinkle in his eye.

Freya ran to the restaurant. Inside, she stopped and looked around her. There was no sign of Mark. A smiling man of about forty welcomed her, but she was not listening.

'I'm looking for Mr Hunter,' she told him curtly.

'Mr Hunter, yes. Are you part of his group of friends?' said the man, a frown forming on his brow. 'It's just that we only expected six people…'

But Freya had stopped listening to him. She had noticed the courtyard and recognised Mark's back. She walked around the man and ran to the back of the restaurant in front of astounded customers and waiters.

'Mark!' she said as she walked into the courtyard.

All eyes were suddenly on her as Luca stepped right behind her. Freya had not imagined that there would be all these people. In her mind, it had just been him and his new amour. But here were Alex and Martha, Max and Mrs Hunter. She bit her lip. And then she saw that Mark was holding Léa's hand. It was true then. He had lied to her about not having a new love here. A burning anger overtook her.

Alex had stood up. 'Freya, what are you doing here?'

'I didn't come to see you Alex but to speak to Mark. I've got something important to tell him.'

'It's not the place or time to do that,' said Alex as Mark was walking towards her, his blue gaze almost black, a sure sign that he was furious.

'It's all his fault,' she shouted, pointing to him, 'he only had to agree to see me!'

'Freya, we've already had this discussion. If it's going over the same stuff, we've already discussed ten days ago, I don't see why you are here or what is urgent—'

'I'm pregnant. And it's yours.'

The silence was deafening in the courtyard after the commotion she had caused. Freya could not help a cruel smile when she saw Mrs Hunter's horrified face. Léa's reaction though disappointed her. She had expected her to say something, but she stayed silent, just watching her, a sad look in her eyes that Freya could not fathom.

Mark stood still and silent. She had expected something else, maybe that he would take her in his arms, telling her that everything would be fine, that he would be there for her. But he was just standing there, staring at her, trying to guess if what she was saying was true or false.

Nobody saw Max got up, but all of a sudden, he was in front of her, his fists up, shouting.

'You're a liar! I don't believe what you say for a minute! Get out! All you want is my father's money! It's you who sent the fake photos to Léa to make her believe that you were still going out with my Dad. Fuck off!'

She thought for a second that he was about to hit her, but Alex and Mark embraced him, pulling him back. His face was red and distorted as he kept shouting to her that she was a liar.

The rest happened so quickly that she did not see it coming. Mark caught her wrist and dragged her away. She moaned that he was hurting her, but he did not loosen his grip. When he finally found a place away from the crowds in a small lane at the back of the Cathedral, she complained that he could not do that to a pregnant woman.

'Shut up! I don't believe a word you say. So first you'll prove to me that you're pregnant and second that this baby is mine, if there is a baby.'

'How dare you accusing me of lying!'

'Because I know you and I know that you're only here because I told you it was over between us ten days ago. You're

225

hoping that by telling me you're pregnant I'll change my mind, but it's not going to happen. Never. It's over between us. You need to get that into your head, Freya.'

The hatred with which he had said that was reflected in his eyes and it hurt her.

'You can't do that to me, Mark. This baby needs you and me…'

'If there is a baby, I'll ask for the exclusive right to look after this child because I believe you're incapable of doing that yourself. But first, you'll take a pregnancy test as soon as possible and my lawyer will get in touch regarding the paternity test.'

He was about to walk away, but he turned around one last time.

'If I ever learn that you tried to get in touch with Léa in any way whatsoever, I promise you I'll get you convicted for harassment so I advise you to go home and stay away from us. Do you hear me?'

She had no time to respond as he walked away and disappeared from view. A bell chimed somewhere. She stood there, in that dark lane, tears running freely, wondering how her well-thought plan could have gone so wrong.

48

When Mark came back to the courtyard, only Alex was there waiting for him.

'Where are they?'

'Your mother asked Martha to drive her home and as Martha doesn't know the area, she asked Max to go with her. It wasn't easy to convince him to go. He wanted to go with Léa.'

'And Léa?' he said, looking around.

'She's just left. You must have seen her. She…'

But Mark was not listening anymore. 'I'll be back. Order whatever you like.'

From here, there was only one way she could have gone home. He started running, pushing people aside as he increased his speed. It was getting dark. Would he recognise her? And then he saw her as he turned a corner.

'Léa!' he shouted, but she did not turn around.

The urgency in his voice the second time he uttered her name made a middle-aged woman who was walking her dog nearby looked at her with worry. Léa stopped, smiling to the lady before turning around. The fear she had kept under control in the last few days was coming back. He had lied to her. He had seen Freya in London. She walked slowly back towards him, stopping only a few steps away.

'Léa, I'm so sorry about tonight. I had no idea Freya would turn up. I'm not even sure half of it is true. She's nothing, nothing to me anymore.'

'But you saw her in London and didn't tell me.'

'It was two weeks ago when I went back the first time. Before us, before… It's not what you think. She had got into my house, she wanted to get back together, but I said no.'

She looked distant again, like she did not want him to come any closer and it bit into him. He extended his hand, but she did not take it.

'Léa, it's over between Freya and I, and a baby won't change that. I told her tonight, and I warned her not to approach you. Why didn't you tell me about the photos?'

She shook her head.

'I'm not good at playing these games. I thought… I thought we were getting somewhere, you and I, that we had something special. But how can we live with suspicion?'

He got closer to her. His voice was low, and he found it difficult to speak.

'Léa, please. I want to be with you. Forget Freya. I swear that there's nothing left between us. I was even going to tell you tonight that I have made a decision for me and the boys.'

She was looking at him, a look of deep sadness in her eyes.

'I can't Mark. Not after this.'

She paused, pulling a curl behind her ear.

'It won't work between us. I'll always be asking myself if there's someone else in your life. We had an enjoyable time, but it's just a holiday romance, it'll fade away with time. You'll forget me once you're back home.'

She could read the pain she was inflicting on his face. His hand around his mouth, this gesture she had seen him do so many times when he was looking for something to say, broke her heart.

'Léa please, just tell me what I can do to make you change your mind.'

'Go home. Look after Max and Tom. Find someone to love and forget about me.'

'I can't do that. I can't forget about you.'

'You'll forget about me.'

'No Léa, you may forget about us but I won't. You're stronger than me.'

She breathed deeply. It had to stop. She could feel her will crumbling against his. She was not strong. She knew before she was about to say it that it would mark a point of no return. She looked him straight in the eyes.

'Maybe you're right. I probably don't love you as much as you love me.'

'I don't believe you. Not now, not ever. There's nothing I can do about Freya if you don't believe me, but I know, I know that I have done nothing wrong. I don't understand why you're doing this, but it's got nothing to do with Freya.'

'It doesn't matter. It's over between us.'

She saw the defeat in his eyes and forced herself not to go to him. He had not convinced her about Freya, but she knew in that moment that she loved him. But it was an impossible love, one that had no future. Her decision, as heart-wrenching as it was, was setting them free again.

'Goodbye Mark,' she said softly before walking away.

She was shaking so much when she reached her house; it took her several attempts before she could turn the key and open the door. She stumbled along the corridor in the dark and went out in the little courtyard. She sat slowly on one of the iron-wrought chairs and put her head on her arms on the table. She cried for a long time. For him, for her, for Max, for them, for having believed that everything would work out like in the fairy tales she loved so much as a child. But more than anything, she cried because she had finally understood that she was in love, in love like she had never been before. And it hurt. It hurt so bad.

She stayed outside for a very long time. Stunned by what had happened, too lost in herself to comprehend why he had done that to her. He had sounded sincere when he had said that he was not with Freya. She had seen something in his eyes. Had she been deceived again or had it be genuine? She almost hoped that he had cheated on her as otherwise. She was the one who was in the wrong. She had pushed him away without giving him a chance. But they could never make it together. Their lives were too different.

And then there was this baby. It could have happened before Mark left Freya; it was not so long ago, after all. But he could not abandon her, he would need to look after her and this child.

She finally understood that she was staying there, in the courtyard, listening to the noises, hoping against hope that someone would ring the bell. If he loved truly her, as he had said, why had he not run after her? She checked her phone again, but there was nothing. No message, no call. Nothing.

Had he left already and gone back to London? Or would he pretend that nothing happened and stayed at the bastide for the last week of the holidays?

Léa took her phone to her bedroom and laid down on the bed. She let her hand caress the soft sheets and buried her head in the pillow, crying silent tears until she fell asleep.

49

Left on his own, Alex called his goddaughter. She answered almost immediately.

'Which hotel?' he asked curtly.

'Have you talked to him?'

But Alex had hung up. He had no wish to start a discussion until he was in front of her.

He paid the bill despite Luca's protestations that he trusted Mr Hunter and that he could come and pay the next day. As he apologised for the drama, Alex hoped they had not pushed away this charming man's clients.

Following Luca's directions to get to the hotel Freya was staying at, Alex took his time. He wanted to let her stew a little. She knew he would not be nice with her.

At the hotel, the receptionist gave him the room number, and he went up the sculpted stone staircase whistling. When she opened her bedroom door, she was wearing a white bathrobe and her eyes were red-rimmed. It did not move him. He had learnt a long time ago, when she was still a little girl, that Freya was a born manipulator.

'Has he said anything to you? I was hoping he'd come with you.'

He sat on a plush chair and crossed his arms.

'Freya, I know Mark has been very clear with you. It's over, *fini, finito*. Whether you like it or not, he won't take you back, whatever the circumstances.'

231

'He has no right to abandon me when I need him…'

'Spare me your idiotic daydream, please! You convinced yourself that if you told him you were pregnant with his child, he'd stop everything and come back to you, but have you thought this through for a minute?'

She did not reply, her eyes fixed on a tissue she was destroying with her long polished fingernails.

'I love him Alex. It's true that I wasn't in love at first and that I used him but he did…'

'The same. I know. But you knew that before you took up with him. I had told you beforehand, and you told me it didn't matter because you weren't looking for a husband. So what changed?'

She kept quiet, continuing to rip apart the tissue in tiny little pieces.

'I'm going to tell you what has changed. You suddenly realised once he had told you he didn't want to be with you anymore than being with him wasn't that bad after all and that if he married you, you'd end up much richer than you are at the moment. I think you probably even told yourself that you wouldn't have to be married to him for too long—'

'You haven't got the right to say that Alex, I love him!'

'No Freya, you don't love him, no more that you're pregnant.'

Anger was burning in her eyes when she finally looked at him.

'I'm pregnant.'

'If that's the case then you'll have no objections to doing this pregnancy test,' he said taking a box out of his jacket pocket.

The surprise was such that she was speechless for a moment.

'I won't—'

'Oh yes, you will! This way we'll know straight away if it's a lie or not. Then, if you are, you'll also have to prove it's his.'

'He's already told me…'

'Good. Let's go,' he said, extending the box to her.

Freya went into the bathroom. She hesitated. She could admit to Alex that there was no baby, that she had just said that to regain Mark's love. To do the test would change nothing. She had lied. And she could not lie for much longer.

Without thinking, she opened the box and took out the tube. She had not done a test until now, but it would not hurt to try. You never knew. And it was not like she had been careful in the last couple of weeks.

50

I don't believe it. I can't believe it. All I hoped for, everything that was in reach, has just crashed because of that bitch.

She turned up claiming she is pregnant and that the baby is my Dad's. But I don't believe her. She is lying. She lies like she breathes. And then she dared trying to intimidate Léa by sending her fake photos of her and Dad.

I can't sleep and Dad isn't back yet. I hope he went to talk to Léa. I wanted to stay with her tonight but Alex, Martha and my grandmother ganged up on me. They wanted me to come home, to leave my Dad, to speak to Léa alone.

Martha did try to tell me that whatever Freya had said or done wouldn't amount to anything much in the end, that my Dad looked very in love with Léa, that he'd find the words, that all of this was just a moment in time and that it would pass. I know she was trying to reassure me. And I wish I could believe her. Granny didn't try to reassure anyone. She's shocked, though. She doesn't like Freya one bit, but she was probably right the other day when she said that she wouldn't let my father go easily. Except that she hadn't thought that Freya could stoop so low as pretending to be pregnant.

There's some noise downstairs. A car. Alex, probably. Maybe I should talk to him, ask him if he's spoken to Dad. No, he probably knows nothing.

I've thought of sending a message to Léa, but I don't know what to say to her. She looked so sad when Dad went out with Freya. I asked her to stay until his return; I pleaded with her even, but she said it was better to let them sort that out without her. I worry she's going to abandon us when we need her most. I don't want that. I want to stay here with her here forever.

I'll go and see her tomorrow. That's for sure. They won't stop me. I'll walk all the way if I have to. I'll tell her I love her, that Freya is a liar, that it's not even true, that she only did this to separate her from my Dad and that they can't let her do that. I'll bring them back together if I have to. I'll do it.

51

When Mark got to the bastide, he thought of getting the whisky out, but he knew that if he started, he would not stop. Something ached in him like it never had before. He walked slowly out into the garden towards the pool. The stars were out in force and the memory of their night in Léa's courtyard came back to him. How could it have gone so wrong?

The pool was unlit, and he walked down the steps, not knowing what he was doing. He took his clothes off one by one and plunged into the dark inky water. It was still warm from the day's heat. He moved to the deeper side and sat on the floor, pushing himself down, feeling the weight of water against him. He finally released himself back up and laid on his back looking at the stars. The stars. They had always been a form of consolation to him. Ever since he was a child. He used to tell them things, releasing his innermost thoughts into the air towards them. He did that now. He told them what he felt; who he loved; asked them why it hurt too much. It was childish, but the pain in his chest felt higher, less cutting.

A noise at the top of the pool made him turn around. Alex was coming down the stairs. He looked alarmed.

'Here you are! Geez, man! When I didn't see you downstairs, I...' He was pushing his sandy hair backward, a worried look on his face.

'I wouldn't top myself, Alex. You know that.'

They looked at each other, and Alex started taking his clothes off.

'How's the water?'

'Lovely,' said Mark, swimming to the further side of the pool as he dived in.

They swam on their backs in silence for a while.

'Do you want to tell me what happened tonight?'

'Not really.'

'You love her?'

There was a silence. 'I do.'

'What are you going to do about it?'

'There's nothing I can do. She doesn't want to see me anymore. Thanks to Freya, I seemed to have lost the only woman who means something to me.'

There was a bitterness in his voice that worried Alex. He could feel him sinking again in the sombre moods that had plagued him for months. They had had little to do with Sarah's death and more with Mark's inherent unhappiness.

'You could fight for her.'

He snorted. 'Fight for her? And how do you do that Alex when someone has made it clear they don't want to see you ever again?'

Alex sat back in the water. 'You fight.'

'I heard that, but what does it mean?'

'You know what your problem is, Mark? You've had it far too easy with women for too long. You've never had to fight for any single one you dated. From the girls in high school, at university, your wife, Freya. They just come to you and you pick them like you'd pick flowers.'

Mark had sat up in the water, facing him. 'That's not true.'

'Is it not? Give me the name of a single woman you fought for. I've known you for most of my life and I can't think of one.'

'There was Alice.'

'Alice Baxter? The girl who was on the trip we made here over twenty years ago?' Alex shook his head. 'No, Mark, you weren't in love with her. She couldn't be yours because she was with Charlie. It's your ego that took a hit that day, not your heart.'

'So you're going to tell me you fought for your girlfriends

next?'

'Not all of them, no. But I fought for Martha. It wasn't a given. It still not is. Every day is a challenge. But you keep going because there's no one else you want to be with.'

The silence returned between them, only punctuated by the cry of an owl somewhere.

'So what do you think I should do?'

'As I said, fight for her. Go and see her, tell her what she means to you, what you want.'

'She thinks I'm hopeless.' He moved back onto his back again. 'That I'll never leave work or the London for her.'

'Would you do it?'

'I've been thinking about it.'

'But the question: is would you do it?'

He pondered the question while looking at the stars. 'Yes. Yes, I would.'

'Then that's your answer. Tell her that. Now I'll race you to the other end.'

'Dream on! I've got several weeks' practice on you.'

They raced for a while before getting out, giggling like schoolboys and running on the grass back to the house. There were towels on the seats drying, and they wrapped themselves in them. Mark went to fetch the Lagavullin and poured two glasses. They sprawled on the sofa side by side, looking at the night sky. Alex rose his glass.

'To your happiness!'

* * * * *

By the time Alex, Martha, his mother and the children were up, Mark was in a car on his way to Marseille airport. He had slept little and, during those long hours, he had decided that he could not go to Léa. The words she had said playing over and over in his mind. He was not angry with her, just angry with himself for having believed that he could change, that he could move here and be with her. He could see how ludicrous the idea was as dawn broke over the fields. He made a call and booked himself on the first flight from Marseille to London.

In the car, on the way to the airport, looking at the sun coming up, he thought of turning back, of going straight to Léa's little house in Uzès, of having it out. Several times he almost told the driver to turn back. But reason got the better of him. She did not want him as he wanted her. And there was nothing he could do to make her love him. No matter what Alex had said last night, there was no point fighting for something that would never happen. Better to cut his losses and take himself back to London, away from her. He would have a week to recover before the children were back. And there was work. Something to focus his mind and his frustration on.

Alex called as he was about to board the plane. He hesitated but decided to answer as he walked down the gangway.

'Mark, where the hell are you?'

'About to fly back to London.'

'What happened to fighting for—'

'Alex, I realised last night that she doesn't want me. I don't see the point of rubbing it in her face. She doesn't deserve this and I've never been one to fight losing battles.'

'Bollocks! If you don't fight, you'll certainly lose.'

He did not answer and put his travel bag in the overhead locker.

'Dude, I think you should come back here and stand up to her. Tell her how you feel.'

'Alex, I don't want to talk about it.'

'What do I tell your son? Max is distraught this morning.'

Mark closed his eyes and rested his head against the headrest. 'I'll call him tonight and explain. He has nothing to worry about. I won't pull the plug on him seeing Léa while he's in France.'

'And after?'

'He'll be back here and, as all teenagers, he'll forget about her.'

There was no reply from Alex and he checked his phone to see if it was on.

'You're making a mistake, a huge one, you know that?'

Mark cut the communication. Somehow, now that he was on the plane, it felt like it was a mistake. But it would pass. Things would get back to normal. Normal life would resume again.

52

The bell rang as Léa was putting the kettle on. It was not even nine o'clock yet; she had had a dreadful night and did not want to talk. She stayed put, hoping that whoever it was would go away. But the shrill noise of the bell broke the silence again. Her heart beat faster. And if it was him?

The disappointment on her face must have shown when she opened the door.

'Oh dear! It's not going well. I've brought you croissants and pains au chocolat,' Luca said, showing her the paper bag as if it would cheer her up.

He waited for her to close the door and for them to be in the lounge, to take her in his arms and kiss her.

'Léa, I'm so sad for you.'

'It wasn't meant to be,' she said, drying her tears with the back of her hand.

'I don't know. I believe that you're just going through a bad patch and that you'll find a way through together.'

She smiled. 'The eternal optimist!'

'Don't knock it! What can I do!' he said with a shrug, 'I believe in love me, that's the only true thing in life. With cooking and good food, of course!'

They sat in the courtyard in the sunshine. He told her how the night had finished after she had left. He made her smile when he called Alex, Monsieur Alex. She realised she did not know Alex's family name either.

'I don't believe that story, this girl getting pregnant. He isn't a man to get caught like that.'

Léa shook her head. 'I'd love to believe that, but I don't know. She also sent me some pictures of them yesterday, which Max called fake. Maybe you're right. Maybe she didn't accept him leaving her,' she mused.

'Did you talk to him last night?'

Léa felt her throat tightened and lowered her eyes. She did not want to go back over what she had said to Mark the night before. She hoped Luca would not insist.

'So it's what I think then, he found you and talked to you?'

She looked at him, surprised.

'He came back to the restaurant once he had spoken to the young lady and then left again in a hurry. I thought that was because he wanted to talk to you. I was hoping you'd both have...'

He did not finish his sentence, but she knew what he meant.

'What happened Léa?'

'It's me who told him it wasn't possible. It was too good to be true from the start. It was just a holiday romance, fleeting...'

She did not finish her sentence. She felt incapable of going any further. Luca was fixing her, pouting.

'He'd never have left London for me, Luca. What could he do here, anyway?'

'Oh, I don't know, buy some vines for example.'

That stopped her right in her tracks.

'He talked to me about a vineyard I know a little about the other night. Apparently it's for sale and he's interested.'

Monsieur de Daujac's vineyard, she thought. She had forgotten about it. 'He knows nothing about vines or winemaking.'

'You weren't a French teacher before you taught French to Max.'

'It's much more complicated...'

'It's not if you get the right people to help you. I think that's what he was thinking of doing.'

Her gaze wandered over the roofs above them. 'It doesn't

matter. He's about to become a dad again and even if he doesn't live with… the mother,' she said with difficulty, 'he must look after that child. It wouldn't make any sense to come and live here in such a situation.'

'If there's a baby. Max doesn't seem to believe that's the case.'

'Max is thirteen and wants to live here. He'd do anything for that dream to come true. And he could never stand Freya. She…. She bullied him.'

Luca was looking at her with the beginning of a smile, and his arms crossed over his chest.

'Right so you convinced yourself that it wasn't worth fighting for the man you've fallen in love with.'

'It's not true, Luca.'

'It's the true my love. I know you well enough now to know that he touched something deep inside in you, Mr Hunter. I can see it in your eyes. You're not happy, Léa.'

'It'll pass,' she said without conviction.

'Or not.'

After Luca left, Léa hung out the washing in the courtyard. All those domestic tasks were doing her good, grounding her. The bell rang again, and her heart flipped. She called out as she walked to the door.

'Who is it?'

'It's Max.'

She opened the door and saw immediately that something troubled him. Mark must have made a decision.

'Dad left for London this morning,' he said before saying hello.

The news almost knocked her out, but she smiled to him and took him by the hand, pulling him gently inside. They sat in the courtyard, a glass of orange juice in front of them. She did not want to hear the rest, but she could see he needed to be reassured.

'I don't understand what happened. I thought you had talked to each other after we left Granny, Martha and I.'

His hair slightly longer than it had been, and the resemblance with his father was striking that morning. She lowered her eyes but did not answer. What could she say to him? What did you understand of relationships when you were thirteen?

'It's because of Freya, isn't it?'

'Yes, and no.'

'I know she lied Léa. It's just like the photos. She did all this on purpose. Alex said that Dad will ask for a paternity test if she's pregnant. I don't want a half-brother or sister with her,' he said before tears overcome him.

She took his hand. 'Max, whether or not she lied isn't the only issue. There are others. Your dad and I live very different lives.'

He shook his head, not wanting to hear about reasons. 'But you know he doesn't love her, right?'

She nodded silently, sure her voice would betray her if she spoke. Yes, she knew, but she also knew that the trust between them was gone. It had been destroyed by the revelation of the night before. Strangely, the chirping of the birds and the buzz of the bees felt loud in the silence between them.

'But I know he loves you and that you love him,' he continued in a small voice, holding her hand tight, his blue eyes full of tears.

'Max, there are things that happened sometimes between adults.' She found it hard to contain the emotions she felt. 'We hope that something's going to work and then suddenly, we see that it won't.'

She breathed slowly before continuing, trying to calm the beating of her heart. 'It's nobody's fault. It's just that it isn't meant to be.'

When she looked up to him, tears were running down his cheeks and on their hands.

She took him back to the Place aux Herbes, where he was to meet up again with Martha and Alex. On the way, she promised that even if he was going back to London, she would always be there for him, even though she thought he would probably forget her once back home. She felt lost as they walked the familiar lanes together.

Alex and his wife were sat in a café having an espresso when they arrived. Martha asked Max to show her where some shops were, leaving Léa alone with Alex. She knew they had planned it. He ordered two more espressos, and they talked about the prices in Provence compared to London and about the weather. It was like she had entered a parallel universe where she could have an innocent conversation while her heart was breaking in a million pieces. She shivered. She did not know why, but something important was about to be revealed.

'I wanted to apologise for this whole mess. You may not know it, but I'm Freya's godfather. We aren't related but her father was a good friend and asked me to look after her if he was to... Anyway that's another story,' he said making a gesture with his hand as he was pushing away a fly.

She nodded, unable to say anything. She was not sure she wanted to hear what was to follow, but she had no choice.

'It's not me who introduced her to Mark, she did that all on her own.'

Freya's life still hold not interest but she tried not to show it.

'I told Mark when I learnt that they were going out together that it wasn't a good idea but...' He seemed to hesitate before continuing. 'Mark does what Mark wants. Tell him he can't have something and he'll go after it with all his might. He's always been like that.'

Except for me. He will not fight for me.

'How long have you known each other?' It was all she could think of asking him.

'A very long time. We were are school together, and then we both studied law at Cambridge. He went into finance and me advertising. We did some very naughty things together.'

He nodded, smiling, reminiscing about things she could not know.

'The thing is, Mark's never loved Freya. I knew it from the start and she knew it too. And it suited her then. What she wanted was to be seen with a rich man, even if she earns more than enough money to be happy. She'll never reach the heights he got to, but I'm sure she'll meet someone at some point that will give her whatever it is she feels she still needs. Anyway, what she wanted then is to be with the guy every other girls were after in the City.'

Léa was dying to ask him what Mark wanted, but she could not do it. Alex, who had just put back his sunglasses, took them off again.

'Since his wife's death, he… How can I explain? He's been looking for something. Just after it happened, he worked like a madman because he couldn't deal with the emptiness his kids felt after their mum's death. I've always thought they would have divorced one day. They weren't made for each other, and it was painful to watch. But he was loyal to her. He stayed with her until the end.'

She knew all this, but she appreciated Alex for having told her. She could tell he loved and worried about his friend in equal amounts. She could have kissed him for it.

'I knew something had changed when I saw him two weeks ago. He was looking so much better than he had only a month before. First, I thought it was the holidays. He had taken none really since his wife's death.'

He looked her straight in the eyes before continuing. 'But I could see there was more to it than just that. It's the way he speaks about you, you see? He loves you. It's clear.'

Tears burned her eyes behind her sunglasses and she looked for a tissue in her handbag, pretending to wipe the sweat off her face.

'Now I will tell you something that you won't like. Freya's pregnant. I didn't believe her last night, no more than Max or Mark did, so I went to see her at her hotel and asked her to take a test. I think she didn't know herself that she was pregnant. It had all been for show. This doesn't mean Mark is the father of this baby. I know she didn't go back to London after Mark asked her to leave. He'll ask for a paternity test.'

Léa swallowed with difficulty. 'Why are you telling me all this?'

'Because you've got a right to know, even if I would have preferred for Mark to tell you.'

Léa nodded but kept quiet.

'I can't prejudge what the results of the paternity test will be and I can understand that you're angry with him but before deciding, wait until we get an answer. Please.'

Léa tried to smile, not sure she was strong enough to answer.

'Are you going to tell Max about all this?'

Alex sighed and ran a hand through his hair. 'I don't know. What do you think?'

'I think he's got the right to know. He's old enough to understand.'

Alex nodded silently. 'Listen, I don't know what I can do to help you but if there's anything I can do, anything, you will tell me right?'

He took a business card in his wallet and put it on the table. 'You can call me anytime.'

His smile was back, and he put his hat on, ready to stand up.

'I better find my wife before she buys the whole shop.'

She smiled, happy for the chat. 'Could you tell Max that I'll be waiting for him Monday at 10 in our usual spot?'

'You bet,' he said, putting his hand on her shoulder as he left. Léa watched him disappear among the crowd, lost in her thoughts.

Her mobile rang as she opened her front door. She saw it was her mum and hesitated. She did not feel like talking to her, but maybe they had news about the house.

'Hi Mum.'

'Hello darling. I'm calling you because I spoke to Mathilde earlier. She wanted to know if you'd given any thought to her offer?'

It was the last thing she wanted to talk about. She had given no thought to it since they had spoken of her aunt's offer in her parents' kitchen. It had always been a no in her head. She rubbed her fingers on the bridge of her nose, trying to think about what she could say to deflect the offer.

'It's very generous of her, you know. And they've got connections. It could be ideal for—'

'I can't do it.'

'Of course you can. Mathilde's delighted to have you around and help you get back on your feet. I—'

'Why do you always think I'm not doing what I want? Or that I want to be this high-flying executive, Mom? I don't. I've tried it, and it just doesn't work for me. It's not me. Can you please understand and let me be?'

'But what do you want to be, Léa? Surely you don't want to go from one small job to another? You need to get a grip!'

'I am getting a grip. I know what I want.'

There was a silence. The force with which she had said that stunned Léa. It had come out of her before she could control her thoughts. There was no going back.

'What is it then?'

'I want to write.'

'Like for companies? Marketing, you mean?'

'No, I want to write for myself. I want to be a writer.'

She could hear her mum's breathing and she worried she would be sick. Yet she felt lighter for having told her. It was like a weight had lifted off her shoulders.

'Mom?'

'You need to see someone. I'll text you some names of people you should see.'

'I'm not ill.'

'You're not yourself. You haven't been for a while now. I don't know what happened in London but it had to be serious for you to just refuse all help we are providing you with.'

'You have no right to tell me this.'

'I'm your mother, I—'

Léa cut the connection. There was no point going round in circles trying to explain herself today of all days. She did not need anyone else putting her down any more than she felt already.

The phone rang again, but she did not pick up. She cut a bit of lavender from the border and crushed it between her fingers before breathing it in. Things would get better, eventually.

Later, as she sat in the courtyard, she reflected that it was the people who she met recently that had been most enthusiastic about her new career. Luca, Mark, even Michel had told her to do it. It was like they could see who her authentic self was. She did not need to hide or be someone else with them to please them. If they had ideas about what she could be, they had not projected their desires onto her. They had let her be, accepting her in all her possibilities. Since moving to Uzès, she had finally accepted herself for who she was and the people around had responded in kind. It was her life. She was responsible for it and for her own happiness. No one could tell her what to do. If this writing career did not work out, she would be the only one to blame, but she knew that she would never feel that empty again. She was hurting tonight, hurting for a love that was gone, but she felt alive. She had made an important life choice.

Instinctively she opened her laptop, which had been lying closed for the best part of two hours and opened a new document. There was only one thing she could do to relieve the pain she felt. Something her grandmother had taught many years before when she had been angry and crushed by another love affair. She would write a letter to him, a letter he would never receive. Just pour her heart out onto the page. Maybe it will all make sense afterwards. Maybe.

53

The weather matched Mark's mood when he landed in London. It was overcast and by the time he was driven home, it was drizzling. The house felt gloomy, and he knew he did not want to be there. He left his bag in the hallway and moved to the living room. He poured himself a glass of whisky and sat on the sofa, remembering the night he had spoken to Léa. It was only three days ago, but it felt like an eternity.

He took his phone out and searched for her number. He suddenly felt the urge to talk to her, to understand what it had all been about the night before. The thought of Freya came back to him, and he put the phone down. How could he convince her it was over between them? That he had no feeling, no desire, nothing left for Freya?

The glass went flying against the wall before he knew what he was doing, tears streaming down his face as he whispered Léa's name over and over again, his head in his hands.

He had no idea how long he had been there when the bell rang. No-one knew he was back, not even his housekeeper, to whom he had happily given a week off the day before. He did not move, but it rang again and he went wearily to the front door.

'Here you are!' said Tim, Caroline's husband, as he opened the door.

'How did you know I was back?'

'Oh! I heard it on the grapevine, you know. Your sister

thought you'd like to have lunch with us.'

Mark looked at Tim. He had never been able to stand up to his sister, and he could see that the situation slightly embarrassed him. Having lunch with the entire family was the last thing he wanted, but he felt like he could not let his brother-in-law down.

'Let me find my keys,' he said, walking back into the house, catching a glimpse of his red-rimmed eyes in the Venetian mirror in the hallway.

They drove in silence, neither of them knowing quite what to say.

'How's business?' said Mark, more to say something than because he wanted to know.

'Not bad. The courts never stop, you know.'

Tim was a criminal lawyer. He was the one who had introduced Mark to his first wife as they had studied together at Cambridge. A brilliant barrister, he had been one of the youngest lawyer to make Queen's Counsel, but outside of the courtroom he was just one of those quiet types who want a quiet life. Passion and upheaval were not his cup of tea. But Mark liked him well enough. He and his sister formed one of these couples who look ill-assorted but are rock solid which had been a blessing as their first child, Sophie, Mark's god-daughter, had been born with cerebral palsy. Thankfully, the next two had not been affected.

Sitting there in his car, Mark envied him. His life might not be as exciting as his, but at least he had a family, a wife and children who cared. For the first time in his life, he missed that. The family unit. But there was only Léa he could envisage it with. But it was about as far away from reality as it was possible to be and it hurt. Despite what she had said, it was not a fling he had wanted with her, but something else, something much deeper. He wanted a bond, companionship, an understanding. Love.

'Mark, I don't want to pry but if there's anything we can do…' Tim's voice trailed off before he continued, 'I know Caroline will say the same thing to you and she met…'

'Léa,' said Mark, his throat tightening up as he told her name out loud.

'Léa,' said Tim in that soft voice of his.

'Thanks Tim but there's nothing to be done.'

They had arrived at the house the couple owned in Hampstead and the kids were out and running towards them before Mark was out of the car. The two boys had grown again and Sophie was at the door in her wheelchair, her mother behind her as always. She was smiling brightly, and Mark smiled back. He kissed her on the cheek, asking how her trip to Florida had been.

'It was so good, thank you, thank you, thank you,' she said taking his hand and kissing it, 'I did sky-diving and kayaking, and met lots of new people! But I want to know about Léa. Mum keeps speaking about her and how good she had been to Max. I'm so jealous that he now speaks French better than me.'

Mark saw his sister winced and pressed her arm. It was okay. He would be okay.

'Let's go in darling,' her mother said, 'let Mark catch his breath, he only got back a few hours ago.'

But Sophie would not let go and asked many questions about Léa and Max and the house in the south of France, and he replied because he could not bear to break her heart as she looked so happy. The trip had boosted her self-confidence, and he hoped that it would last well into the academic year. Not that she lacked confidence by any means. It was one thing Sophie had in spades. It had never bothered her not to be like the others, and she had flourished in whatever environment she had been in. But she was a teenager now. And just like children, they can be cruel. He wished Léa was there. He could see her there at the table having Sunday lunch with them. The feeling was so strong that, at one point, he was almost sure she was sat next to him.

The sun was out by the time lunch was over and they moved out into the garden for coffee. Tim excused himself by pretending he had files to look over before tomorrow, and the kids opted to stay indoors. For once, Caroline decided not to say anything; she wanted some time alone with her brother.

She watched him sipping his coffee. He was deeply unhappy. She knew him too well not to notice the drawn eyes and the deepening of the fine lines around them.

'Mark, what happened?'

He looked at her and chuckled softly. 'Who told you?'

She smiled back, compassion in her eyes. 'Mum. She's worried about you.'

'She needs not be. There's nothing to worry about. I won't top myself because I…' He stopped and moved his fingertips to his lips. The bravado suddenly left him, and he wondered if he would ever kiss Léa again. 'Sorry that was crass.'

'It's fine. But you're not.'

They looked at each other.

'What did she tell you?'

'That Freya had turned up yesterday in Uzès.'

He nodded. He looked towards the edge of the garden.

'Léa and I…'

'You got together,' said Caroline.

'I thought we were going somewhere. I care about her Caroline. More than I can remember caring for any woman I've ever been with.'

There was a silence between them, punctuated by the cries of the birds in the trees.

'But I don't know. Maybe it wasn't to be. Freya turning up last night didn't help, obviously. Léa thought I was back with her.'

'And what did you say?'

'That it wasn't true, but it didn't matter. She thinks it'll never work between us, that there are far too many differences for us to overcome.'

'What do you think?'

He breathed deeply. 'I was ready to sell the house and re-locate out there for her.'

He saw Caroline's eyes open wide, and she whistled, which made him laugh and cleared the air a little.

'So why are you here then?'

'Ah no! Not you as well!' he said, exasperation in his voice.

'Has someone else said something?'

They said it together, 'Alex!' She laughed. 'Good old Alex! But he's right, you know. If you want that woman as much as you say, then you need to show it to her.'

'She made it clear she didn't want me.'

'No Mark, she didn't. She's scared. Look at it from her point-of-view. She probably didn't believe that you'd do what you said. Not to mention that with Freya back on the scene…'

'I didn't ask her to come! I threw her out!'

'I know but put yourself in Léa's shoes for a minute. One week you're with Freya, and the next you want to be with her. She isn't stupid, and she's old enough to have been hurt before. I'm sure you didn't exactly strike her as the face of constancy.'

'Thanks,' he said, deflated. But he knew Caroline was right. 'What did you think of her?'

'She's lovely and I'd be thrilled to have her as my sister-in-law.'

'Don't buy a dress just yet,' he said bitterly.

'You need to get back on a plane and go back there, little brother of mine.'

He shook his head. 'No, she made it clear—'.

'No Mark, no more she made it clear. What do you want? If you want her, then bloody fight for her! Show her. Shit! You have the money and the means to do something pretty spectacular.'

'She won't be swayed. She's too intelligent for that.'

'You're going to have to work at it. Obviously it's not something you've done before.'

'Here we go again! I feel like I'm listening to Alex.'

'Well, he's right whatever it is he said to you. You've had it so good with women, with every single one of them falling for you.'

'I was married for fourteen years and I didn't stray.'

'True, but you didn't fight for Sarah, she fell for you. Just like every other woman you've been with before and since.'

'They could have said no.'

'To money and power? Some women, Freya is the perfect example, love that you know. And it's never bothered you because as a man you can do that and still be seen as a beacon of respectability.'

She saw him about to say something but stopped him with her hand. 'That's the truth Mark and you know it. The thing with you is that you can be charming when you want to, and I suspect that you're probably a talented lover too.'

'Caroline!'

'That's a compliment. But here's the rub, you've forgotten that not everyone will fall for you because of your money or your power. But what seems incredible to me is that you're such a fighter in all other areas of your life and yet here, what do you do, you fall at the first hurdle. You're like a child who gets stuck on a piece of homework and just give up. Damn Mark! Stand up. Fight. Show her she means something to you, that she isn't just a plaything.'

She looked at her brother. He looked lost: his eyes fixed on something far away, his fingertips touching his lips. When he looked at her, she knew she had touched a nerve.

'I can't go back there straight away but you've given me an idea.' They smiled at each other. 'Thanks sis.' She threw a cushion playfully at him.

Caroline's words resonated with Mark long after he went home. They echoed what Alex had said to him less than twenty-four hours before. As he sat in his garden, he reflected that if two of the people who knew him best said something similar, there might be some truth in it. As he sipped his Islay whisky, he tried to put himself in Léa's shoes. What had she seen in him and what did she make of him? He could see he had possibly rushed things in the last week or so. He had got so caught up in her and his own vision of her he had not checked whether she was happy to be in his life the way he wanted her to be. He had gone back to Uzès fully expecting her to be waiting for him just like he had and that they would just pick up where they had left off. That was presumptuous at best. He could hear now the fear in her voice on the phone the night he had come back to London after the financial markets crisis. One minute they were making love and the next he was miles away working all hours.

And then Freya. Bloody Freya had just added the last nail in the coffin by turning up at the worse moment. But then, would things have been different? It may have taken slightly longer, but they would probably have come to the same crossroad. Their lives were too different not to diverge at some point. It did not matter that he was prepared to give up a lot of his current life for her. If she did not believe him, it made no difference.

So they had come to that crossroad because of circumstances rather than their relationship, but of the two, it was him who had given up first. She had questioned him and he had just given up. He should have followed her the night before, not let her go without looking back - that hurt him the most somehow - or he should have gone back and spoken to her that morning. Alex and Caroline were right, he had just stumbled at the first hurdle. Was he as unused as they said about being rejected? He tried to remember the last time it had had happened to him. And the only time that came back to him was the girl he had travelled to Provence with together with Alex and her boyfriend all these years ago. He had been infatuated rather than in love then - too much booze, freedom, sun - and Alex had been right that he had not stood a chance with her and he knew it then. Before and after that, he had always had whoever he wanted, from his wife to the string of women that had shared his bed in the last couple of years since Sarah's death. None of them had resisted him, and yet they all knew that he would not go further than just a casual relationship. There had been no fight, no trying to seduce a reluctant participant, and he had probably forgotten the pain of being rejected.

He drank a little more of his whisky. Actually, he had never experienced the pain. He had been infatuated, but never in love. And now that he was, it hurt. Like hell. And going back to Léa would mean more pain. Of that he was fairly certain. She was as stubborn as he was. He admired her for it.

He sighed and looked at the dusk falling around him. You could not see the stars here despite the fine evening. He felt strangely out of place in his own house. He missed Léa, the bastide, the warmth in the air, the stars. What many saw as a successful life felt hollow.

He needed to get back to her, to show her he cared. Truly. Madly. Deeply. But how? How could he do to make her want to take a chance on him again?

54

The week had been morose. Alex had confirmed to Max that Freya was pregnant, which had made him rage against his father. He had sworn that he would not go back to London, and it had taken all of Léa's diplomatic skills and his grandmother's firm stance to make him accept the inevitable. The effects of this had been that Max had lost all joy and hope and, no matter what Léa had tried, she had not got him to recover his sense of fun.

Friday was the day she feared the most both for him and for her, but she had promised herself that she would stand tall and had asked him to spend the day with her in Uzès. They would have a wander in town before she would take him back to the bastide from where he was going back home the next day with his brother, Martha, and his grandmother.

He turned up, his hands deep in his pockets at their meeting point. She could see the sadness in his blue eyes. Léa took him by the arm and they walked in silence should against shoulder for a while. When he finally said something, they were passing the high school.

'Dad has agreed not to enrol me in the same school as last year,' he said in a monotone voice.

'That's splendid news, Max! Where are you going?'

'The Lycée français in London. The letter you wrote for me helped according to him.'

She kissed him on the cheek. 'I'm sure they didn't need my letter to accept you! Ok, it's not the high school here but at least it's a French school and with this one, you still have all your chances to get into Cambridge.'

'I don't want to go to Cambridge,' he said dejected.

'It's too early to say that. But it's good to have options, no?'

He shrugged. 'I don't have options, Léa. The only option is to go back to London and to wait and see if I'll have a half-brother or half-sister that I don't want. I don't understand why Dad doesn't want to let me come and live here with you.'

'Because you're his son and it's for him to look after you.'

She bit her lip when she saw the hurt in his eyes.

'I mean nothing to you, is that it?'

'Max, stop. You know that you mean the world to me but that I've got no legal right over you and you're too young to go against your Dad's decision. You know that if I could, I would've agreed straightaway to you coming to live with me.'

At lunchtime, they stopped to eat a pizza, but even Luca's antics could not make Max smile. Before they left, she asked him what he wanted to do before she drove him back to the bastide.

'I'd like to go back to your house. One last time.'

At the house, she watched him took photos. She could feel him both sad and happy.

'Do you know if you'll be able to buy it? Have you heard from the bank?'

'They are still waiting for the surveyor to check the house structure. We're in August, it's complicated. And then, my flat in London still hasn't sold, so whatever happens I don't have the money for the deposit.'

He nodded. 'I hope you'll get it. Maybe I could come back and spend some time with you during the next holidays?'

She smiled. She wanted to tell him she hoped so too, but the more she thought about it and the more impossible it seemed to her. His father had not called her or asked about her. How could he agree to this without talking to her?

When he had finished going round, it was almost time to take him back to the bastide. She took a box from one of drawers of the kitchen and extended it to him, her hands shaking a little.

'It's for you. For you to remember me by.'

He pulled apart the wrapping paper delicately and opened the pretty box. Inside, she had put several coloured notebooks and a fountain pen.

'For your journal or school. You choose!' she said with a joy she did not feel.

He kissed her, and she held him tight in her arms. She felt his sobs and rocked him gently.

'It's going to be ok Max, you'll see.'

'I want to stay here, I don't want to go back.'

'I know my love, but you'll be back. We'll speak to your Dad. We'll find a way you'll see.'

She had no idea how they would find a solution and it felt wrong to give him a hope that she knew she had little chance of honouring.

'Let's go to the bastide, otherwise your grandma will think I've kidnapped you,' she said wiping a tear from his face.

Max rang the bell at the gate and Léa parked the car where she had seen Mark's car parked so often under the large oak tree. She did not want to go in, but he insisted his grandmother wanted to see her before they left.

In the bastide, everything was silent. Manuela came to meet them. Mrs Martha was upstairs with trying to get Tom to sleep, she told them. The heat was tiring the poor boy. She was about to tell Léa that Lady Hunter was on the terrace, but the old lady was quicker than she was.

'Come and say hello to me, my dear Léa,' she said from somewhere inside the house.

Léa found her in a comfortable armchair, facing the view, a magazine on her knees and a glass of lemonade on a small table next to her.

They shook hands and Léa saw the start of a thin smile on her lips.

'I'm very sorry about my son, my dear. Truly.'

She looked sincere, and Léa tried to return her smile.

'I know it's no consolation but I know he likes you very much. He just doesn't think about the consequences of his actions, unfortunately. It's his job, you know, he's been like that since his wife passed away.'

The elderly lady stopped, and Léa was sure she saw a tear fall and disappear among the lines of her face.

'It's not all his fault, Madam. He was very generous with me. I...'

She lowered her eyes. She was not sure she could go any further. Lady Hunter patted her hand.

'There's no need for you to make excuses. I've always said that this woman was bad news,' she said, shaking her head sadly. 'But you, what are you going to do now that you've finished looking after my grandson? Are you going to teach full time?'

'Oh no! It's not for me teaching, even if I loved looking after him,' she said looking at Max. 'No, I want to write.'

She hesitated and then said out loud the name of this job she did not dare to name. 'I want to be a writer.'

When she looked up, she saw that Mrs Hunter was looking at her, a mischievous glint in her eyes.

'Go for it! And please send me the book when it's finished. You see I love reading,' she said, tapping with the tips of her manicured fingers the pile of books on a table next to her. 'I read everything.'

Léa was not sure that she would like her novel, but she promised she would send it to her. Her grandmother had told her to never presume what other people's tastes were. It was a habit she had to learn to unlearn fast.

She wanted to ask Mrs Hunter to tell her son she wished him the best, but the words just refused to come out of her mouth. Maybe if Lady Hunter read her book one day, Mark would learn that she had published it. Maybe he would feel proud too that she had followed his advice. It was a tiny ray of hope to cling to, but it was better than no hope at all.

The goodbyes with Max were as hard as she had expected them to be, despite the two of them doing their best not to cry.

'This is for you,' said Max, giving her small carefully wrapped box. 'Don't open it now. Only once you're home. It's so you don't forget about me.'

She held him tight. How could I forget you, my love, she thought, kissing him on the cheek before getting in the car.

He closed the door and walked with her to the gate. Tears were running down her cheeks when she turned on the road that led back to Uzès.

PART FOUR

55

London, Monday 24th August

London, Monday 24th August

Mum,

I've been so angry lately that I have been unable to write, but I need to tonight.

We came back from Uzès with Gran and Tom yesterday. I didn't want to. I wanted to stay there with Léa, but all the adults, even her, said it was not possible. I still believe it is. I just need to convince Dad. You'd be pleased though because he has agreed to remove me from my previous school. Léa had written a letter of recommendation for me to the French lycée in London, the one in Kensington near the Natural History Museum. Do you remember the place? Anyway, I start on Thursday. I don't want to go, but as Léa said, it's a start. Now I only need to get Dad to agree to send me back to France during half-term in October. Léa had said she'd be happy to have me, and I don't see why he would say no.

He is not happy. He has this frown on his forehead, the one he gets when he is worried or upset. He's trying though, but I told him I'd like to spend the days before school at aunty Caroline's rather than at home, so I'm off to stay with her tonight. She comes and picks me up in half an hour. I don't know if I'll be able to write once I'm there. I don't want them to find out, though I think Sophie would like it. I may tell her. What do you think? You used to love Sophie. Do you know that she went to Florida to a place where she could do many dangerous sports? She even went sky-diving! I can't wait to hear about it.

Léa had put a note for me in one of the notebooks she gave me before I left. It's a list of all the maxims her grandmother used to tell her when she was alive. Some reminded me of you and what you used to say. I love it. I'll copy it and have it up in my room once I'm back home. I've printed a photo of Léa and of you, and I've put them above my desk. You're like my guardian angels. I don't think Dad was too pleased when he saw it, but I don't care. If he hadn't messed things up with Léa, we wouldn't be here but in Uzès now. I'm so angry, Mum. What can I do to change things? How can I get them to speak to each other again? This is so stupid.

I've got to go Aunty Caroline has just arrived.

Until next time,

I love you.

56

It was the Monday after the children had come back home and Mark had just put Tom to bed when the bell rang. He was tired and unhappy and thought for a minute of not answering the door. But the bell rang again and not wanting Tom to wake up - he had been fretful since they got back - he opened the door. Alex was standing at the gate, a bottle of whisky in his hand.

'Alex. You…'

Alex did not listen and walked past him. 'I've come in the spirit of peace, bearing a gift,' he said, showing the bottle. 'We need to talk.'

'About what?'

Alex gave him a look. 'I'm sure you can guess.'

'There is nothing to talk about.'

'Oh yes, there is! Where's Max?'

'At Caroline's. I'm not his favourite person at the moment.'

Alex looked at his friend. He had black circles under his eyes, and his skin looked grey. He looked like he had not been sleeping well for quite some time. Probably since the day he had left Provence behind. He wished he had come sooner.

They moved to the lounge and Alex shut the door and went to get two tumblers from a cupboard. He poured two large measures in each glass and extended a glass to Mark. They clinked and drank in silence.

'Did you have a delightful time in France?' He almost said Provence, but stopped himself just in time.

Alex did not reply straightaway and took another sip from his glass. 'I didn't come here to talk about my holiday Mark. I came here to talk about you.'

Mark sighed and let his head fall on the back of the armchair. 'Alex I don't need this.'

'You do brother. Because you don't know that I met with Léa and that I promised her you weren't the idiot you appeared to be.'

Mark looked at him, holding his glass high. 'Thank you. I'm chuffed.'

Alex dismissed the reply. He could see the interest in Mark's eyes now that Léa's name had been uttered. He was still pinning for her.

'I told her she shouldn't take it on you, that you weren't back with Freya.'

Mark did not reply but kept his eyes on Alex.

'I think she knew that already. Whether you had convinced her...'

'I doubt that very much.' He remembered only too well the anger in her eyes that night in Uzès.

'Or Max had told her. But she knew there was nothing between you and Freya, and I made it clear that Freya is a troublemaker.'

'She's your god-daughter.'

'It doesn't alter the fact that she's a troublemaker and I've had some harsh words with her since.'

There was a silence.

'Thanks Alex. You didn't need to do this. But it doesn't...'

Alex was on the edge of his seat, bristling. 'It changes everything. Léa is as in love with you as you are with her. The question is: what are you going to do about it? Killing yourself at work, avoiding my calls and pretending that everything's fine when it isn't, are not options I'm prepared to accept.'

'It's not your choice.'

'It is because you're my best friend and Max is my god-son and neither of you are happy with the situation.'

'She said she thought our lives were too different and...'

'You said to me you were prepared to move to Provence for her.' He stopped before continuing. 'Anyway, don't you think you owe it to her to fight for her a bit?'

'Owe her?'

'Yes, owe her. You fall in love with her, make her feel like she's the centre of your world and when she's worried that this won't work because you abandon her for your work, you just expect her to pick up where you left off. So yes, you owe it to her to fight for her. Otherwise don't tell me you're in love with her.'

Mark got up and almost smashed the glass on the table. 'You've no right to tell me this, Alex! You weren't party to the discussion we had Léa and I before this.'

'I know what Max told me.'

'Max told you what?'

'That you kissed her that night he slept over at her place and then that you spent the next night together.'

Mark put his hands to his face. It did not matter to him that Max had caught them kissing, but the fact that he had hoped they would get together explained the attitude he had been getting from his son since he had got back home from Uzès. It also explained so many things Max had done to get them together. He smiled sadly at Alex.

'I guess I knew it.'

Alex did not reply and got up. He put his hand on Mark's shoulder. 'Mate, I want the best for you. I don't know many things, but I know that this woman makes you happy. So, you can either hope that the memory of her will go away and that you'll get over her at some point, or as I suspect, suffer for many years and regret not doing something when you still could. And I believe you still can. Go out there. Talk to her. What have you got to lose?'

'Everything.' He had said that without thinking, but he knew it to be true. He had been unable to face Léa since that night because he was terrified of losing her forever. But there was always the possibility that something could happen. She could call or speak to Max, or he could do something. But if she said no a second time, he knew that it would be final. And that he could not face.

'But at least you'll know, Mark. Right now, you're in limbo, hoping for something that you're not prepared to put in motion.'

Mark chuckled. 'Still good with the old words, hey?'

'That's my job, remember?'

Alex left an hour later. As he went to bed, Mark looked into Tom's bedroom. His youngest son was fast asleep, and he stayed there looking at him for a while. Tom had met Léa in France, but too briefly to have the same relationship with her as Max. But he suspected that Max had told Tom that he hoped Léa could become their stepmom. Maybe this was why his happy, bubbly boy had been grouchy and tetchy since they got back, which was so unlike him. He felt his heart breaks at the thought that both his sons hoped to find a mother and that he had possibly denied them one.

He had asked Léa to believe that they could have a future together without explaining what that future could be. His rush to go back to London after sleeping with her had been a mistake. She had every right to wonder what he had done for all these hours. He had had the same thoughts about her since he had got back here, wondering if she was seeing someone, kissing them, sleeping with them. He winced at the thought in the semi-darkness of the room. But maybe this was just his mind playing tricks on him. Alex had implied that she still cared about him. He thought of Max, who had caught them kissing and smiled. Of that he was not sorry. Not at all.

And then the idea that he had had in her courtyard that magical night came back to him. The house. If there was one thing he could do for Léa that would prove her he cared was to buy her the house in Uzès. Hell, he could buy both houses. He could not believe that he had forgotten about that. As he closed the door, he knew this was his way back. Alex and Caroline had been right: he had to take a risk.

57

Léa walked into the *maison de retraite* and was greeted by a cheerful young woman at reception.

'Can I help you?' she said with a big smile.

'I come to see Monsieur de Daujac.'

"At this hour, you'll find him with his friends in the lounge. They play cards at the same time every day. It's at the end of the corridor on your right."

Léa thanked her and walked slowly down the corridor. The place, its smell, the people in white coats evoked memories of her grandmother she had kept buried for close to fifteen years. She had been in one of these at the end of her life. She had pretended it was because she wanted to be independent, but Léa knew it was also because she had not wanted to be a burden for her children. She had came in a joyful woman, but it had not lasted. Ill-health and her own idiosyncrasies had not endeared her to the other residents, and she had soon found herself spending most of her time in her room. Léa had only seen her a few times - she had left for the bright lights of London by then - and she had found every single visit more painful than the one before. Her only consolation was that it had not lasted too long.

She saw the sign 'salle de séjour' on a little white board by a double set of glass doors and stopped. Should she tell him the truth? Maybe it was better for him to believe that they were still interested in the castle. What wrong did it do? And what if Mark had already called him?

She was lost in her thoughts when she felt someone touch her arm delicately.

'Are you alright, my dear? Are you looking for someone?' a feminine voice said behind her.

She turned around to see a small elderly lady with short white hair and pale grey eyes behind her glasses. She wore a little make-up and Léa noticed her lipstick was assorted to her cardigan.

'I'm looking for Monsieur de Daujac.'

'Ah, Monsieur de Daujac! A charming man. I'm sure he's in here playing cards. Let's go and find him, shall we?'

Léa gave her arm to the old lady, and they went in. The room was L-shaped with tables and chairs on one side and a large TV set on the other. Card players occupied two tables and Léa recognised Monsieur de Daujac even though he had his back to her.

'*Cher ami*, you've got company,' said Léa's companion as she put a hand on his shoulder. His friends had stopped playing and were looking at her eagerly. She remembered that look well, it was the one the other residents would give her when she would visit her grandmother, that hope in their eyes that soon, they too, would have someone to visit them. Léa made a little wave with her hand.

'Do I?' said Monsieur de Daujac turning around in his chair. '*Ah Madame!* What a pleasure to see you! *Vous êtes seule?*'

Léa was grateful to him not to call her Madame Hunter or ask where her 'husband' was. She wondered if it was just his natural elegance or if he had guessed.

'I don't want to bother you. I can wait until you have finished your game—'

'*Non, non, non!* A man should never make a woman wait. My friend, Paulette, will take over from me.' He turned around to his friends. 'Gentlemen, please excuse me, business calls but I'll be back.'

He turned around and led the way to the terrace, where he found a couple of chairs in the shade by a small fountain. Léa was amazed at how green the garden behind them was. There were colourful flowers in the beds that surrounded the alleyways.

'It's pretty, isn't it?'

She smiled to him. 'It is. It's so lovely to find so much greenery in this heat. Are you sure you won't be too hot?'

'I'm used to it and I've always been good with heat. How are you? Has Monsieur Hunter gone back to London for work? Not that I'm complaining, it's so nice to get visits you see,' he said smiling, a glint of curiosity in his eyes.

She suddenly felt very foolish. He was obviously delighted to see someone, and she was going to tell him that this had all been what? A hoax? A crazy dream? She was not sure, but all she knew was that it would not happen.

'He has. I came to see you because I...' She stopped, not wanting to disappoint him.

'You want to have another look at the castle on your own? I understand that. I'll give you the keys and you bring them back to me when you can or with Monsieur Hunter when he's back.'

Léa shook her head, trying to smile. 'It's not about that. It's a lovely place and we would be delighted to buy it. It's just that we...' She paused. 'We are not married you see and...'

'Oh, my dear! This isn't a problem for me at all. Marriage isn't for everyone you know. I was lucky to have found the love of my life so it worked out for me, but I'd never expect other people to be just like me. Life's so difficult for young people like you nowadays.'

Léa smiled. She was not sure she was as young as he thought she was, but his talk made her feel better somehow. She had not told him they would not be buying the castle, but she was not sure it mattered.

His watery eyes were looking at her with mischief in them. 'Monsieur Hunter called me only this morning.'

Léa was so taken aback that she could only manage a 'Did he?'

'He said he had something to sort out before he makes me an offer but, as I said to him, I'm in no rush. It's not like I've got anywhere else to go these days. Ah, I remember now! I promised to give him the name of the winemaker who looks after my vines.' He was looking for something in his shirt pocket and took out a small piece of paper folded in half. 'Here it is. Will you be so kind as to give it to him? Your English is so much better than mine,' he said, extending a folded piece of paper to her.

She took it, not knowing how she could do that, given they had not spoken to each other since that fateful night over ten days ago.

'He shouldn't hesitate to give the guy a call and ask all the questions he needs answers to. Better he should go and see him and try the wines, see what he thinks. I think he's done a suitable job, but my taste isn't as sure as it was before. Maybe young people want something different now.'

'I wouldn't know. I'll let Mark know. Thank you.'

'My love, whatever is the issue, there's nothing wrong in someone like your…,' he hesitated before continuing, 'partner taking his time and asking questions about a property. Everybody should do it, and not just when one is thinking of buying a castle. Let's go back inside, it's starting to be too hot for me here.'

They walked back in and he reiterated his offer for her to give the keys so she could check out of the books in the library. The temptation was great, but the idea of being where she had been with Mark was too hard to bear. Maybe in a few months' time when this idyll would just be a memory, she thought.

She wandered back slowly to the town centre, deep in her thoughts. She felt a bit like a fraud for not having told him that this sale would not happen, but then Mark had called and said he needed a little more time. What did that mean? Was he coming back? She felt the little piece of paper in her pocket. It was like a connection to him, something she could use to get in touch. Her heart beat faster at the thought.

58

On Friday morning, Léa walked in the small office she shared with Michel and a few others and settled at the desk next to her friend.

'You look happy today,' he said with a wry smile.

'I had a look at my bank account.'

'Yep, he paid us and we even got a bonus, thanks to you. I don't like the guy, but I've got to say on this one I'd happily buy him a drink.'

She chuckled, pulling her laptop out of her bag.

'How's the book going?'

Michel was with Luca and Mark, one of the few people she had told about her writing ambitions, and she was close to regretting it as he had been relentless in checking how far she was every time he saw her.

'Almost finished,' she said, plugging the lead into the socket on the wall.

'When do I get to read it?'

She shook her head as she switched on her computer. 'Patience Michel, patience.'

'You know I want you to do well right?'

She looked at him sideways. 'I know but you have to trust me. It's a process. You'll read it when I feel it's ready and not before.'

He went back to typing on his computer and she tried to focus on the job at hand, writing a 500-word piece for the local newspaper. Another job Michel had got for her. She felt guilty.

He was trying his best to help, after all. It was just that sometimes he was too… insistent.

They worked in silence with only the buzz of the fan for company. Alicia and Romain, two other desk sharers, were outside smoking their morning cigarette. Focus did not come easily today. Her phone rang. Dad, it said. She picked it up and went outside, smiling to the other two.

'Hi Dad!'

'Hi darling, how are you?'

There was something in his voice that told her all was not well. 'What's wrong?' She heard him sigh at the other end.

'I've got some unwelcome news for you. I just spoke to my neighbours. They have sold the house.'

She felt like someone had punched her in the stomach. She tried to breathe. Tears prickled behind her eyes. 'Who? Who bought the house?'

'The estate agent told her it was a company. They don't know more. They were offered more than the asking price, you see. They couldn't say no.'

'They could have called and said Dad.'

'I know. I said that but, apparently, it all went very fast. They said they would give you money for all the work you did in the courtyard.'

She did not reply.

'You still there?'

'Yes. Yes, I am. Sorry. I just got to love that house.'

It was his turn to stay silent.

'When do I have to leave?'

'You have three months. But they can put you in touch with the new owners. Maybe they would accept you renting the house a little while longer.'

Léa looked at her feet and closed her eyes. 'I don't think so. I'll start looking for something. Do you mind if I go, Dad, I've got a deadline?'

'Sure. Come and see us this weekend. Your Mum would love to see you. We'll have a chat about things.'

'I don't know. I'll call you back.'

She ended the call, and stayed there, hands on hips, tears running down her face. This was the one blow she was not sure she could take. It was not so much that she did not have the money to find somewhere else - with what Mark had paid her; she had more than enough - but she had just got attached to the house. It was where they... She tried to put him out of her mind. He was the last thing she needed to think about.

'Are you ok?' said Michel behind her.

She did not reply, not trusting her voice. She stayed back to him, sobbing quietly.

'Babe, what happened?' He took her in his arms. He smelt of cheap aftershave, mint and cigarettes and she found it curiously calming. 'What's wrong?'

People passed them by, but she could not have cared less.

'I lost the house.'

'How's that you lost the house? They're evicting you?'

She giggled through her tears, her head on his shoulder.

'They found a buyer.'

'But they had promised it to you!'

She turned around and looked up at him. He looked perplexed.

'Not really. They had just said that they were happy to sell it to me if I could get the money together. But the bank wanted a surveyor and this being August, we couldn't get one until next week. It didn't worry me as...'

She stopped mid-sentence and looked at him.

'What?'

'It's strange. No-one came to see the house.'

'No-one?'

'No. I would have known. I think. Unless the estate agent... But they would have contacted me, asked me to tidy up.'

'Have they said who it is?'

'A company apparently, Dad didn't know the name.'

She saw Michel bristled.

'I hate these people, these developers who turn houses that should be for local people into luxury flats or holiday homes that none of us can buy.' He spat.

277

'We don't know that.'

He threw his hands in the air, pent-up anger getting the better of him. 'Can't you see? This has to be it. They don't even need to see the house. They just buy, spend a fortune on it and will sell it to some rich people who want a pied-à-terre in Provence and will only be here two weeks a year at most. Or it'll become a rental property for tourists.'

'There's nothing wrong with tourists. We need them.'

But he kept shaking his head, unconvinced. 'We do babe, but we also need people to be able to live somewhere. The only good news is that the house is in the protected area, so they won't be able to have it all their way.'

Her heart broke when he said that. Her house. This is how she thought of it. The place where she had been at her happiest for the first time in so many years. Things had not turned out how she would have liked them to, but the idea of giving it up just tore her apart. Max came into her head, he would be devastated.

Michel was ranting, but she was only half listening until something he said caught her attention and she asked him to repeat.

'I said that maybe it's him, your ex, that bought the house. To hurt you for not giving him what he wanted.'

She was so shocked by what he had just said that she stayed silent, gawping at him.

'Mark?'

'Yes Hunter. I wouldn't put it past him, you know.'

She shook her head and burst out of laughing. 'No Michel, he wouldn't do that.'

'How do you know?'

She looked at him from under her eyelashes. He would not have been gay that she would have thought him jealous.

'He's not that kind of man.'

'Look at the facts. A company buying the house so we don't know it's him. The whole thing wrapped up in no time. Hell, we know he can! He has the money and the means.'

She could see his reasoning, but something in her just refused to believe it. 'He left Michel. And that's not his kind of house.

Why would he do that?'

There was a sadness in his eyes that touched her. 'Because he wants to hurt you.' There was a pause. 'And I hate him for it. He's got no right to do that.'

She breathed in deeply. 'I think you'll find that it's not him but some developer as you said.'

He hugged her again. 'How about I take you out for lunch today and we finish early?'

'I can't. I've got this deadline. But why don't you come with the others to my house around 5? We'll have some drinks in the courtyard to celebrate our little windfall.'

He kissed her on the forehead. 'Now you're talking, I'll bring the booze.'

They smiled at each other, and he wiped something under her eyes. 'Just a little smudge. They need not know,' he said, making a gesture towards their co-workers.

Léa went home around four. The little office was too hot by then, and she needed some fresh air. She bought some *fougasse* and some bread from her favourite bakery and picked up a *paté* and some cheese from an épicerie[6] she liked.

At home, a few letters were on the doormat. Bills mainly, and an envelope with an English stamp. Her heart missed a beat when she saw it. Hands shaking, she opened it, hoping beyond hope that he would have added a word to Max's letter.

He had not, but the words from Max were so sweet that she felt her heart break. He had written most of it in French. It was upbeat about home and the new school he would be going to and full of questions about the house and the town and the people he knew.

She felt the urge to speak to him. There was still an hour before the others would turn up; she had time. She opened her computer to check if he was online and clicked on his name. He answered almost straight away.

'Léa!' he screamed, arms open wide. 'I was thinking of you. Did you get my card?'

---

[6] Grocery shop.

'I did, this is why I'm calling you. *Pour te dire merci!*' she said, making a heart shape sign with her fingers.

He grinned. 'How did I do? Not too many mistakes?'

'Nope. It's very good and I'll treasure it.'

They talked about London and Uzès and she gave him some news of the various people he had met and some boys he had befriended. Some had asked her about him today when she had crossed the place. She asked about Tom, but they both skirted lightly around Mark.

'Have you bought the house yet?' he asked excitedly. 'I can't wait to come back and stay with you this time.'

She did not ask how he would do this given that his father and her had still not spoken to each other, but she avoided the subject. She wondered if she should tell him about the house, but the words were out before she could stop herself.

'The house's been sold.'

'You bought it?' he asked, clapping his hands.

'Unfortunately no, someone else bought it. They had the money, you see, and I didn't.'

He looked crushed, but then an idea seemed to take hold of him.

'Why didn't you ask Dad for the money? He'd have bought it for you.'

She was so surprised that she was speechless for a while. 'I couldn't have asked him that. It wouldn't have been fair.'

'I'll talk to him. Ask him if he can do something. I'm sure he can. You'll see.'

She smiled. Only children could believe in fairytales. 'I don't think there is much he can do. How is he anyway?'

He made a face. 'He's okay with us. He tries, I know he does.'

She felt he wanted to say something else but did not dare. She did not push him. He had not said where his father was. Was he home? The desire to see him overcame her fear.

'Is he around?'

'He left for New York in a hurry today. Granny and our governess are looking after us.'

The hope that had risen in her came crashing down, but she

kept smiling. 'Say hello to your granny for me.' She paused as he said yes, then continued. 'Could you do me a favour?'

'Yes! Anything!'

'When you see your Dad, could you tell him I called?'

'Do you want him to call you back?'

She shook her head, trying to hold the tears that she could feel coming on. 'He'll know what to do. Just let him know that I called ok?'

The door bell rang, and they promised to call each other again soon. She wiped the tears from her eyes and went to the door.

59

'Mr Hunter,' said his personal assistant as he came back from his business lunch, 'this arrived for you. I was told it was urgent.' She handed him a large envelope, and he walked into his office, shutting the door behind him and throwing it on his desk. He slumped in his chair. The time on his watch said 2pm. He wondered what Léa was doing. What she was wearing? What was the weather down in Uzès? Did she think of him sometimes?

He picked up the envelope and opened it absent-mindedly. Inside was a note from his lawyer, together with another envelope with her name typed in capital letters. His heart missed a beat. The sale. He could send the envelope to her or he could... Yes, he could.

It was only once he was on the plane he wondered if this was such a good idea. He had not thought it through, just acted on pure instinct when he had got out of his office and barked orders at his assistant to get him a flight to Nîmes as soon as possible. What if she did not want to see him? What if she had moved on? The thought made him flinched, but he put it out of his mind.

He needed to know. He needed to know where he stood, and he needed her to know what she meant to him. They needed to have it out. They should have had it out before. Alex had been right. He should have driven back to Léa's that night and have it out with her. He should have told her that he loved her, that they would find a way, that he was ready to sell up and move to Uzès. He just needed her to listen to him.

A car was waiting when he landed and he drove out of the airport with his heart in his mouth. His phone was buzzing somewhere, but he ignored it. Something to do with work, probably. If things were going according to plan, they would have to learn to live without him, so they might as well start now. He put the radio on. Cheesy pop songs played on the pre-set channel, but he did not mind.

The drive back to Uzès felt oddly like coming home. A weight that had been there since that fateful night seemed to dissipate as he drove in the late sunshine, windows opened, taking in the golden colours and the smells of the *garrigue*. It was just over six thirty when he drove into Uzès. He went straight to the open-air car park he knew and strolled through the town. He felt both happy and tense. His phone buzzed again, and he saw that Max had left a message. He called his voicemail as he walked towards the *Place aux Herbes* but he could not make out what Max was saying. He had lied to him earlier, telling him he had to go to New York on urgent business and would not be back for a few days. He was not proud of it, but he could not tell him what he was doing. There was always the possibility that things would not go the way he hoped. He shrugged and smiled to himself. Who would have thought that Mark Hunter would one day have doubts about succeeding at something?

Outside Léa's door, Mark stood still. His heart was pounding in his chest and his palms sweaty. What would she say? How would she react? He had played the scenario many times in his head and thought he had come up with all the possible answers to convince her to speak to him. He had just not thought that she would not be the one opening the door.

He looked at the man with the short black hair and the goatee and frowned. The guy looked cocky and Mark's natural assurance took over. He could hear music in the background and people talking.

'Is Léa here?' he said in shaky French.

'Maybe. What do you want with her?'

'I have something important to give her.' He hesitated about saying it was about the house, but felt no one needed to know except her.

The man shrugged. 'Sorry I don't know who you are and she's busy.'

He did not move, and Mark did not either. He felt himself becoming cross and hoped that Léa would appear at the door.

'My name's Mark Hunter. I'm a friend of Léa's.'

The guy seemed to recognise him - had they met before? - and he thought, at last, he would allow him to speak to Léa. The idea to say what he had to say to her in front of him was out of the question but, hopefully, she would agree to come with him for a drink.

'Then it's probably best that you leave,' said the man, crossing his arms on his chest.

'Why? Who are you?'

'It doesn't matter who I am. But you've done enough damage to Léa for a lifetime, so now if you excuse me, I'd like to return to my friends.'

'Hold on! I didn't do any harm to Léa. I—'

'Well, that may be your point-of-view, but it's not mine or any of her friends. She doesn't want to see you ever again.'

'I want to see Léa.'

'And I've told you, you won't. Bye-bye.' He went to slam the door but Mark shouted, 'Wait!'

The skinny man looked exasperated. 'What now?'

Mark hesitated, he had so wanted to give her the piece of paper himself. 'Please give her this. It's important. Very important, you understand.'

A tanned hand took the envelope before closing the door.

It was the most painful blow. He could have lived with Léa telling him she did not want to see him, but he had hoped that he could convince her to give him one last chance. But now there was nothing. He thought of calling her. But what was the point? That weasel of a man had said that she did not want to see him - he still could not place him, although he must have been from around here given the atrocious accent. She did not want to see him ever again. There was nothing left to hope, so he made his way towards the centre of town, turning over a few times, hoping that the door would open and that she would come running after him. But she did not.

* * * * *

It was Luca who discovered the envelope on the kitchen counter near the door, neatly placed again the wall. It looked official as her name was typed neatly with a notary's stamp on the right-hand corner.

'Have you got the house?' he asked her, a glass of wine in one hand and a piece of pizza in the other.

Léa looked at him, puzzled. 'Michel did not tell you? It was sold to someone else. I was told this morning.'

'What's this then?' he said, nodding to the envelope before taking a large bit of his pizza.

Lea's heart stopped. 'Michel?'

'Yes darling,' he said walking in from the courtyard. 'What a party! That was so much fun! We need to do that more often.' He kissed Léa on the cheek and saw that she was holding the envelope.

'What is this? Did that come through earlier?' Despite the couple of glasses of wine she had drunk, she remembered that someone had rung the bell.

'Oh yes, it was our ex-employer. What's his name again? He gave me that and said it was important.'

'Mark? Mark Hunter?' she said, her voice breaking.

'Yeah, that's him,' he said while finishing his beer.

'He was here?' asked Luca.

Michel looked at both of them, surprised. 'Yeah, he was. But honestly, he's done enough damage to you, darling. I don't know what this is, but it should probably go in the bin. Save yourself the pain.'

She swallowed with difficulty. 'He... He didn't want to come in?'

'Oh, he did! But I put my foot down and said no. I thought

he'd left, anyway. Are you okay?'

Léa was frenziedly looking for her handbag and her sunglasses.

'What are you doing?'

'I need to see him.' Then she looked at him again. 'Oh Michel, if you only knew how lovely he's been to me and how awful I've been to him.'

'Babe, just forget it! This guy's bad news. You told me yourself he was an annoying prat.'

'That was… That was a lifetime ago. Can I borrow your car?'

'Take mine,' said Luca, handing her his car keys. 'It's much more reliable. It's parked by the house.'

She kissed him on the cheek. 'Help yourself to whatever you want and just slam the door when you leave. Bye!' she said as she closed the door.

She ran to Luca's car. She was not sure she was supposed to drive, but this was an emergency. Where was he? Where did he go from here? He could not have left already.

Breathe Léa. Think.

She tried to evaluate how long it had been since he had rung the bell. Pictures of him standing there kept flashing through her mind as she joined the Friday afternoon traffic out of Uzès. 'Mark, Mark, Mark,' she said ruefully, 'why didn't you call me you fool?'

* * * * *

As Mark walked to his car, he tried to make sense of what he had been told, that Léa did not want to see him. She must have been in the house, maybe even seen or heard him. The pain of the rejection bit at him.

By the time he got back to the bastide, anger had taken over. He stopped the car brutally, wheels screeching on the gravel, slamming the steering wheel. Why could he not have stayed in London and forgotten about her? Why?

Inside the house, he grabbed a glass, and an opened bottle of whisky and poured himself a stiff one. He drank it in one go, feeling the heat burn his throat. He expected the alcohol to hit, but it did not come. He poured himself another glass and walked onto the terrace. The clouds he had seen while driving back were advancing like a giant rolling wave on the horizon. There was a metallic taste in the air. He almost wished the rain was here now. He needed something, anything to take this pain away.

He took out his phone and was about to dial the number of the private jet company to make a booking when the bell rang. He thought of ignoring it, but it rang again. Who could that be? Manuela? He went to the door and saw her on the little screen.

Léa.

He hesitated in pushing the button to open the gate. He was not sure he wanted to speak to her anymore, and yet something in him still wanted to have it out, if only to strike back. He pressed the button and opened the front door, glass in hand.

60

Getting out of Uzès had taken no time, although it felt like an eternity to Léa. She felt that every minute that passed was another chance for him to leave. It was just after eight o'clock when she found herself on the road to Arpaillargues. The light was fading and on the horizon, a band of low ominous clouds were visible. She drove as fast as she dared on the narrow road, wishing cars in front of her would go away. Would he still be there? Was he staying somewhere else? Questions to which she had no answers swirled around in her head, and she almost missed the turning for the lane that went to the house.

She parked in front of the gate and rang the bell. There was no answer. She tried again, peering through the iron-wrought gate to see if a car was there. But she could see nothing, and she felt her hope fading. She took a deep breath and pressed the button one last time. She just had to be sure. Suddenly, there was a buzz. She pushed through the gate and ran towards the house. Her heart felt like it would explode. She saw him as she turned the corner of the path that led to the house and slowed down. He was wearing dark blue chinos, a white shirt and had a glass in his hand. He was leaning against the jamb of the front door and, as she got closer, she noticed the tightness of his jaw and the thin line of his lips.

'Mark, I'm so glad I didn't miss you, I was so scared you'd be gone by now.'

He looked at her but said nothing before turning around.

Shaken, she stopped before following him through the house and onto the terrace, bare of all furniture except for a couple of armchairs bare of their cushions. It was the end of summer. The holiday was over.

He kept his back to her. 'What do you want, Léa?'

She did not know what to say. Where should she start? Should she talk about Max, or Alex, or just the fact that she had missed him terribly?

He turned around. There was sarcasm in his eyes and in the smile that was forming at the corner of his mouth. It pained her, but she kept her gaze levelled with his.

'I didn't know you came to my house until half an hour ago.'

He raised his glass. 'Don't worry, a funny little man told me you didn't want to see me, that I had hurt you enough. Bye-bye, I was told.'

She would have burst out laughing at the perfect imitation of Michel if she had not wanted to cry. 'That was Michel.'

'I don't care who that was. All I know is that he made it very clear that I wasn't to see you again, that you didn't want to see me,' he said, pointing his index finger at her.

'Michel's the guy from the agency. He got it wrong. I never said that.'

'Yes, you did! You said it to me in Uzès.' He had pounced, smashing the glass on the terrace with a violence that startled her. There was a silence, only broken by the sound of the water running into the swimming pool below.

'But not to Michel. He's upset because someone bought the house I live in. I learned about it earlier today. He was with me and thought it was probably you. I told him it couldn't be, but nothing I said could change his mind.'

She shook her head. 'I came because you left this.' She took the envelope out of her handbag. 'I can't take this.'

'Have you checked what it is?'

'No, but I can't take it.'

'You have too. I can't take it back,' he said bitterly. He turned slightly and looked at the sky. 'Open it.'

She broke the seal and opened the couple of pieces of paper

slowly. She knew what it was; the stamp had given it away. It was the *compromis de vente* to her house. What she did not expect was that it also included the house next door. Her name was on it too. She was the buyer of both houses. Which she could not be. She looked up to him and saw him watching her.

He could see Léa's eyes glistening with tears. She might have guessed, but she had not known for sure or about the second house until she had opened the envelope which was just how he had wanted it to be. He would have liked to go to her, but the wound had reopened and the bitterness seeping out of it redoubled.

'Why?' she said.

'Does it matter? They're yours. You can do whatever you want with them.' He had said that with more resentment that he had wanted too.

'I can't accept it. Not now.'

'There's nothing either of us can do. It's done and dusted.'

He turned his back to her, not wanting to see in her eyes the pain he was causing. He knew that if she stayed any longer, he could not resist her. He could feel his body pulling him to her. But theirs was a relationship that was doomed. She had been right in that dark alley two weeks before, and he should have seen that from the start.

'Did you come back here because of this?'

He smirked and tilted his head back. 'I didn't come back for you if that's your question.'

The sky had darkened considerably. The clouds on the horizon seemed to move faster, and thunder rolled somewhere. He waited, but nothing came back. He turned around, but she was gone. He saw in that second that this was it. If he did not run after her, it would be over. She had come back and explained, and he had just hurt her again and again.

He started running through the house, shouting her name.

61

The wheels of the car skidded on the soft wet gravel as Léa braked just before the road. A couple of minutes later, the rain started falling heavily, blurring the windscreen. She drove as fast as she could, tears flowing freely down her face. She kept checking her mirror to see if the big black Range Rover she had seen at the bastide was following, but there was nothing. Once again he was letting her go without trying to hold her back.

She tried to focus on the road. She could hear the thunder not far off and the sky which had become very dark was lit by strikes of lightning. She felt small against the elements and once again alone.

As she arrived in Uzès, she parked near Michel and Luca's house. As she cut the engine, she wondered where to go. The rain was still heavy, and the wind whipped around the car. Their house was the closest, but she knew she could not bear to hear Michel's I-told-you-so speech. Her house was too far to reach on foot in this weather. She waited for the rain to abate a little before checking the road she had followed for his car.

She would have like to talk to her grandmother, to tell her that although she had found the one, she had lost him again, that she was hurting like hell, that she felt lost. She thought of Monsieur de Daujac. She had to tell him the truth. There was no chance that things would finally get better. She could not live with those lies any longer.

She got out of the car and ran to the retirement home. It was not far, but by the time she got there she was drenched. The lady at reception who she had met once before recognised her.

'It's just awful, isn't it? Are you parked far?'

Léa shook her head, and tiny drops of water fell on the surrounding floor. The woman continued. 'I have to leave in a minute but I think I may wait a little longer. Are you here to see Monsieur de Daujac? It's getting late…'

'It won't take long. Has he had dinner?'

'I saw him got out of the dining room with Paulette ten minutes ago. You'll find him in his room. He likes to read in the evening. He told me he has an incredible book collection, you know?'

In front of his room on the first floor, she knocked softly.

'Who is it?'

'It's Léa Pasquier,' she said, opening the door and waiting on the threshold. 'Could I speak to you?'

'Of course, darling, of course!' said Armand de Daujac getting up and coming towards her. He was wearing a blue shirt and a light cotton jumper with dark grey trousers. 'Oh my, you're wet, put this blanket over your shoulders, we don't want you to catch a cold.'

He stopped speaking, fixing her with his pale blue eyes. 'Something's the matter, isn't it? Come in and tell me.'

He moved back to his chair, and she sat on the sofa next to him, her thoughts all jumbled in her head. How was she going to explain it all?

'I need to tell you that… That Mr Hunter and I are not together anymore…' As the truth of her statement hit her, she started sobbing uncontrollably, her head on the arm of the sofa.

'My dear, dear child, I'm so sorry to hear that. You were the most beautiful couple that I had seen in a long while,' he said, putting a hand on her shoulder. 'Are you sure it's truly over? Maybe it's just a hiccup, you know, a lovers' tiff?'

She raised her head. 'I wish it was only that, I so wish it was but no it's a lot more serious…'

'Maybe this is what you think but believe me at my age I've seen everything and what may feel like the end of the world to you may just be a silly misunderstanding,' he said putting a box of tissues on the small table by Léa.

She shook her head, grabbing one to blow her nose and dry her eyes.

'He loves you, you know?' said Monsieur de Daujac without warning. 'But he's like all of us men, we're just not very good at showing our feelings. We think it makes us weak or look like fools. It doesn't matter where we come from, we're all the same.'

Léa smiled through her tears. 'I bet you were the most romantic of men with your late wife.'

'I tried, but it took me a lifetime to show her I loved her. Like others, I just assumed that she knew, that I didn't need to say it. I understood that I had to change when she was about to leave me.'

Monsieur de Daujac nodded, his eyes lost somewhere above Léa's head. 'I was taken with the work on the estate, the politics of it all. I just assumed she would be here always, that she knew I loved her. I did not see that she felt abandoned. She didn't come from a family like mine, she had left her friends in Paris to come and settle down with me in my isolated castle. I just assumed that it was normal, that things would always stay the same. I was wrong.'

There was a silence. 'You worry too much about the differences between you. It doesn't matter. What matters is what you and he are prepared to do for each other.'

'He bought the house for me and the one next door too.'

'That's very generous.'

'It is but we just don't seem to be able to speak without hurting each other. Surely that just shows it cannot work.'

'I don't believe that people need to be similar to have a long life together. It must be boring after a while, don't you think? Maybe all you need is a little time to adjust.'

'He isn't speaking to me anymore. And I...'

She was not sure what she wanted. Him, them, Max, nothing. Her head hurt of trying to arrange and re-arrange the pieces to make them stick.

'Stop thinking about it. Think about you. What, in your heart, do you want? It's the only truth to follow.'

Léa tightened the blanket around her. It was made of colourful squares sewn together. Her grandmother used to have one just like that in her house in Nîmes.

'Why don't you stay here for a while? You look exhausted, my dear child.'

It was like he had read her mind. She felt safe here with him. She kissed his liver-spotted hand. 'Thank you,' she said in a breath.

'I'll read you a passage of this book by Stendhal that I love. Have you read *The Chartreuse de Parme*?'

Léa settled herself more comfortably on the sofa and let his voice soothed her. The rain was still falling hard outside.

62

Mark heard the car start as he reached the front door. She was at the end of the lane when he realised he did not have his car keys on him.

Thunder roared to the south, and a large raindrop fell on his hand. He ran back to the house, closed the doors to the terrace, grabbed his keys. The storm broke out as he was climbing into his car. He was off like a shot and almost smashed into the gate that was opening slowly. He raged against it. Lightning strikes lit up the sky, and the rain lashed the windscreen. He could not see further than a few metres. The few cars present on the narrow road that led to Uzès were moving cautiously, their back lights blurred by the rain. He would have liked to overtake them, but it was just too dangerous.

The wind had risen up and the plane trees on the side of the road seemed to sway. Just after one of the bends, he braked hard and missed the car in front of him by a hair's breadth. A tree had fallen on it, crushing the front of the car. He parked as best as he could and got out. By the time he reached the car, he was soaked to the bone. There was no passenger, just a middle-aged man who was stuck behind the driving wheel. He walked around the car and tried to open the driver's door, but it was stuck. The tree that had fallen had twisted the windscreen frame, which blocked part of the door. He tried to pull the door open once again using all his strength, but nothing moved. He walked around the car and opened the passenger's door.

'Please, please help me. My leg, my leg,' said the injured man, his voice barely audible through the noise made by the wind and the rain.

Mark returned to his car and tried to call the emergency services. When he finally got hold of someone, he tried in bad French to explain the situation. The woman on the other side did not seem to understand what he was saying and in an English that he could barely understand, told him that they would send a fire crew. He tried to ask her when, but she hung up before he could finish his sentence. He looked around. But on this part of the road between the village and Uzès, there were few houses. The only solution was to take the car and look for a house where he could get help.

The rain was still falling, and the wind swirled around the tall trees as he exited his car again to inform the injured man of his plan. A car slammed on the brakes behind him. A man got out as white as his t-shirt and Mark recognised him as the guy who had told him to get lost at Léa's. Michel. They stared at each other. The other man looked like he had seen a ghost and did not move. Mark could have punched him in the face, but that would have served no purpose.

'There's a man in the car, he needs help,' he shouted as he got closer to Michel. 'I can't open the door and he can't exit on the passenger side.'

'What about the emergency services?'

Mark shrugged. 'I don't know when they'll turn up.'

'We shouldn't stay here, it's dangerous', said Michel, moving towards his car.

He had never been courageous, and the situation looked risky.

'We can't leave him here. He's complaining about his leg.'

It was Michel's turn to shrug. 'I don't see what we can do'.

'I do. We need to find someone with a chainsaw or something that could help us move the tree to open the door. You must know someone in the area.'

Michel pushed away the strand of hair that was sticking to his forehead. He seemed to think about it, and Mark was close to boiling point.

'Do you know someone around here?'

'Is there anything at the bastide?'

Mark looked at him and decided to take charge. 'It's too far. Take your car and knock on the door of the first house you find. And please bring someone back. I'll stay with the gentleman.'

Michel hesitated, but the dark look the Brit gave him told him it would be better for him to do as he was told. He would probably accuse him of failing to assist a person in danger. He turned on his heels and heard Mark say, 'And hurry, please!'.

While Michel was gone, Mark spoke to the man in the car at length. Thunder had stopped, but the rain and the wind still whipped the crushed car.

Michel was back fifteen minutes later with a man he said was a winemaker. The guy was built like a lumberjack and first took out a triangle he put at the entrance of the bend before picking up his chainsaw and moving towards the tree.

'We'll get you out!' he shouted to the man in the car before turning to Mark. 'Can you help me? Hold the trunk here. If your friend could help us...'

'I don't know him,' Mark started but did not continue. Pettiness would achieve nothing. He would have ample time later to tell Michel what he thought of him. He made a sign to Michel to come and help them. He was now wearing a yellow plastic poncho but did not feel much more inclined than earlier to come and help. The winemaker placed them around the trunk and told them to be careful of shards.

In a few minutes, the man had cut the tree in three sections that they moved as quickly as they could to the side of the road.

On the other side of the tree, a car had stopped. A tall, well-dressed man with small round glasses and a large moustache got out.

'Can I help you?' he shouted to the others before joining Mark and Michel in pushing the bits of trunks and branches in the ditch. As he walked back to the car, he saw the injured man.

'What are you doing?' shouted Mark when he saw him ran to his car and come back with a black satchel.

'I'm a surgeon. If the emergency services take too long, this man is likely to lose his leg. Please help me to open the door.'

'I tried without success earlier,' said Mark doubtfully.

'Let's try once again together. We have to act fast.'

The man in the car was moaning faintly now, and Mark wondered if it was not already too late. The surgeon, as if he was reading his thoughts, smiled to him and in perfect English told him he would make it. He sincerely hoped that it would be the case.

After several tries and the help of the winemaker, they finally prised the door open. The front of the car had been crushed by the tree and the man's left leg was stuck under the driving wheel as Mark had suspected. There was blood all over the man's leg and Mark prayed for him to get out alive. He saw Michel almost faint and told him to try the emergency services one more time. Maybe he would have more luck being a local and all that. The surgeon looked up to him and smiled. 'Natural born leader.'

'No choice,' said Mark while glancing at Michel, who was speaking to someone.

He soon was back and announced that the emergency services would be here any minute now. He was almost jumping for joy.

Mark had gone behind the man and was holding him by his shoulders while the surgeon was applying a tourniquet to the leg. The fire crew turned up just a couple of minutes later.

While they were cutting the man out of the car with the surgeon's help, Mark thought of Léa. Was she safe? Had she got home? The storm had gone, and the wind had stopped as suddenly as it had started. The rain was still falling lightly. The night was almost there and there was now a coolness in the air. A fireman gave him a survival blanket. A voice came behind him.

'Monsieur Hunter…'

He turned around and found Michel looking at him, his arms hanging loosely around his body. 'I wanted to apologise… for what I said to you earlier. I was angry without knowing the truth. I shouldn't have…'

It was rather light in terms of excuses, but Mark was just too tired and worried to ask for more. He nodded.

'Did Léa come to see you at the bastide? She ran out the door about half an hour after you turned up. She was looking for you… I didn't know when I saw you…'

'She came to find me, but I pushed her away. I was furious. I was following her when…,' Mark said, looking around him.

'She was on the road?' Michel said, clasping his hands on his cheeks.

'I couldn't hold her back. I hope…'

Michel looked terrified, and then suddenly his hands were looking for something. 'My phone… Where's my phone?'

He found it in one of his pockets and fumbled to find Léa's number. Mark was looking at him, his heart in his mouth.

Just pick up the phone, darling, please.

'She's not answering!'

He tapped the digits again on his phone and listened. He was stamping his feet while biting the fingernails of his free hand before slicking his wet hair. 'And Luca isn't answering either!'

'You know Luca?'

Michel looked at Mark with suspicion. 'He's my partner. How do you know him?'

'I had dinner at his restaurant with Léa. Was he with her?'

'No! He lent her his car so that she could get to you. He went to check on his parents. His father isn't well. Shit!'

Mark was trying to stay calm, but his own fears were rising, not helped by Michel's restlessness. He looked at the road. It was now free of the tree.

'Listen, go and find your partner while I'll look for Léa.'

Michel did not wait for Mark to change his mind and ran to his car. Mark was about to do the same when the surgeon stopped him.

'He isn't well your friend?'

'He's fine but we can't reach two people we love.'

'Go then. There's nothing for you to do here. I'll follow the emergency services to the hospital, but our man should make a full recovery. Thank you for your help earlier. I couldn't have done it without you.'

They smiled to each other before shaking hands.

'My name's Jean-Rémi Dufour. I'm a surgeon at Nîmes hospital. Don't forget to have that wound on your head looked at quickly.'

Mark touched his head and saw blood on his fingers. He had not noticed or even felt the cut.

'Mark Hunter. Thank you.'

They shook hands again with more warmth and Mark drove slowly to Uzès. The rain had finally stopped, and the road to the city was clear. Only strewn leaves and bits of branches testified to the violence of the storm. He did not see any car on the side of the road and started hoping that Léa had reached her house safely.

The city was like empty of his inhabitants. He crossed the *Place of Herbes* where they had met all these weeks ago without seeing another human being. It was only nine thirty, but everything appeared closed. He found himself in Léa's lane and walked cautiously up to her door. There was no light in her house and worry rose in him again. What if he had missed her car in the ditch along the road? Rain had started to fall again, and his clothes were sticking to him.

He rang the bell, but no noise came back from inside. He rang again. He knocked on the door and shouted Léa's name. There was still no movement inside the house. He took a few steps back to see if there was a light on the first floor, but there was nothing. The other houses seemed to be dark too. There seemed to be no-one around. Maybe people hid in their houses, worried about that man screaming in the street? Despair was threatening to overwhelm him.

He took out his phone. There was almost no hope that she would answer, but he had to try. There were several messages from Max, but he ignored them. His hands were shaking so much that it took him a couple of tries before he could find her number. He leant against the door as he pressed the green button and closed his eyes.

'Answer, please answer,' he whispered.

Against all hopes, someone answered. 'Allo? Monsieur

Hunter?'

He knew this man's voice but could not place it. The man was whispering.

'It's Monsieur de Daujac.'

What was Léa's phone doing at Monsieur de Daujac's?

'Léa is here with me. She's asleep. You need to come and pick her up.'

There was a silence, and he wondered if the line was dead, but then the old man whispered, 'It's you she's waiting for.'

63

When Mark arrived at the retirement home, he had to negotiate with the porter to get in. At reception, the night receptionist looked at him suspiciously too.

'Visits are over, sir.'

'I'm well aware of that but I just spoke to Monsieur de Daujac who's waiting for me.'

'He must be sleeping at that hour.'

'He wasn't when I spoke to him fifteen minutes ago.'

'I can't let you go up, it's against the rules…'

Mark could feel his anger returning, but he tried to keep a hold of himself.

'Let me call him,' he said, taking his phone out just as the phone on the reception desk rang. The receptionist picked it up and listened intently, nodding.

'You can go up. Room 104 on the first floor.'

Mark ran as the guy told him he could not stay long, that Monsieur de Daujac was tired.

There was no-one in the corridors, but he found the room easily. He knocked softly before going in. The room was in darkness, except for a lamp set on a mahogany table next to the old man's armchair. They looked at each other and Monsieur de Daujac put a finger over his lips.

Mark walked around the sofa and found Léa asleep, curled up on herself, a colourful blanket over her.

'I was waiting for you since she turned up tonight but I see you must've had an arduous night,' said the old man nodding to Mark's head wound.

Mark smiled. 'You can say that. That storm was violent.'

Monsieur de Daujac was looking at Léa with the eyes of a father. 'For her too, for her too,' he said softly.

There was a silence only punctuated by the ticking of an old clock set on an imposing chest of drawers, remnant without a doubt of his previous life at the castle.

'Do we still see each other tomorrow?' he asked Mark, his eyes shining in the dark.

'Of course,' Mark said with a smile.

'Good, good. I think it's time for you to bring our friend home.' He stopped gazing at Mark. 'She needs you to reassure her.'

Mark nodded before kneeling next to Léa and shaking her shoulder softly.

'Léa,' he said in her ear, 'it's time to go home.'

She did not move straightaway and looked stunned when she opened her eyes.

'What are you doing here?' she asked, her eyes on the wound above his right eyebrow, her hand almost ready to touch it before falling back on her knees as she sat up.

'It's nothing. Only a scratch. The storm's gone, we need to go home.'

She looked lost, like she was unsure whether or not she should follow him. She looked at Monsieur de Daujac, took the hand he was extending to her.

'Armand.'

'Go home, my love. We'll see each other again soon.'

She stooped to kiss him, and he gripped her hand. 'Don't be angry with him. Men are weak. But he loves you. He came back for you.'

She kissed him on the cheek and he looked at them until they closed the door.

They went out the building under the night watchman's surprised look. She looked fragile with just a light scarf on her shoulders. He saw her shiver and regretted not having kept the survival blanket the fireman had given him. They walked through the streets side-by-side without speaking. Inside Léa's house, a few abandoned glasses here and there showed that a party had taken place a few hours before. She switched on the light and went into the kitchen. He stayed up not knowing what to do.

64

In the kitchen, Léa grabbed the emergency box she kept in a cupboard by the door and filled a bowl with tepid water. Thoughts of what Mark had said at the bastide collided with Armand's soothing words in her head. Who was she supposed to believe? She thought of Max too, of his dreams. Were they even compatible with hers?

When she walked back into the lounge, Mark was still standing up. He seemed to wait for her to say something.

'Sit down. Here,' she said, nodding to a wooden chair by a tall lamp. His clothes were still damp, and she saw that there were bits of wood and leaves on them. What had he been doing all this time since she had left the bastide?

She dipped a bit of cotton-wool in the bowl of water and dabbed it gently onto the wound he had on his forehead. The blood had dried, and it took her a few attempts before it was finally clean. He had his eyes closed and did not move, not even when she applied some disinfectant. She could feel the warmth of his body through his clothes, his woody scent. Memories came back to her of another time in this house, but she pushed them back. Now was not the time. As she raised her eyes, she saw the letter from her grandmother. It was sticking out from the notebook she wrote in on the mantelpiece. What would she say?

Have no regrets. Take a chance.

'The wound is not deep, but you'd better get it seen by

someone tomorrow,' she said as she applied a small plaster to protect it. As she finished, she took a step back. It was as much about resistance as protection from him, from the desire she felt of just letting herself go to him, of trying one more time.

'You should go home,' she said, putting the plasters and disinfectant back in the box and avoiding his eyes.

'Léa,' he said as he got up slowly.

She finally looked up to him but did not reply. She could feel tears coming on.

'Léa, I'm sorry for what I said to you earlier. Michel's words…' He did not finish and she shook her head. She did not want to hear the rest, she just wanted him to go.

'It was like poison. It drove me mad. I couldn't understand why—'

'There's nothing to understand. It just can't work, you and I. Please go.'

She turned on her heels, ready to take flight, but his hand grabbed her arm, pulling her gently back to him. She resisted, trying to break free, but he was stronger than she was and did not let go. She turned to face him, angry at his domination.

'What do you want Mark?'

'You. Only you,' he whispered, 'I only want you.'

'What about Freya and the baby?'

She had forgotten about them earlier when she had run to the bastide, but she just could not ignore them now.

'The baby isn't mine.'

'But you slept with her after us?' she retorted.

'No, I didn't. She came to see me when I went back to London before us.'

She was still resisting, unable to let go of her fears and her doubts. She had been there before, being lied to by someone she had loved. She could not let that happen to her again, no matter what Armand had said about Mark. Yet she could not set herself free from his embrace as he wrapped his other arm around her.

'Léa, Léa, Léa, I've been an idiot from the start but it's over.'

She looked up to him, shaking her head.

'Mark, don't tell me you're going to stay, we both know it

won't happen—'

'I'll stay. That's what I came here to tell you.'

'Why did you buy the houses then?' she sobbed.

'I wanted to make you a present so you could forgive me going to London after our first night together. I should've told you a long time ago—'

She did not let him finish and kissed him. He had come back for her.

Epilogue

Uzès, Monday 21st September

Mum,
*Today was my first day at school in Uzès. School started three
weeks ago, so I'm the new boy and all eyes were on me when I got into
class this morning. But that's okay because they don't know yet who
my father is. And anyway, he is not that powerful finance guy
anymore. Apparently he wants to become a winemaker. We are off to
visit the vines he wants to buy next weekend. And Dad and Léa said,
there will also be a surprise.*

*For now, we all live in Léa's little house that Dad bought for her.
It's cramped but great fun. Dad is getting used to life in France, but
his French is just awful. He has also bought the house next door, but
we can't live in it. They're looking for a bigger house to rent while they
look for the perfect home for us. The house in London is on the market
and our stuff is being shipped soon. Despite the happy times I had there
with you, I don't miss it.*

*I've decided to call Léa Maman. I hope you don't mind. I asked her
before I did. She asked me if I had thought about it. I told her that, as
much as I loved you, you aren't here anymore and won't ever be again.
I told her it was you who told me we can't live in the past, that we have
to live in the present. She is my present. And my future, too. The star I
have to follow.*

Printed in Great Britain
by Amazon